PRAISE FOR THE NOVELS OF
#1 *NEW YORK TIMES*
BESTSELLING AUTHOR NICHOLAS SPARKS

THE WEDDING

"Sparks's fans have from the very beginning eagerly anticipated a sequel to the romantic tale of Allie and Noah Calhoun.
The wait is now over....Sparks tells his sweet story...[with] a
gasp-inducing twist at the very end. Satisfied female readers
will close the covers with a sigh."
—*Publishers Weekly*

"Nicholas Sparks follows up his beloved bestseller *The
Notebook* with a touching novel about one man's attempt to save
a failing marriage."
—*BookPage*

"Sure to leave you breathless....In this stunning follow-up to
The Notebook, readers new and old will remember the joy of
falling in love and the challenge of staying in love."
—RoundTableReviews.com

"Sparks, a master of description, does not fail....This is a
thoughtfully written account of a man's search into his past in
an effort to revive a lost love...a story filled with reality,
romance, and anticipation."
—ReviewingTheEvidence.com

"Excellent....After reading this book you really will want to
convey your feelings to someone you care about before it's too
late!"
—BestsellersWorld.com

Please turn this page for more reviews and turn to the back
of this book for an excerpt from *The Notebook*.

"A story of renewed efforts to make a man's personal life better. Sparks has the ability to tell a simple story with rich emotion and give his readers a sense of fulfillment."
—Bookreporter.com

"THE WEDDING left me with a smile on my face. The ending surprised me, and left my heart all aflutter. This is a book that will forever have a spot on my bookshelf."
—TheRomanceReadersConnection.com

"A lovely, involving tale."
—BookLoons.com

"Mr. Sparks is one of the few authors who has been able to get his readers to cry and laugh in the same book....This is an incredible story about the evolution of love....This reader continues to hope that Sparks does not stop writing his beautiful love stories."
—MyShelf.com

THE GUARDIAN

"Surprising...hair-raising....Thanks to the spiced-up, suspenseful new recipe, readers will be in for a little heat."
—*Denver Post*

"An involving love story...an edge-of-your-seat, unpredictable thriller."
—*Booklist*

"Compelling action....Sparks's fans clamor for his brand of love story, and, with the added punch of suspense, this one will be another bestseller."
—*Publishers Weekly*

"An exciting mystery....Fans of Sparks won't be disappointed."
—*Southern Pines Pilot* (NC)

"Fans everywhere are familiar with Nicholas Sparks's poignant, emotionally driven novels....Sparks's latest is proof that he's just as proficient writing suspenseful fiction as he is writing classic tearjerkers."
—*Romantic Times*

NIGHTS IN RODANTHE

"Bittersweet...romance blooms....You'll cry in spite of yourself."
—*People*

"Passionate and memorable...smooth, sensitive writing....This is a novel that can hold its own."
—Associated Press

"Extremely hard to put down...a love story, and a good love story at that."
—*Boston Herald*

A BEND IN THE ROAD

"Sweet, accessible, uplifting...expect instant bestsellerdom."
—*Publishers Weekly*

"A powerful tale of true love."
—*Booklist*

"A charming and thoughtful love story....Don't miss it; this is a book that's light on the surface but with subtle depths."
—BookLoons.com

more...

THE RESCUE

"A modern master of fateful love stories."
—Bookpage.com

"A romantic page-turner....Sparks's fans won't be disappointed."
—*Glamour*

"All of Sparks's trademark elements—love, loss, and small-town life—are present in this terrific read."
—*Booklist*

A WALK TO REMEMBER

"An extraordinary book...touching, at times riveting...a book you won't soon forget."
—*Sunday New York Post*

"A sweet tale of young but everlasting love."
—*Chicago Sun-Times*

"Bittersweet...a tragic yet spiritual love story."
—*Variety*

MESSAGE IN A BOTTLE

"The novel's unabashed emotion—and an unexpected turn—will put tears in your eyes."
—*People*

"Glows with moments of tenderness...has the potential to delve deeply into the mysteries of eternal love."
—*Cleveland Plain Dealer*

THE NOTEBOOK

ALSO BY NICHOLAS SPARKS

THE
WEDDING

Nicholas Sparks

WARNER BOOKS

NEW YORK   BOSTON

This book is a work of fiction. Names, characters, places and incidents are the product of the author's imagination or are used fictitiously. Any resemblance to actual events, locales, or persons, living or dead, is coincidental.

Copyright © 2003 by Nicholas Sparks
Excerpt from *The Notebook* © copyright 1996 by Nicholas Sparks
All rights reserved.

Warner Books

Time Warner Book Group
1271 Avenue of the Americas, New York, NY 10020
Visit our Web site at www.twbookmark.com.

Originally publishing in hardcover by Warner Books, Inc.

Printed in the United States of America

First Trade Printing: July 2004

10 9 8 7 6 5 4 3 2 1

ISBN: 0-446-53245-2 (hardcover)
ISBN: 0-446-69333-2 (pbk.)
LCCN: 2003107400

Book design by Giorgetta Bell McRee

For Cathy,
Who made me the luckiest man alive
when she agreed to be my wife.

Acknowledgments

Thanking people is always fun,
And something that I like to do,
I'm no poet, I'll admit that first,
So forgive me if the rhymes go askew.

I'd like to thank my children first,
Because I love each and every one,
Miles, Ryan, Landon, Lexie and Savannah are great,
And they make my life a source of fun.

Theresa helps me constantly, and Jamie never falters,
I'm lucky I get to work with them, and I hope that never
    alters.

To Denise, who made movies about my books,
And Richard and Howie, who negotiated the deals,
Scotty would work the contracts,
All are friends, and it's the way I'll always feel.

To Larry, the boss and a really great guy,
And Maureen who's sharp as a tack,
To Emi, Jennifer and Edna the pros,
In selling books, they all have a knack.

There are others too, who make my days
A grand and wonderful adventure,
So to all my friends and family I thank you,
Because of you, my life is a treasure.

Prologue

*I*s it possible, I wonder, for a man to truly change? Or do character and habit form the immovable boundaries of our lives?

It is mid-October 2003, and I ponder these questions as I watch a moth flail wildly against the porch light. I'm alone outside. Jane, my wife, is sleeping upstairs and she didn't stir when I slipped out of bed. It is late; midnight has come and gone, and there's a crispness in the air that holds the promise of an early winter. I'm wearing a heavy cotton robe, and though I imagined it would be thick enough to keep the chill at bay, I notice that my hands are trembling before I bury them in my pockets

Above me, the stars are specks of silver paint on a charcoal canvas. I see Orion and the Pleiades, Ursa Major and Corona Borealis, and think I should be inspired by the realization that I'm not only looking at the stars, but staring into the past as well. Constellations shine with light that was emitted aeons ago, and I wait for something to come to me, words that a poet might use to illuminate life's mysteries. But there is nothing.

This doesn't surprise me. I've never considered myself a sentimental man, and if you asked my wife, I'm sure she would agree. I do not lose myself in films or plays, I've never been a dreamer, and if I aspire to any form of mastery at all, it is one defined by rules of the Internal Revenue Service and codified by law. For the most part, my days and years as an estate lawyer have been spent in the company of those preparing for their own deaths, and I suppose that some might say that my life is less meaningful because of this. But even if they're right, what can I do? I make no excuses for myself, nor have I ever, and by the end of my story, I hope you'll view this quirk of my character with a forgiving eye.

Please don't misunderstand. I may not be sentimental, but I'm not completely without emotion, and there are moments when I'm struck by a deep sense of wonder. It is usually simple things that I find strangely moving: standing among the giant sequoias in the Sierra Nevadas, for instance, or watching ocean waves as they crash together off Cape Hatteras, sending salty plumes into the sky. Last week, I felt my throat tighten when I watched a young boy reach for his father's hand as they strolled down the sidewalk. There are other things, too: I can sometimes lose track of time when staring at a sky filled with wind-whipped clouds, and when I hear thunder rumbling, I always draw near the window to watch for lightning. When the next brilliant flash illuminates the sky, I often find myself filled with longing, though I'm at a loss to tell you what it is that I feel my life is missing.

My name is Wilson Lewis, and this is the story of a wedding. It is also the story of my marriage, but despite the thirty years that Jane and I have spent together, I suppose I should begin by admitting that others know far more about marriage than I. A man can learn nothing by asking my advice. In the course of my marriage, I've been selfish and stubborn and as ignorant as a goldfish, and it pains me to realize this about myself. Yet, looking back, I believe that if I've done one thing right, it has been to love my wife throughout our years together. While this may strike some as a feat not worth mentioning, you should know that there was a time when I was certain that my wife didn't feel the same way about me.

Of course, all marriages go through ups and downs, and I believe this is the natural consequence of couples that choose to stay together over the long haul. Between us, my wife and I have lived through the deaths of both of my parents and one of hers, and the illness of her father. We've moved four times, and though I've been successful in my profession, many sacrifices were made in order to secure this position. We have three children, and while neither of us would trade the experience of parenthood for the riches of Tutankhamen, the sleepless nights and frequent trips to the hospital when they were infants left both of us exhausted and often overwhelmed. It goes without saying that their teenage years were an experience I would rather not relive.

All of those events create their own stresses, and when two people live together, the stress flows both ways. This, I've come to believe, is both the blessing and the curse of marriage. It's a blessing because there's an outlet for the everyday strains of life; it's a curse because the outlet is someone you care deeply about.

Why do I mention this? Because I want to underscore that throughout all these events, I never doubted my feelings for my wife. Sure, there were days when we avoided eye contact at the breakfast table, but still I never doubted us. It would be dishonest to say that I haven't wondered what would have happened had I married someone else, but in all the years we spent together, I never once regretted the fact that I had chosen her and that she had chosen me as well. I thought our relationship was settled, but in the end, I realized that I was wrong. I learned that a little more than a year ago—fourteen months, to be exact—and it was that realization, more than anything, that set in motion all that was to come.

What happened then, you wonder?

Given my age, a person might suppose that it was some incident inspired by a midlife crisis. A sudden desire to change my life, perhaps, or maybe a crime of the heart. But it was neither of those things. No, my sin was a small one in the grand scheme of things, an incident that under different circumstances might have been the subject of a humorous anecdote in later years. But it hurt her, it hurt us, and thus it is here where I must begin my story.

It was August 23, 2002, and what I did was this: I rose and ate breakfast, then spent the day at the office, as is my custom. The events of my workday played no role in what came after; to be honest, I can't remember anything about it other than to recall that it was nothing extraordinary. I arrived home at my regular hour and was pleasantly surprised to see Jane preparing my favorite meal in the kitchen. When she turned to greet me, I thought I saw her eyes flicker downward, looking to see if I was holding something other than my briefcase, but I was empty-handed. An hour later we ate dinner together, and afterward, as Jane began collecting the dishes from the table, I retrieved a few legal documents from my briefcase that I wished to review. Sitting in my office, I was perusing the first page when I noticed Jane standing in the doorway.

She was drying her hands on a dish towel, and her face registered a disappointment that I had learned to recognize over the years, if not fully understand.

"Is there anything you want to say?" she asked after a moment.

I hesitated, aware there was more to her question than its innocence implied. I thought perhaps that she was referring to a new hairstyle, but I looked carefully and her hair seemed no different from usual. I'd tried over the years to notice such things. Still, I was at a loss, and as we stood before each other, I knew I had to offer something.

"How was your day?" I finally asked.

She gave a strange half smile in response and turned away.

I know now what she was looking for, of course, but at the time, I shrugged it off and went back to work, chalking it up as another example of the mysteriousness of women.

Later that evening, I'd crawled into bed and was making myself comfortable when I heard Jane draw a single, rapid breath. She was lying on her side with her back toward me, and when I noticed that her shoulders were trembling, it suddenly struck me that she was crying. Baffled, I expected her to tell me what had upset her so, but instead of speaking, she offered another set of raspy inhales, as if trying to breathe through her own tears. My throat tightened instinctively, and I found myself growing frightened. I tried not to be scared; tried not to think that something bad had happened to her father or to the kids, or that she had been given terrible news by her doctor. I tried not to think that there might be a problem I couldn't solve, and I placed my hand on her back in the hope that I could somehow comfort her.

"What's wrong?" I asked.

It was a moment before she answered. I heard her sigh as she pulled the covers up to her shoulders.

"Happy anniversary," she whispered.

Twenty-nine years, I remembered too late, and in the corner of the room, I spotted the gifts she'd bought me, neatly wrapped and perched on the chest of drawers.

Quite simply, I had forgotten.

I make no excuses for this, nor would I even if I could. What would be the point? I apologized, of course, then apologized again the following morning; and later in the evening, when she opened the perfume I'd selected carefully with the help of a young lady at Belk's, she smiled and thanked me and patted my leg.

Sitting beside her on the couch, I knew I loved her then as much as I did the day we were married. But in looking at her, noticing perhaps for the first time the distracted way she glanced off to the side and the unmistakably sad tilt of her head—I suddenly realized that I wasn't quite sure whether she still loved me.

Chapter One

It's heartbreaking to think that your wife may not love you, and that night, after Jane had carried the perfume up to our bedroom, I sat on the couch for hours, wondering how this situation had come to pass. At first, I wanted to believe that Jane was simply reacting emotionally and that I was reading far more into the incident than it deserved. Yet the more I thought about it, the more I sensed not only her displeasure in an absentminded spouse, but the traces of an older melancholy—as if my lapse were simply the final blow in a long, long series of careless missteps.

Had the marriage turned out to be a disappointment for Jane? Though I didn't want to think so, her expression had answered otherwise, and I found myself wondering what that meant for us in the future. Was she questioning whether or not to stay with me? Was she pleased with her decision to have married me in the first place? These, I must add, were frightening questions to consider—with answers that were possibly even more frightening—for until that moment, I'd always assumed that Jane was as content with me as I'd always been with her.

What, I wondered, had led us to feel so differently about each other?

I suppose I must begin by saying that many people would consider our lives fairly ordinary. Like many men, I had the obligation to support the family financially, and my life was largely centered around my career. For the past thirty years, I've worked with the law firm of Ambry, Saxon and Tundle in New Bern, North Carolina, and my income—while not extravagant—was enough to place us firmly in the upper middle class. I enjoy golfing and gardening on the weekends, prefer classical music, and read the newspaper every morning. Though Jane was once an elementary school teacher, she spent the majority of our married life raising three children. She ran both the household and our social life, and her proudest possessions are the photo albums that she carefully assembled as a visual history of our lives. Our brick home is complete with a picket fence and automatic sprinklers, we own two cars, and we are members of both the Rotary Club and the Chamber of Commerce. In the course of our married life, we've saved for retirement, built a wooden swing set in the backyard that now sits unused, attended dozens of parent-teacher conferences, voted regularly, and contributed to the Episcopal church each and every Sunday. At fifty-six, I'm three years older than my wife.

Despite my feelings for Jane, I sometimes think we're an unlikely pair to have spent a life together. We're different in almost every way, and though opposites can and do attract, I've always felt that I made the better choice on our wedding day. Jane is, after all, the kind of person I always wished to be. While I tend toward stoicism and logic, Jane is outgoing and kind, with a natural empathy that endears her to others. She laughs easily and has a wide circle of

friends. Over the years, I've come to realize that most of
my friends are, in fact, the husbands of my wife's friends,
but I believe this is common for most married couples our
age. Yet I'm fortunate in that Jane has always seemed to
choose our friends with me in mind, and I'm appreciative
that there's always someone for me to visit with at a dinner
party. Had she not come into my life, I sometimes think
that I would have led the life of a monk.

There's more, too: I'm charmed by the fact that Jane
has always displayed her emotions with childlike ease.
When she's sad she cries; when she's happy she laughs;
and she enjoys nothing more than to be surprised with a
wonderful gesture. In those moments, there's an ageless
innocence about her, and though a surprise by definition
is unexpected, for Jane, the memories of a surprise can
arouse the same excited feelings for years afterward.
Sometimes when she's daydreaming, I'll ask her what she's
thinking about and she'll suddenly begin speaking in
giddy tones about something I've long forgotten. This, I
must say, has never ceased to amaze me.

While Jane has been blessed with the most tender of
hearts, in many ways she's stronger than I am. Her values and
beliefs, like those of most southern women, are grounded
by God and family; she views the world through a prism
of black and white, right and wrong. For Jane, hard decisions are reached instinctively—and are almost always
correct—while I, on the other hand, find myself weighing
endless options and frequently second-guessing myself.
And unlike me, my wife is seldom self-conscious. This lack
of concern about other people's perceptions requires a
confidence that I've always found elusive, and above all
else, I envy this about her.

I suppose that some of our differences stem from our

respective upbringings. While Jane was raised in a small town with three siblings and parents who adored her, I was raised in a town house in Washington, D.C., as the only child of government lawyers, and my parents were seldom home before seven o'clock in the evening. As a result, I spent much of my free time alone, and to this day, I'm most comfortable in the privacy of my den.

As I've already mentioned, we have three children, and though I love them dearly, they are for the most part the products of my wife. She bore them and raised them, and they are most comfortable with her. While I sometimes regret that I didn't spend as much time with them as I should have, I'm comforted by the thought that Jane more than made up for my absences. Our children, it seems, have turned out well despite me. They're grown now and living on their own, but we consider ourselves fortunate that only one has moved out of state. Our two daughters still visit us frequently, and my wife is careful to have their favorite foods in the refrigerator in case they're hungry, which they never seem to be. When they come, they talk with Jane for hours.

At twenty-seven, Anna is the oldest. With black hair and dark eyes, her looks reflected her saturnine personality growing up. She was a brooder who spent her teenage years locked in her room, listening to gloomy music and writing in a diary. She was a stranger to me back then; days might pass before she would say a single word in my presence, and I was at a loss to understand what I might have done to provoke this. Everything I said seemed to elicit only sighs or shakes of her head, and if I asked if anything was bothering her, she would stare at me as if the question were incomprehensible. My wife seemed to find nothing unusual in this, dismissing it as a phase typical of young

girls, but then again, Anna still talked to her. Sometimes I'd
pass by Anna's room and hear Anna and Jane whispering to
each other; but if they heard me outside the door, the
whispering would stop. Later, when I would ask Jane what
they'd been discussing, she'd shrug and wave a hand mysteriously, as if their only goal were to keep me in the dark.

Yet because she was my firstborn, Anna has always
been my favorite. This isn't an admission I would make to
anyone, but I think she knows it as well, and lately I've
come to believe that even in her silent years, she was
fonder of me than I realized. I can still remember times
when I'd be perusing trusts or wills in my den, and she'd
slip through the door. She'd pace around the room, scanning the bookshelves and reaching for various items, but if
I addressed her, she'd slip back out as quietly as she'd come
in. Over time, I learned not to say anything, and she'd
sometimes linger in the office for an hour, watching me as
I scribbled on yellow legal tablets. If I glanced toward her,
she'd smile complicitly, enjoying this game of ours. I have
no more understanding of it now than I did back then, but
it's ingrained in my memory as few images are.

Currently, Anna is working for the *Raleigh News and
Observer*, but I think she has dreams of becoming a novelist.
In college she majored in creative writing, and the stories
she wrote were as dark as her personality. I recall reading
one in which a young girl becomes a prostitute to care for
her sick father, a man who'd once molested her. When I
set the pages down, I wondered what I was supposed to
make of such a thing.

She is also madly in love. Anna, always careful and
deliberate in her choices, was highly selective when it
came to men, and thankfully Keith has always struck me
as someone who treats her well. He intends to be an

orthopedist and carries himself with a confidence that comes only to those who've faced few setbacks in life. I learned through Jane that for their first date Keith took Anna kite flying on the beach near Fort Macon. Later that week, when Anna brought him by the house, Keith came dressed in a sports coat, freshly showered and smelling faintly of cologne. As we shook hands, he held my gaze and impressed me by saying, "It's a pleasure to meet you, Mr. Lewis."

Joseph, our second-born, is a year younger than Anna. He's always called me "Pop," though no one else in our family has ever used that term, and again, we have little in common. He's taller and thinner than I, wears jeans to most social functions, and when he visits at Thanksgiving or Christmas, he eats only vegetables. While he was growing up, I thought him quiet, yet his reticence, like Anna's, seemed directed at me in particular. Others often remarked on his sense of humor, though to be honest, I seldom saw it. Whenever we spent time together, I often felt as if he were trying to form an impression of me.

Like Jane, he was empathetic even as a child. He chewed his fingernails worrying about others, and they've been nothing but nubs since he was five years old. Needless to say, when I suggested that he consider majoring in business or economics, he ignored my advice and chose sociology. He now works for a battered women's shelter in New York City, though he tells us nothing more about his job. I know he wonders about the choices I've made in my life, just as I wonder about his, yet despite our differences, it's with Joseph that I have the conversations that I always wished to have with my children when I held them as infants. He is highly intelligent; he received a near perfect score on his SATs, and his interests span the spectrum from the history of Middle Eastern dhimmitude to theoretical applications of fractal geometry. He is also honest—sometimes painfully so—and it goes without saying that these aspects of his personality leave me at a disadvantage when it comes to debating him. Though I sometimes grow frustrated at his stubbornness, it's during such moments that I'm especially proud to call him my son.

Leslie, the baby of our family, is currently studying biology and physiology at Wake Forest with the intention of becoming a veterinarian. Instead of coming home during the summers like most students, she takes additional classes with the intention of graduating early and spends her afternoons working at a place called Animal Farm. Of all our children, she is the most gregarious, and her laughter sounds the same as Jane's. Like Anna, she liked to visit me in my den, though she was happiest when I gave her my full attention. As a youngster, she liked to sit in my lap and pull on my ears; as she grew older, she liked to wander in and share funny jokes. My shelves are covered with the gifts she made me growing up: plaster casts of her handprints, drawings in crayon, a necklace made from macaroni. She was the easiest to love, the first in line for hugs or kisses from the grandparents, and she took great pleasure in curling up on the couch and watching romantic movies. I was not surprised when she was named the homecoming queen at her high school three years ago.

She is kind as well. Everyone in her class was always invited to her birthday parties for fear of hurting someone's feelings, and when she was nine, she once spent an afternoon walking from towel to towel at the beach because she'd found a discarded watch in the surf and wanted to return it to its owner. Of all my children, she has always caused me the least worry, and when she comes to visit, I drop whatever I'm doing to spend time with her. Her energy is infectious, and when we're together, I wonder how it is I could have been so blessed.

Now that they've all moved out, our home has changed. Where music once blared, there is nothing but stillness; while our pantry once shelved eight different types of sugared cereal, there is now a single brand that promises extra fiber. The furniture hasn't changed in the bedrooms where our children slept, but because the posters and bulletin boards have been taken down—as well as all other reminders of their personalities—there is nothing to differentiate one room from the next. But it was the emptiness of the house that seemed to dominate now; while our home was perfect for a family of five, it suddenly struck me as a cavernous reminder of the way things ought to be. I remember hoping that this change in the household had something to do with the way Jane was feeling.

Still, regardless of the reason, I couldn't deny that we were drifting apart, and the more I thought about it, the more I noticed how wide the gap between us had become. We'd started out as a couple and been changed into parents—something I had always viewed as normal and inevitable—but after twenty-nine years, it was as if we'd become strangers again. Only habit seemed to be keeping us together. Our lives had little in common; we rose at different hours, spent our days in different places, and followed our own routines in the evenings. I knew little of her daily activities and admitted to keeping parts of mine secret as well. I couldn't recall the last time Jane and I had talked about anything unexpected.

Two weeks after the forgotten anniversary, however, Jane and I did just that.

"Wilson," she said, "we have to talk."

I looked up at her. A bottle of wine stood on the table between us, our meal nearly finished.

"Yes?"

"I was thinking," she said, "of heading up to New York to spend some time with Joseph."

"Won't he be here for the holidays?"

"That's not for a couple of months. And since he didn't make it home this summer, I thought it might be nice to visit him for a change."

In the back of my mind, I noted that it might do us some good as a couple to get away for a few days. Perhaps that had even been the reason for Jane's suggestion, and with a smile, I reached for my wineglass. "That's a good idea," I agreed. "We haven't been to New York since he first moved there."

Jane smiled briefly before lowering her gaze to her plate. "There's something else, too."

"Yes?"

"Well, it's just that you're pretty busy at work, and I know how hard it is for you to get away."

"I think I can clear up my schedule for a few days," I said, already mentally leafing through my work calendar. It would be tough, but I could do it. "When did you want to go?"

"Well, that's the thing . . . ," she said.

"What's the thing?"

"Wilson, please let me finish," she said. She drew a long breath, not bothering to hide the weariness in her tone. "What I was trying to say was that I think I might like to visit him by myself."

For a moment, I didn't know what to say.

"You're upset, aren't you," she said.

"No," I said quickly. "He's our son. How could I get upset about that?" To underscore my equanimity, I used my knife to cut another bite of meat. "So when were you thinking about heading up there?" I asked.

"Next week," she said. "On Thursday."

"Thursday?"

"I already have my ticket."

Though she wasn't quite finished with her meal, she rose and headed for the kitchen. By the way she avoided my gaze, I suspected she had something else to say but wasn't quite sure how to phrase it. A moment later, I was alone at the table. If I turned, I could just see her face in profile as she stood near the sink.

"Sounds like it'll be fun," I called out with what I hoped sounded like nonchalance. "And I know Joseph will enjoy it, too. Maybe there's a show or something that you could see while you're up there."

"Maybe," I heard her say. "I guess it depends on his schedule."

Hearing the faucet run, I rose from my seat and brought my dishes to the sink. Jane said nothing as I approached.

"It should be a wonderful weekend," I added.

She reached for my plate and began to rinse.

"Oh, about that . . . ," she said.

"Yes?"

"I was thinking about staying up there for more than just the weekend."

At her words, I felt my shoulders tense. "How long are you planning to stay?" I asked.

She set my plate off to the side.

"A couple of weeks," she answered.

Of course, I didn't blame Jane for the path our marriage seemed to have taken. Somehow I knew I bore a greater portion of the responsibility, even if I hadn't yet put together all the pieces of why and how. For starters, I have to admit that I've never been quite the person my wife wanted me to be, even from the beginning of our marriage. I know, for instance, that she wished I were more romantic, the way her own father had been with her mother. Her father was the kind of man who would hold his wife's hand in the hours after dinner or spontaneously pick a bouquet of wildflowers on his way home from work. Even as a child, Jane was enthralled by her parents' romance. Over the years, I've heard her speaking with her sister Kate on the phone, wondering aloud why I seemed to find romance such a difficult concept. It isn't that I haven't made attempts, I just don't seem to have an understanding of what it takes to make another's heart start fluttering. Neither hugs nor kisses were common in the house where I'd grown up, and displaying affection often left me feeling uncomfortable, especially in the presence of my children. I talked to Jane's father about it once, and he suggested that I write a letter to my wife. "Tell her why you love her," he said, "and give specific reasons." This was twelve years ago. I remember trying to take his advice, but as my hand hovered over the paper, I couldn't seem to find the appropriate words. Eventually I put the pen aside. Unlike her father, I have never been comfortable discussing feelings. I'm steady, yes. Dependable, absolutely. Faithful, without a doubt. But romance, I hate to admit, is as foreign to me as giving birth.

I sometimes wonder how many other men are exactly like me.

While Jane was in New York, Joseph answered the phone when I called.

"Hey, Pop," he said simply.

"Hey," I said. "How are you?"

"Fine," he said. After what seemed like a painfully long moment, he asked, "And you?"

I shifted my weight from one foot to the other. "It's quiet around here, but I'm doing okay." I paused. "How's your mom's visit going?"

"It's fine. I've been keeping her busy."

"Shopping and sightseeing?"

"A little. Mainly we've been doing a lot of talking. It's been interesting."

I hesitated. Though I wondered what he meant, Joseph seemed to feel no need to elaborate. "Oh," I said, doing my best to keep my voice light. "Is she around?"

"Actually, she isn't. She ran out to the grocery store. She'll be back in a few minutes, though, if you want to call back."

"No, that's okay," I said. "Just let her know that I called. I should be around all night if she wants to give me a ring."

"Will do," he agreed. Then, after a moment: "Hey, Pop? I wanted to ask you something."

"Yes?"

"Did you really forget your anniversary?"

I took a long breath. "Yes," I said, "I did."

"How come?"

"I don't know," I said. "I remembered that it was coming, but when the day arrived, it just slipped my mind. I don't have an excuse."

"It hurt her feelings," he said.

"I know."

There was a moment of silence on the other end. "Do you understand why?" he finally asked.

Though I didn't answer Joseph's question, I thought I did.

Quite simply, Jane didn't want us to end up like the elderly couples we sometimes saw when dining out, couples that have always aroused our pity.

These couples are, I should make clear, usually polite to each other. The husband might pull out a chair or collect the jackets, the wife might suggest one of the specials. And when the waiter comes, they may punctuate each other's orders with the knowledge that has been gained over a lifetime—no salt on the eggs or extra butter on the toast, for instance.

But then, once the order is placed, not a word passes between them.

Instead, they sip their drinks and glance out the window, waiting silently for their food to arrive. Once it does, they might speak to the waiter for a moment—to request a refill of coffee, for instance—but they quickly retreat to their own worlds as soon as he departs. And throughout the meal, they will sit like strangers who happen to be sharing the same table, as if they believed that the enjoyment of each other's company was more effort than it was worth.

Perhaps this is an exaggeration on my part of what their lives are really like, but I've occasionally wondered what brought these couples to this point.

While Jane was in New York, however, I was suddenly struck by the notion that we might be heading there as well.

When I picked Jane up from the airport, I remember feeling strangely nervous. It was an odd feeling, and I was relieved to see a flicker of a smile as she walked through the gate and made her way toward me. When she was close, I reached for her carry-on.

"How was your trip?" I asked.

"It was good," she said. "I have no idea why Joseph likes living there so much. It's so busy and noisy all the time. I couldn't do it."

"Glad you're home, then?"

"Yes," she said. "I am. But I'm tired."

"I'll bet. Trips are always tiring."

For a moment, neither of us said anything. I moved her carry-on to my other hand. "How's Joseph doing?" I asked.

"He's good. I think he's put on a little weight since the last time he was here."

"Anything exciting going on with him that you didn't mention on the phone?"

"Not really," she said. "He works too much, but that's about it."

In her tone I heard a hint of sadness, one that I didn't quite understand. As I considered it, I saw a young couple with their arms around each other, hugging as if they hadn't seen each other in years.

"I'm glad you're home," I said.

She glanced at me, held my eyes, then slowly turned toward the luggage carousel. "I know you are."

This was our state of affairs one year ago.

I wish I could tell you that things improved in the weeks immediately following Jane's trip, but they did not. Instead, our life went on as it had before; we led our separate lives, and one unmemorable day passed into the next. Jane wasn't exactly angry with me, but she didn't seem happy, either, and try as I might, I was at a loss as to what to do about it. It seemed as though a wall of indifference had somehow been constructed between us without my being aware of it. By late autumn, three months after the forgotten anniversary, I'd become so worried about our relationship that I knew I had to talk to her father.

His name is Noah Calhoun, and if you knew him, you would understand why I went to see him that day. He and his wife, Allie, had moved to Creekside Extended Care Facility nearly eleven years earlier, in their forty-sixth year of marriage. Though they once shared a bed, Noah now sleeps alone, and I wasn't surprised when I found his room empty. Most days, when I went to visit him, he was seated on a bench near the pond, and I remember moving to the window to make sure he was there.

Even from a distance, I recognized him easily: the white tufts of hair lifting slightly in the wind, his stooped posture, the light blue cardigan sweater that Kate had recently knitted for him. He was eighty-seven years old, a widower with hands that had curled with arthritis, and his health was precarious. He carried a vial of nitroglycerin pills in his pocket and suffered from prostate cancer, but the doctors were more concerned with his mental state. They'd sat Jane and me down in the office a few years earlier and eyed us gravely. He's been suffering from delusions, they informed us, and the delusions seem to be getting worse. For my part, I wasn't so sure. I thought I knew him better than most people, and certainly better than the doctors. With the exception of Jane, he was my dearest friend, and when I saw his solitary figure, I couldn't help but ache for all that he had lost.

His own marriage had come to an end five years earlier, but cynics would say it had ended long before that. Allie suffered from Alzheimer's in the final years of her life, and I've come to believe it's an intrinsically evil disease. It's a slow unraveling of all that a person once was. What are we, after all, without our memories, without our dreams? Watching the progression was like watching a slow-motion picture of an inevitable tragedy. It was difficult for Jane and me to visit Allie; Jane wanted to remember her mother as she once was, and I never pressed her to go, for it was painful for me as well. For Noah, however, it was the hardest of all.

But that's another story.

Leaving his room, I made my way to the courtyard. The morning was cool, even for autumn. The leaves were brilliant in the slanting sunshine, and the air carried the faint scent of chimney smoke. This, I remembered, was Allie's favorite time of year, and I felt his loneliness as I approached. As usual, he was feeding the swan, and when I reached his side, I put a grocery bag on the ground. In it were three loaves of Wonder Bread. Noah always had me purchase the same items when I came to visit.

"Hello, Noah," I said. I knew I could call him "Dad," as Jane had with my father, but I've never felt comfortable with this and Noah has never seemed to mind.

At the sound of my voice, Noah turned his head.

"Hello, Wilson," he said. "Thanks for dropping by."

I rested a hand on his shoulder. "Are you doing okay?"

"Could be better," he said. Then, with a mischievous grin: "Could be worse, though, too."

These were the words we always exchanged in greeting. He patted the bench and I took a seat next to him. I stared out over the pond. Fallen leaves resembled a kaleidoscope as they floated on the surface of the water. The glassy surface mirrored the cloudless sky.

"I've come to ask you something," I said.

"Yes?" As he spoke, Noah tore off a piece of bread and tossed it into the water. The swan bobbed its beak toward it and straightened its neck to swallow.

"It's about Jane," I added.

"Jane," he murmured. "How is she?"

"Good." I nodded, shifting awkwardly. "She'll be coming by later, I suppose." This was true. For the past few years, we've visited him frequently, sometimes together, sometimes alone. I wondered if they spoke of me in my absence.

"And the kids?"

"They're doing well, too. Anna's writing features now, and Joseph finally found a new apartment. It's in Queens, I think, but right near the subway. Leslie's going camping in the mountains with friends this weekend. She told us she aced her midterms."

He nodded, his eyes never leaving the swan. "You're very lucky, Wilson," he said. "I hope you realize how fortunate you are that they've become such wonderful adults."

"I do," I said.

We fell into silence. Up close, the lines in his face formed crevices, and I could see the veins pulsing below the thinning skin of his hands. Behind us, the grounds were empty, the chilly air keeping people inside.

"I forgot our anniversary," I said.

"Oh?"

"Twenty-nine years," I added.

"Mmm."

Behind us, I could hear dried leaves rattling in the breeze.

"I'm worried about us," I finally admitted.

Noah glanced at me. At first I thought he would ask me why I was worried, but instead he squinted, trying to read my face. Then, turning away, he tossed another piece of bread to the swan. When he spoke, his voice was soft and low, an aging baritone tempered by a southern accent.

"Do you remember when Allie got sick? When I used to read to her?"

"Yes," I answered, feeling the memory pull at me. He used to read to her from a notebook that he'd written before they moved to Creekside. The notebook held the story of how he and Allie had fallen in love, and sometimes after he read it aloud to her, Allie would become momentarily lucid, despite the ravages of Alzheimer's. The lucidity never lasted long—and as the disease progressed further, it ceased completely—but when it happened, Allie's improvement was dramatic enough for specialists to travel from Chapel Hill to Creekside in the hopes of understanding it. That reading to Allie sometimes worked, there was no doubt. Why it worked, however, was something the specialists were never able to figure out.

"Do you know why I did that?" he asked.

I brought my hands to my lap. "I believe so," I answered. "It helped Allie. And because she made you promise you would."

"Yes," he said, "that's true." He paused, and I could hear him wheezing, the sound like air through an old accordion. "But that wasn't the only reason I did it. I also did it for me. A lot of folks didn't understand that."

Though he trailed off, I knew he wasn't finished, and I said nothing. In the silence, the swan stopped circling and moved closer. Except for a black spot the size of a silver dollar on its chest, the swan was the color of ivory. It seemed to hover in place when Noah began speaking again.

"Do you know what I most remember about the good days?" he asked.

I knew he was referring to those rare days when Allie recognized him, and I shook my head. "No," I answered.

"Falling in love," he said. "That's what I remember. On her good days, it was like we were just starting out all over again."

He smiled. "That's what I mean when I say that I did it for me. Every time I read to her, it was like I was courting her, because sometimes, just sometimes, she would fall in love with me again, just like she had a long time ago. And that's the most wonderful feeling in the world. How many people are ever given that chance? To have someone you love fall in love with you over and over?"

Noah didn't seem to expect an answer, and I didn't offer one.

Instead, we spent the next hour discussing the children and his health. We did not speak of Jane or Allie again. After I left, however, I thought about our visit. Despite the doctors' worries, Noah seemed as sharp as ever. He had not only known that I would be coming to see him, I realized, but had anticipated the reason for my visit. And in typical southern fashion, he'd given me the answer to my problem, without my ever having had to ask him directly.

It was then that I knew what I had to do.

Chapter Two

$\mathscr{I}$ had to court my wife again.

It sounds so simple, doesn't it? What could be easier? There were, after all, certain advantages to a situation like ours. For one thing, Jane and I live in the same house, and after three decades together, it's not as though we had to start over. We could dispense with the family histories, the humorous anecdotes from our childhoods, the questions of what we did for a living and whether or not our goals were compatible. Furthermore, the surprises that individuals tend to keep hidden in the early stages of a relationship were already out in the open. My wife, for instance, already knew that I snore, so there was no reason to hide something like that from her. For my part, I've seen her when she's been sick with the flu, and it makes no difference to me how her hair looks when she gets up in the morning.

Given those practical realities, I assumed that winning Jane's love again would be relatively easy. I would simply try to re-create what we had had in our early years together—as Noah had done for Allie by reading to her.

Yet upon further reflection, I slowly came to the realization that I'd never really understood what she saw in me in the first place. Though I think of myself as responsible, this was not the sort of trait women considered attractive back then. I was, after all, a baby boomer, a child of the hang-loose, me-first generation.

It was 1971 when I saw Jane for the first time. I was twenty-four, in my second year of law school at Duke University, and most people would have considered me a serious student, even as an undergraduate. I never had a roommate for more than a single term, since I often studied late into the evenings with the lamp blazing. Most of my former roommates seemed to view college as a world of weekends separated by boring classes, while I viewed college as preparation for the future.

While I'll admit that I was serious, Jane was the first to call me shy. We met one Saturday morning at a coffee shop downtown. It was early November, and due to my responsibilities at the *Law Review*, my classes seemed particularly challenging. Anxious about falling behind in my studies, I'd driven to a coffee shop, hoping to find a place to study where I wouldn't be recognized or interrupted.

It was Jane who approached the table and took my order, and even now, I can recall that moment vividly. She wore her dark hair in a ponytail, and her chocolate eyes were set off by the hint of olive in her skin. She was wearing a dark blue apron over a sky blue dress, and I was struck by the easy way she smiled at me, as if she were pleased that I had chosen to sit in her section. When she asked for my order, I heard the southern drawl characteristic of eastern North Carolina.

I didn't know then that we would eventually have dinner together, but I remember going back the following day and requesting the same table. She smiled when I sat down, and I can't deny that I was pleased that she seemed to remember me. These weekend visits went on for about a month, during which we never struck up a conversation or asked each other's names, but I soon noticed that my mind began to wander every time she approached the table to refill my coffee. For a reason I can't quite explain, she seemed always to smell of cinnamon.

To be honest, I wasn't completely comfortable as a young man with those of the opposite sex. In high school, I was neither an athlete nor a member of the student council, the two most popular groups. I was, however, quite fond of chess and started a club that eventually grew to eleven members. Unfortunately, none of them were female. Despite my lack of experience, I had managed to go out with about half a dozen women during my undergraduate years and enjoyed their company on those evenings out. But because I'd made the decision not to pursue a relationship until I was financially ready to do so, I didn't get to know any of these women well and they quickly slipped from my mind.

Yet frequently after leaving the coffee shop, I found myself thinking of the ponytailed waitress, often when I least expected it. More than once, my mind drifted during class, and I would imagine her moving through the lecture hall, wearing her blue apron and offering menus. These images embarrassed me, but even so, I was unable to prevent them from recurring.

I have no idea where all of this would have led had she not finally taken the initiative. I had spent most of the morning studying amid the clouds of cigarette smoke that drifted from other booths in the diner when it began to pour. It was a cold, driving rain, a storm that had drifted in from the mountains. I had, of course, brought an umbrella with me in anticipation of such an event.

When she approached the table I looked up, expecting a refill for my coffee, but noticed instead that her apron was tucked beneath her arm. She removed the ribbon from her ponytail, and her hair cascaded to her shoulders.

"Would you mind walking me to my car?" she asked. "I noticed your umbrella and I'd rather not get wet."

It was impossible to refuse her request, so I collected my things, then held the door open for her, and together we walked through puddles as deep as pie tins. Her shoulder brushed my own, and as we splashed across the street in the pouring rain, she shouted her name and mentioned the fact that she was attending Meredith, a college for women. She was majoring in English, she added, and hoped to teach school after she graduated. I didn't offer much in response, concentrating as I was on keeping her dry. When we reached her car, I expected her to get in immediately, but instead she turned to face me.

"You're kind of shy, aren't you," she said.

I wasn't quite sure how to respond, and I think she saw this in my expression, for she laughed almost immediately.

"It's okay, Wilson. I happen to like shy."

That she had somehow taken the initiative to learn my name should have struck me then, but it did not. Instead, as she stood on the street with the rain coming down and mascara running onto her cheeks, all I could think was that I'd never seen anyone more beautiful.

My wife is still beautiful.

Of course, it's a softer beauty now, one that has deepened with age. Her skin is delicate to the touch, and there are wrinkles where it once was smooth. Her hips have become rounder, her stomach a little fuller, but I still find myself filled with longing when I see her undressing in the bedroom.

We've made love infrequently these last few years, and when we did, it lacked the spontaneity and excitement we'd enjoyed in the past. But it wasn't the lovemaking itself I missed most. What I craved was the long-absent look of desire in Jane's eyes or a simple touch or gesture that let me know she wanted me as much as I longed for her. Something, anything, that would signal I was still special to her.

But how, I wondered, was I supposed to make this happen? Yes, I knew that I had to court Jane again, but I realized that this was not as easy as I'd originally thought it would be. Our thorough familiarity, which I first imagined would simplify things, actually made things more challenging. Our dinner conversations, for instance, were stilted by routine. For a few weeks after talking to Noah, I actually spent part of my afternoons at the office coming up with new topics for later discussion, but when I brought them up, they always seemed forced and would soon fizzle out. As always, we returned to discussions of the children or my law firm's clients and employees.

Our life together, I began to realize, had settled into a pattern that was not conducive to renewing any kind of passion. For years we'd adopted separate schedules to accommodate our mostly separate duties. In the early years of our family's life, I spent long hours at the firm— including evenings and weekends—making sure that I would be viewed as a worthy partner when the time came. I never used all my allotted vacation time. Perhaps I was overzealous in my determination to impress Ambry and Saxon, but with a growing family to provide for, I didn't want to take any chances. I now realize that the pursuit of success at work combined with my natural reticence kept me at arm's length from the rest of the family, and I've come to believe that I've always been something of an outsider in my own house.

While I was busy in my own world, Jane had her hands full with the children. As their activities and demands grew more numerous, it sometimes seemed that she was a blur of harried activity who merely rushed past me in the hallways. There were years, I had to admit, in which we ate dinner separately more often than together, and though occasionally it struck me as odd, I did nothing to change this.

Perhaps we became used to this way of life, but once the children were no longer there to govern our lives, we seemed powerless to fill in the empty spaces between us. And despite my concern about the state of our relationship, the sudden attempt to change our routines was akin to tunneling through limestone with a spoon.

This is not to say I didn't try. In January, for instance, I bought a cookbook and took to preparing meals on Saturday evenings for the two of us; some of them, I might add, were quite original and delicious. In addition to my regular golf game, I began walking through our neighborhood three mornings a week, hoping to lose a bit of weight. I even spent a few afternoons in the bookstore, browsing the self-help section, hoping to learn what else I could do. The experts' advice on improving a marriage? To focus on the four As—attention, appreciation, affection, and attraction. Yes, I remember thinking, that makes perfect sense, so I turned my efforts in those directions. I spent more time with Jane in the evenings instead of working in my den, I complimented her frequently, and when she spoke of her daily activities, I listened carefully and nodded when appropriate to let her know she had my full attention.

I was under no illusions that any of these remedies would magically restore Jane's passion for me, nor did I take a short-term view of the matter. If it had taken twenty-nine years to drift apart, I knew that a few weeks of effort was simply the beginning of a long process of rapprochement. Yet even if things were improving slightly, the progress was slower than I'd hoped. By late spring, I came to the conclusion that in addition to these daily changes, I needed to do something else, something dramatic, something to show Jane that she was still, and always would be, the most important person in my life. Then, late one evening, as I found myself glancing through our family albums, an idea began to take hold.

I awoke the next day filled with energy and good intentions. I knew my plan would have to be carried out secretly and methodically, and the first thing I did was to rent a post office box. I didn't progress much further on my plans right away, however, for it was around this time that Noah had a stroke.

It was not the first stroke he'd had, but it was his most serious. He was in the hospital for nearly eight weeks, during which time my wife's attention was devoted fully to his care. She spent every day at the hospital, and in the evenings she was too tired and upset to notice my efforts to renew our relationship. Noah was eventually able to return to Creekside and was soon feeding the swan at the pond again, but I think it drove home the point that he wouldn't be around much longer. I spent many hours quietly soothing Jane's tears and simply comforting her.

Of all I did during that year, it was this, I think, that she appreciated most of all. Perhaps it was the steadiness I provided, or maybe it really was the result of my efforts over the last few months, but whatever it was, I began to notice occasional displays of newfound warmth from Jane. Though they were infrequent, I savored them desperately, hoping that our relationship was somehow back on track.

Thankfully, Noah continued to improve, and by early August, the year of the forgotten anniversary was coming to a close. I'd lost nearly twenty pounds since I'd begun my neighborhood strolls, and I'd developed the habit of swinging by the post office box daily to collect items I'd solicited from others. I worked on my special project while I was at the office to keep it a secret from Jane. Additionally, I'd decided to take off the two weeks surrounding our thirtieth anniversary—the longest vacation I'd ever taken from work—with the intention of spending time with Jane. Considering what I'd done the year before, I wanted this anniversary to be as memorable as possible.

Then, on the evening of Friday, August 15—my first night of vacation and exactly eight days before our anniversary—something happened that neither Jane nor I would ever forget.

We were both relaxing in the living room. I was seated in my favorite armchair, reading a biography of Theodore Roosevelt, while my wife was leafing through the pages of a catalog. Suddenly Anna burst through the front door. At the time, she was still living in New Bern, but she had recently put down a deposit on an apartment in Raleigh and would be moving in a couple of weeks to join Keith for the first year of his residency at Duke Medical School.

Despite the heat, Anna was wearing black. Both ears were double pierced, and her lipstick seemed at least a few shades too dark. By this time, I had grown used to the gothic flairs of her personality, but when she sat across from us, I saw again how much she resembled her mother. Her face was flushed, and she brought her hands together as if trying to steady herself.

"Mom and Dad," she said, "I have something to tell you."

Jane sat up and set the catalog aside. I knew she could tell from Anna's voice that something serious was coming. The last time Anna had acted like this, she'd informed us that she would be moving in with Keith.

I know, I know. But she was an adult, and what could I do?

"What is it, honey?" Jane asked.

Anna looked from Jane to me and back to Jane again before taking a deep breath.

"I'm getting married," she said.

I've come to believe that children live for the satisfaction of surprising their parents, and Anna's announcement was no exception.

In fact, everything associated with having children has been surprising. There's a common lament that the first year of marriage is the hardest, but for Jane and myself, this was not true. Nor was the seventh year, the year of the supposed itch, the most difficult.

No, for us—aside from the past few years, perhaps—the most challenging years were those that followed the births of our children. There seems to be a misconception, especially among those couples who've yet to have kids, that the first year of a child's life resembles a Hallmark commercial, complete with cooing babies and smiling, calm parents.

In contrast, my wife still refers to that period as "the hateful years." She says this tongue-in-cheek, of course, but I strongly doubt she wants to relive them any more than I do.

By "hateful," what Jane meant was this: There were moments when she hated practically everything. She hated how she looked and how she felt. She hated women whose breasts didn't ache and women who still fit into their clothes. She hated how oily her skin became and hated the pimples that appeared for the first time since adolescence. But it was the lack of sleep that raised her ire most of all, and consequently, nothing irritated her more than hearing stories of other mothers whose infants slept through the night within weeks of leaving the hospital. In fact, she hated *everyone* who had the opportunity to sleep more than three hours at a stretch, and there were times, it seemed, that she even hated me for my role in all this. After all, I couldn't breast-feed, and because of my long hours at the law firm, I had no choice but to sleep in the guest room occasionally so I could function at the office the next day. Though I'm certain that she understood this intellectually, it often didn't seem that way.

"Good morning," I might say when I saw her staggering into the kitchen. "How did the baby sleep?"

Instead of answering, she would sigh impatiently as she moved toward the coffeepot.

"Up a lot?" I'd ask tentatively.

"You wouldn't last a week."

On cue, the baby would start to cry. Jane would grit her teeth, slam her coffee cup down, and look as if she wondered why it was that God seemed to hate her so.

In time, I learned it was wiser not to say anything.

Then, of course, there is the fact that having a child transforms the basic marriage relationship. No longer are you simply husband and wife, you are mother and father as well, and all spontaneity vanishes immediately. Going out to dinner? Have to find out whether her parents can watch the baby, or if another sitter is available. New movie playing at the theater? Haven't seen one of these in over a year. Weekend getaways? Couldn't even conceive of them. There was no time to do those things that had encouraged us to fall in love in the first place—walking and talking and spending time alone—and this was difficult for both of us.

This is not to say that the first year was entirely miserable. When people ask me what it's like to be a parent, I say that it's among the hardest things you'll ever do, but in exchange, it teaches you the meaning of unconditional love. Everything a baby does strikes a parent as the most magical thing he or she has ever seen. I'll always remember the day each of my children first smiled at me; I remember clapping and watching the tears spill down Jane's face as they took their first steps; and there is nothing quite as peaceful as holding a sleeping child in the comfort of your arms and wondering how it's possible to care so deeply. Those are the moments that I find myself remembering in vivid detail now. The challenges—though I can speak of them dispassionately—are nothing but distant and foggy images, more akin to a dream than reality.

No, there's no experience quite like having children, and despite the challenges we once faced, I've considered myself blessed because of the family we created.

As I said, however, I've just learned to be prepared for surprises.

At Anna's statement, Jane jumped up from the couch with a squeal and immediately wrapped Anna in her arms. She and I were both very fond of Keith. When I offered my congratulations and a hug, Anna responded with a cryptic smile.

"Oh, honey," Jane repeated, "this is just wonderful! . . . How did he ask you? . . . When? . . . I want to hear all about it. . . . Let me see the ring. . . ."

After the burst of questions, I could see my wife's face fall when Anna began shaking her head.

"It's not going to be that kind of wedding, Mom. We already live together, and neither of us wants to make a big deal about this. It's not like we need another blender or salad bowl."

Her statement didn't surprise me. Anna, as I've mentioned, has always done things her own way.

"Oh . . . ," Jane said, but before she could say anything more, Anna reached for her hand.

"There's something else, Mom. It's kind of important."

Anna glanced warily from me to Jane again.

"The thing is . . . well, you know how Grampa's doing, right?"

We nodded. Like all my children, Anna had always been close to Noah.

"And with his stroke and all . . . well, Keith has really enjoyed getting to know him and I love him more than anything . . ."

She paused. Jane squeezed her hand, urging her to continue.

"Well, we want to get married while he's still healthy, and none of us knows how long he really has. So Keith and I got to talking about possible dates, and with him heading off to Duke in a couple of weeks for his residency and the fact that I'm moving, too, and then Grampa's health . . . well, we wondered if you two wouldn't mind if . . ."

She trailed off, her gaze finally settling on Jane.

"Yes," Jane whispered.

Anna drew a long breath. "We were thinking about getting married next Saturday."

Jane's mouth formed a small O. Anna continued speaking, clearly anxious to get the rest out before we could interrupt.

"I know it's your anniversary—and it's okay if you say no, of course—but we both think it would be a wonderful way to honor the two of you. For everything you've done for each other, for everything you've done for me. And it seems like the best way. I mean, we want something easy, like a justice of the peace at the courthouse and maybe dinner with the family. We don't want gifts or anything fancy. Would you mind?"

As soon as I saw Jane's face, I knew what her answer would be.

Chapter Three

Like Anna, Jane and I didn't have a long engagement. After graduating from law school, I'd started as an associate at Ambry and Saxon, for Joshua Tundle had not yet been made partner. He was, like me, an associate, and our offices were across the hall from each other. Originally from Pollocksville—a small hamlet twelve miles south of New Bern—he'd attended East Carolina University, and during my first year at the firm, he often asked me how I was adapting to life in a small town. It wasn't, I confessed, exactly what I'd imagined. Even in law school, I'd always assumed that I would work in a large city as my parents had, yet I ended up accepting a job in the town where Jane had been raised.

I'd moved here for her, but I can't say I've ever regretted my decision. New Bern may not have a university or research park, but what it lacks in size, it makes up for in character. It's located ninety miles southeast of Raleigh in flat, low country amid forests of loblolly pines and wide, slow-moving rivers. The brackish waters of the Neuse River wash the edges of the town and seem to change color almost hourly, from gunmetal gray at dawn, to blue on sunny afternoons, and then to brown as the sun begins to set. At night, it's a swirl of liquid coal.

My office is downtown near the historic district, and after lunch, I'll sometimes stroll by the old homes. New Bern was founded in 1710 by Swiss and Palatine settlers, making it the second oldest town in North Carolina. When I first moved here, a great many of the historic homes were dilapidated and abandoned. This has changed in the last thirty years. One by one, new owners began to restore these residences to their former glory, and nowadays, a sidewalk tour leaves one with the feeling that renewal is possible in times and places we least expect. Those interested in architecture can find handblown glass in the windows, antique brass fixtures on the doors, and hand-carved wainscoting that complements the heart-pine floor inside. Graceful porches face the narrow streets, harkening back to a time when people sat outside in the early evenings to catch a stray breeze. The streets are shaded with oaks and dogwoods, and thousands of azaleas bloom every spring. It is, quite simply, one of the most beautiful places I've ever seen.

Jane was raised on the outskirts of town in a former plantation house built nearly two hundred years earlier. Noah had restored it in the years following World War II; he was meticulous in the work he did, and like many of the other historic homes in town, it retains a look of grandeur that has only grown with the passage of time.

Sometimes I visit the old home. I'll drop by after finishing at work or on my way to the store; other times I make a special trip. This is one of my secrets, for Jane doesn't know I do this. While I'm certain she wouldn't mind, there's a hidden pleasure in keeping these visits to myself. Coming here makes me feel both mysterious and fraternal, for I know that everyone has secrets, including my wife. As I gaze out over the property, I frequently wonder what hers might be.

Only one person knows about my visits. His name is Harvey Wellington, and he's a black man about my age who lives in a small clapboard house on the adjacent property. One or more members of his family have lived in the home since before the turn of the century, and I know he's a reverend at the local Baptist church. He'd always been close to everyone in Jane's family, especially Jane, but since Allie and Noah moved to Creekside, most of our communication has taken the form of the Christmas cards we exchange annually. I've seen him standing on the sagging porch of his house when I visit, but because of the distance, it's impossible to know what he's thinking when he sees me.

I seldom go inside Noah's house. It's been boarded up since Noah and Allie moved to Creekside, and the furniture is covered, like sheeted ghosts on Halloween. Instead, I prefer to walk the grounds. I shuffle along the gravel drive; I walk the fence line, touching posts; I head around to the rear of the house, where the river passes by. The river is narrower at the house than it is downtown, and there are moments when the water is absolutely still, a mirror reflecting the sky. Sometimes I stand at the edge of the dock, watching the sky in the water's reflection, and listen to the breeze as it gently moves the leaves overhead.

Occasionally I find myself standing beneath the trellis that Noah built after his marriage. Allie had always loved flowers, and Noah planted a rose garden in the shape of concentric hearts that was visible from the bedroom window and surrounded a formal, three-tiered fountain. He'd also installed a series of floodlights that made it possible to see the blooms even in the darkness, and the effect was dazzling. The hand-carved trellis led to the garden, and because Allie was an artist, both had appeared in a number of her paintings—paintings that for some reason always seemed to convey a hint of sadness despite their beauty. Now, the rose garden is untended and wild, the trellis is aged and cracking, but I'm still moved when I stand before them. As with his work on the house, Noah put great effort into making both the garden and the trellis unique; I often reach out to trace the carvings or simply stare at the roses, hoping perhaps to absorb the talents that have always eluded me.

I come here because this place is special to me. It was here, after all, that I first realized I was in love with Jane, and while I know my life was bettered because of it, I must admit that even now I'm mystified by how it happened.

I certainly had no intention of falling for Jane when I walked her to her car on that rainy day in 1971. I barely knew her, but as I stood beneath the umbrella and watched her drive away, I was suddenly certain that I wanted to see her again. Hours later, while studying that evening, her words continued to echo through my mind.

It's okay, Wilson, she had said. *I happen to like shy.*

Unable to concentrate, I set my book aside and rose from the desk. I had neither the time nor the desire for a relationship, I told myself, and after pacing around the room and reflecting on my hectic schedule—as well as my desire to be financially independent—I made the decision not to go back to the diner. This wasn't an easy decision, but it was the right one, I thought, and resolved to think no more on the subject.

The following week, I studied in the library, but I would be lying if I said I didn't see Jane. Each and every night, I found myself reliving our brief encounter: her cascading hair, the lilt of her voice, her patient gaze as we stood in the rain. Yet the more I forced myself not to think of her, the more powerful the images became. I knew then that my resolve wouldn't last a second week, and on Saturday morning, I found myself reaching for my keys.

I didn't go to the diner to ask her out. Rather, I went to prove to myself that it had been nothing more than a momentary infatuation. She was just an ordinary girl, I told myself, and when I saw her, I would see that she was nothing special. I'd almost convinced myself of that by the time I parked the car.

As always, the diner was crowded, and I wove through a departing group of men as I made my way to my regular booth. The table had been recently wiped, and after taking a seat, I used a paper napkin to dry it before opening my textbook.

With my head bowed, I was turning to the appropriate chapter when I realized she was approaching. I pretended not to notice until she stopped at the table, but when I looked up, it wasn't Jane. Instead, it was a woman in her forties. An order pad was in her apron, and a pen was tucked behind her ear.

"Would you like some coffee this morning?" she asked. She had a briskly efficient demeanor that suggested she'd probably worked here for years, and I wondered why I hadn't noticed her before.

"Yes, please."

"Back in a minute," she chirped, dropping off a menu. As soon as she turned away, I glanced around the diner and spotted Jane carrying plates from the kitchen to a group of tables near the far end of the diner. I watched her for a moment, wondering if she'd noticed that I'd come in, but she was focused on her work and didn't look my way. From a distance, there was nothing magical in the way she stood and moved, and I found myself breathing a sigh of relief, convinced that I'd shaken off the strange fascination that had plagued me so much of late.

My coffee arrived and I placed my order. Absorbed in my textbook again, I had read through half a page when I heard her voice beside me.

"Hi, Wilson."

Jane smiled when I looked up. "I didn't see you last weekend," she went on easily. "I thought I must have scared you away."

I swallowed, unable to speak, thinking that she was even prettier than I remembered. I don't know how long I stared without saying anything, but it was long enough for her face to take on a concerned expression.

"Wilson?" she asked. "Are you okay?"

"Yes," I said, but strangely, I couldn't think of anything more to add.

After a moment she nodded, looking puzzled. "Well . . . good. I'm sorry I didn't see you come in. I would have had you sit in my section. You're just about the closest thing I have to a regular customer."

"Yes," I said again. I knew even then that my response made no sense, but this was the only word I seemed able to formulate in her presence.

She waited for me to add something more. When I didn't, I glimpsed a flash of disappointment in her expression. "I can see you're busy," she finally said, nodding to my book. "I just wanted to come over and say hello, and to thank you again for walking me to my car. Enjoy your breakfast."

She was about to turn before I was able to break the spell I seemed to be under.

"Jane?" I blurted out.

"Yes?"

I cleared my throat. "Maybe I could walk you to your car again sometime. Even if it's not raining."

She studied me for a moment before answering. "That would be nice, Wilson."

"Maybe later today?"

She smiled. "Sure."

When she turned, I spoke again.

"And Jane?"

This time she glanced over her shoulder. "Yes?"

Finally understanding the real reason I had come, I put both hands on my textbook, trying to draw strength from a world that I understood. "Would you like to have dinner with me this weekend?"

She seemed amused that it had taken me so long to ask.

"Yes, Wilson," she said. "I'd like that very much."

It was hard to believe that here we were, more than three decades later, sitting with our daughter discussing her upcoming wedding.

Anna's surprise request for a simple, quick wedding was met with utter silence. At first Jane seemed thunderstruck, but then, regaining her senses, she began to shake her head, whispering with mounting urgency, "No, no, no . . ."

In retrospect, her reaction was hardly unexpected. I suppose that one of the moments a mother looks most forward to in life is when a daughter gets married. An entire industry has been built up around weddings, and it's only natural that most mothers have expectations about the way it's supposed to be. Anna's ideas presented a sharp contrast to what Jane had always wanted for her daughters, and though it was Anna's wedding, Jane could no more escape her beliefs than she could her own past.

Jane didn't have a problem with Anna and Keith marrying on our anniversary—she of all people knew the state of Noah's health, and Anna and Keith were, in fact, moving in a couple of weeks—but she didn't like the idea of them getting married by a justice of the peace. Nor was she pleased that there were only eight days to make the arrangements and that Anna intended to keep the celebration small.

I sat in silence as the negotiations began in earnest. Jane would say, "What about the Sloans? They would be heartbroken if you didn't invite them. Or John Peterson? He taught you piano for years, and I know how much you liked him."

"But it's no big deal," Anna would repeat. "Keith and I already live together. Most people act like we're already married anyway."

"But what about a photographer? Surely you want some pictures."

"I'm sure lots of people will bring cameras," Anna would counter. "Or you could do it. You've taken thousands of pictures over the years."

At that, Jane would shake her head and launch into an impassioned speech about how it was going to be the most important day in her life, to which Anna would respond that it would still be a marriage even without all the trimmings. It wasn't hostile, but it was clear they had reached an impasse.

I am in the habit of deferring to Jane in most matters of this sort, especially when they involve the girls, but I realized that I had something to add in this instance, and I sat up straighter on the couch.

"Maybe there's a compromise," I interjected.

Anna and Jane turned to look at me.

"I know your heart is set on next weekend," I said to Anna, "but would you mind if we invited a few extra people, in addition to the family? If we help with all the arrangements?"

"I don't know that we have enough time for something like that . . . ," Anna began.

"Would it be all right if we try?"

The negotiations continued for an hour after that, but in the end, a few compromises resulted. Anna, it seemed, was surprisingly agreeable once I'd spoken up. She knew a pastor, she said, and she was sure he would agree to do the ceremony next weekend. Jane appeared happy and relieved as the initial plans began to take form.

Meanwhile, I was thinking about not only my daughter's wedding, but also our thirtieth anniversary. Now, our anniversary—which I'd hoped to make memorable—and a wedding were going to occur on the same day, and of the two, I knew which event suddenly loomed largest.

The home that Jane and I share borders the Trent River, and it's nearly half a mile wide behind our yard. At night, I sometimes sit on the deck and watch the gentle ripples as they catch the moonlight. Depending on the weather, there are moments when the water seems like a living thing.

Unlike Noah's home, ours doesn't have a wraparound porch. It was constructed in an era when air-conditioning and the steady pull of television kept people indoors. When we first walked through the house, Jane had taken one look out the back windows and decided that if she couldn't have a porch, she would at least have a deck. It was the first of many minor construction projects that eventually transformed the house into something we could comfortably call our home.

After Anna left, Jane sat on the couch, staring toward the sliding glass doors. I wasn't able to read her expression, but before I could ask what she was thinking, she suddenly rose and went outside. Recognizing that the evening had been a shock, I went to the kitchen and opened a bottle of wine. Jane had never been a big drinker, but she enjoyed a glass of wine from time to time, and I thought that tonight might be one of them.

Glass in hand, I made my way to the deck. Outside, the night was buzzing with the sounds of frogs and crickets. The moon had not yet risen, and across the river I could see yellow lights glowing from country homes. A breeze had picked up, and I could hear the faint tings of the wind chime Leslie had bought us for Christmas last year.

Other than that, there was silence. In the gentle light of the porch, Jane's profile reminded me of a Greek statue, and once again, I was struck by how much she resembled the woman I first saw long ago. Eyeing her high cheekbones and full lips, I was thankful that our daughters look more like her than me, and now that one was getting married, I suppose I expected her expression to be almost radiant. As I drew near, however, I was startled to see that Jane was crying.

I hesitated at the edge of the deck, wondering whether I'd made a mistake in trying to join her. Before I could turn, however, Jane seemed to sense my presence and glanced over her shoulder.

"Oh, hey," she said, sniffing.

"Are you okay?" I asked.

"Yes." She paused, then shook her head. "I mean, no. Actually, I'm not sure how I feel."

I moved to her side and set the glass of wine on the railing. In the darkness, the wine looked like oil.

"Thank you," she said. After taking a sip, she let out a long breath before gazing out over the water.

"This is so like Anna," she finally said. "I guess I shouldn't be surprised, but still . . ."

She trailed off, setting the wine aside.

"I thought you liked Keith," I said.

"I do." She nodded. "But a week? I don't know where she gets these ideas. If she was going to do something like this, I don't understand why she didn't just elope and get it over with."

"Would you rather she had done that?"

"No. I would have been furious with her."

I smiled. Jane had always been honest.

"It's just that there's so much to do," she went on, "and I have no idea how we're going to pull it all together. I'm not saying the wedding has to be at the ballroom of the Plaza, but still, you'd think she would want a photographer there. Or some of her friends."

"Didn't she agree to all that?"

Jane hesitated, choosing her words carefully.

"I just don't think she realizes how often she'll think back to her wedding day. She acted like it's no big deal."

"She'll always remember it no matter how it turns out," I countered gently.

Jane closed her eyes for a long moment. "You don't understand," she said.

Though she said no more on the subject, I knew exactly what she meant.

Quite simply, Jane didn't want Anna to make the same mistake that she had.

My wife has always regretted the way we got married. We had the kind of wedding I'd insisted on, and though I accept responsibility for this, my parents played a significant role in my decision.

My parents, unlike the vast majority of the country, were atheists, and I was raised accordingly. Growing up, I remember being curious about church and the mysterious rituals I sometimes read about, but religion was something we never discussed. It never came up over dinner, and though there were times when I realized that I was different from other children in the neighborhood, it wasn't something that I dwelled upon.

I know differently now. I regard my Christian faith as the greatest gift I've ever been given, and I will dwell no more on this except to say that in retrospect, I think I always knew there was something missing in my life. The years I spent with Jane have proved that. Like her parents, Jane was devout in her beliefs, and it was she who started bringing me to church. She also purchased the Bible we read in the evenings, and it was she who answered the initial questions I had.

This did not happen, however, until after we were married.

If there was a source of tension in the years we were dating, it was my lack of faith, and there were times I'm sure she questioned whether we were compatible. She has told me that if she hadn't been sure that I would eventually accept Jesus Christ as my Savior, then she wouldn't have married me. I knew that Anna's comment had brought back a painful memory for her, for it was this same lack of faith that led us to be married on the courthouse steps. At the time, I felt strongly that marrying in the church would make me a hypocrite.

There was an additional reason we were married by a judge instead of a minister, one that had to do with pride. I didn't want Jane's parents to pay for a traditional church wedding, even though they could have afforded it. As a parent myself, I now view such a duty as the gift that it is, but at the time, I believed that I alone should be responsible for the cost. If I wasn't able to pay for a proper reception, my reasoning went, then I wouldn't have one.

At the time, I could not afford a gala affair. I was new at the firm and making a reasonable salary, but I was doing my best to save for a down payment on a home. Though we were able to purchase our first house nine months after we were married, I no longer think such a sacrifice worthwhile. Frugality, I've learned, has its own cost, one that sometimes lasts forever.

Our ceremony was over in less than ten minutes; not a single prayer was uttered. I wore a dark gray suit; Jane was dressed in a yellow sundress with a gladiola pinned in her hair. Her parents watched from the steps below us and sent us off with a kiss and a handshake. We spent our honeymoon at a quaint inn in Beaufort, and though she adored the antique canopy bed where we first made love, we stayed for less than a weekend, since I had to be back in the office on Monday.

This is not the sort of wedding that Jane had dreamed

about as a young girl. I know that now. What she wanted was what I suppose she was now urging on Anna. A beaming bride escorted down the aisle by her father, a wedding performed by a minister, with family and friends in attendance. A reception with food and cake and flowers on every table, where the bride and groom can receive congratulations from those dearest to them. Maybe even music, to which the bride could dance with her new husband, and with the father who had raised her, while others looked on with joy in their eyes.

That's what Jane would have wanted.

Chapter Four

On Saturday morning, the day after Anna's announcement, the sun was already stifling as I parked in the lot at Creekside. As in most southern towns, August slows the pace of life in New Bern. People drive more cautiously, traffic lights seem to stay red longer than usual, and those who walk use just enough energy to move their bodies forward, as if engaging in slow-motion shuffle contests.

Jane and Anna were already gone for the day. After coming in from the deck last night, Jane sat at the kitchen table and started making notes of all that she had to do. Though she was under no illusions that she would be able to accomplish everything, her notes covered three pages, with goals outlined for each day of the following week.

Jane had always been good with projects. Whether it was running a fund-raiser for the Boy Scouts or organizing a church raffle, my wife was usually the person tapped to volunteer. While it left her feeling overwhelmed at times—she did, after all, have three children engaged in other activities—she never refused. Recalling how frazzled she often became, I made a mental note to keep any requests of her time to a minimum in the week to come.

The courtyard behind Creekside was landscaped with square hedges and clustered azaleas. After passing through the building—I was certain Noah wasn't in his room—I followed the curving gravel pathway toward the pond. Spotting Noah, I shook my head when I noticed that he was wearing his favorite blue cardigan despite the heat. Only Noah could be chilled on a day like today.

He'd just finished feeding the swan, and it still swam in small circles before him. As I approached, I heard him speaking to it, though I couldn't make out his words. The swan seemed to trust him completely. Noah once told me that the swan sometimes rested at his feet, though I had never actually seen this.

"Hello, Noah," I said.

It was an effort for him to turn his head. "Hello, Wilson." He raised a hand. "Thanks for dropping by."

"You doing okay?"

"Could be better," he replied. "Could be worse, though, too."

Though I came here often, Creekside sometimes depressed me, for it seemed to be full of people who'd been left behind in life. The doctors and nurses told us that Noah was lucky since he had frequent visitors, but too many of the others spent their days watching television to escape the loneliness of their final years. Noah still spent his evenings reciting poetry to the people who live here. He's fond of the poems of Walt Whitman, and *Leaves of Grass* was on the bench beside him. He seldom went anywhere without it, and though both Jane and I have read it in the past, I must admit that I don't understand why he finds the poems so meaningful.

Studying him, I was struck anew by how sad it was to watch a man like Noah grow old. For most of my life, I'd never thought of him in those terms, but nowadays, when I heard his breath, it reminded me of air moving through an old accordion. He didn't move his left hand, a consequence of the stroke he'd suffered in the spring. Noah was winding down, and while I'd long known this was coming, it seemed that he finally realized it as well.

He was watching the swan, and following his gaze, I recognized the bird by the black spot on its chest. It reminded me of a mole or birthmark, or coal in the snow, nature's attempt to mute perfection. At certain times of the year, a dozen swans could be found on the water, but this was the only one that never left. I've seen it floating on the pond even when the temperature plunged in the winter and the other swans had long migrated farther south. Noah once told me why the swan never left, and his explanation was one of the reasons the doctors thought him delusional.

Taking a seat beside him, I recounted what had happened the night before with Anna and Jane. When I finished, Noah glanced at me with a slight smirk.

"Jane was surprised?" he asked.

"Who wouldn't be?"

"And she wants things a certain way?"

"Yes," I said. I told him about the plans she had outlined at the kitchen table before discussing an idea of my own, something that I thought Jane had overlooked.

With his good hand, Noah reached over and patted my leg as if giving me the okay.

"How about Anna?" he asked. "How's she doing?"

"She's fine. I don't think Jane's reaction surprised her in the least."

"And Keith?"

"He's fine, too. At least from what Anna said."

Noah nodded. "A good young couple, those two. They both have kind hearts. They remind me of Allie and myself. "

I smiled. "I'll tell her you said that. It'll make her day."

We sat in silence until Noah finally motioned toward the water.

"Did you know that swans mate for life?" he said.

"I thought that was a myth."

"It's true," he insisted. "Allie always said it was one of the most romantic things she'd ever heard. For her, it proved that love was the most powerful force on earth. Before we were married, she was engaged to someone else. You knew that, right?"

I nodded.

"I thought so. Anyway, she came to visit me without telling her fiancé, and I took her out in a canoe to a place where we saw thousands of swans clustered together. It was like snow on the water. Did I ever tell you that?"

I nodded again. Though I hadn't been there, the image was vivid in my mind, as it was in Jane's. She often spoke of that story with wonder.

"They never came back after that," he murmured. "There were always a few in the pond, but it was never like that day again." Lost in the memory, he paused. "But Allie liked to go there anyway. She liked to feed the ones that were there, and she used to point out the pairs to me. There's one, she'd say, there's another one. Isn't it wonderful how they're always together?" Noah's face creased as he grinned. "I think it was her way of reminding me to stay faithful."

"I don't think she needed to worry about that."

"No?" he asked.

"I think you and Allie were meant for each other."

He smiled wistfully. "Yes," he finally said, "we were. But we had to work at it. We had our tough times, too."

Perhaps he was referring to her Alzheimer's. And long before that, the death of one of their children. There were other things, too, but these were the events he still found difficult to discuss.

"But you made it seem so easy," I protested.

Noah shook his head. "It wasn't. Not always. All those letters I used to write to her were a way of reminding her not only how I felt about her, but of the vow we'd once made to each other."

I wondered if he was trying to remind me of the time he'd suggested that I do such a thing for Jane, but I made no mention of it. Instead, I brought up something I'd been meaning to ask him.

"Was it hard for you and Allie after all the kids had moved out?"

Noah took a moment to think about his answer. "I don't know if the word was hard, but it was different."

"How so?"

"It was quiet, for one thing. Really quiet. With Allie working in her studio, it was just me puttering around the house a lot of the time. I think that's when I started talking to myself, just for the company."

"How did Allie react to not having the kids around?"

"Like me," he said. "At first, anyway. The kids were our life for a long time, and there's always some adjusting when that changes. But once she did, I think she started to enjoy the fact that we were alone again."

"How long did that take?" I asked.

"I don't know. A couple of weeks, maybe."

I felt my shoulders sag. A couple of weeks? I thought.

Noah seemed to catch my expression, and after taking a moment, he cleared his throat. "Now that I think about it," he said, "I'm sure it wasn't even that long. I think it was just a few days before she was back to normal."

A few *days*? By then I couldn't summon a response.

He brought a hand to his chin. "Actually, if I remember right," he went on, "it wasn't even a few days. In fact, we did the jitterbug right there in front of the house as soon as we'd loaded the last of David's things in the car. But let me tell you, the first couple of minutes were tough. Real tough. I sometimes wonder how we were able to survive them."

Though his expression remained serious as he spoke, I detected the mischievous gleam in his eye.

"The jitterbug?" I asked.

"It's a dance."

"I know what it is."

"It used to be fairly popular."

"That was a long time ago."

"What? No one jitterbugs anymore?"

"It's a lost art, Noah."

He nudged me gently. "Had you going, though, didn't I."

"A little," I admitted.

He winked. "Gotcha."

For a moment he sat in silence, looking pleased with himself. Then, knowing he hadn't really answered my question, he shifted on the bench and let out a long breath.

"It was hard for both of us, Wilson. By the time they'd left, they weren't just our kids, but our friends, too. We were both lonesome, and for a while there, we weren't sure what to do with each other."

"You've never said anything about it."

"You never asked," he said. "I missed them, but of the two of us, I think it was worse for Allie. She may have been a painter, but she was first and foremost a mother, and once the kids were gone, it was like she wasn't exactly sure who she was anymore. At least for a while, anyway."

I tried to picture it but couldn't. It wasn't an Allie that I'd ever seen or even imagined possible.

"Why does that happen?" I asked.

Instead of answering, Noah looked over at me and was silent for a moment. "Did I ever tell you about Gus?" he finally asked. "Who used to visit me when I was fixing the house?"

I nodded. Gus, I knew, was kin to Harvey, the black pastor I sometimes saw when visiting Noah's property.

"Well, old Gus," Noah explained, "used to love tall tales, the funnier the better. And sometimes we used to sit on the porch at night trying to come up with our own tall tales to make each other laugh. There were some good ones over the years, but you want to know what my favorite one was? The tallest tale Gus ever uttered? Now, before I say this, you have to understand that Gus had been married to the same gal for half a century, and they had eight kids. Those two had been through just about everything together. So anyway, we'd been telling these stories back and forth all night, and he said, 'I've got one.' So then Gus took a deep breath, and with a straight face, he looked me right in the eye and said, 'Noah, I under- stand women.' "

Noah chuckled, as if hearing it for the first time. "The point is," he continued, "that there's no man alive who can honestly say those words and mean them. It just isn't pos- sible, so there's no use trying. But that doesn't mean you can't love them anyway. And it doesn't mean that you should ever stop doing your best to let them know how important they are to you."

On the pond, I watched the swan flutter and adjust its wings as I contemplated what he'd said. This had been the way Noah talked to me about Jane during the past year. Never once had he offered specific advice, never once had he told me what to do. At the same time, he was always conscious of my need for support.

"I think Jane wishes I could be more like you," I said.

At my words, Noah chuckled. "You're doing fine, Wilson," he said. "You're doing just fine."

Aside from the ticking of the grandfather clock and the steady hum of the air conditioner, the house was quiet when I reached home. As I dropped my keys on the desk in the living room, I found myself scanning the bookshelves on either side of the fireplace. The shelves were filled with family photographs that had been taken over the years: the five of us dressed in jeans and blue shirts from two summers ago, another at the beach near Fort Macon when the kids were teens, still another from when they were even younger. Then there were those that Jane had taken: Anna in her prom dress, Leslie wearing her cheerleader outfit, a photo of Joseph with our dog, Sandy, who'd sadly passed away a few summers ago. There were more, too, some that went back to their infancy, and though the pictures weren't arranged chronologically, it was a testament to how the family had grown and changed over the years.

In the center of the shelves right above the fireplace sat a black-and-white photograph of Jane and me on the day of our wedding. Allie had snapped the picture on the courthouse steps. Even then, Allie's artistry was apparent, and though Jane had always been beautiful, the lens had been kind to me as well that day. It was how I hoped I would always look when standing by her side.

But, strangely, there are no more photographs of Jane and me as a couple on the shelves. In the albums, there are dozens of snapshots that the kids had taken, but none had ever found its way into a frame. Over the years, Jane had suggested a number of times that we have another portrait made, but in the steady rush of life and work, it never quite claimed my attention. Now, I sometimes wonder why we never made the time, or what it means for our future, or even whether it matters at all.

My conversation with Noah had left me musing about the years since the children left home. Could I have been a better husband all along? Unquestionably, yes. But looking back, I think it was during the months that followed Leslie's departure for college that I truly failed Jane, if an utter lack of awareness can be characterized that way. I remember now that Jane seemed quiet and even a bit moody during those days, staring sightlessly out the glass doors or sorting listlessly through old boxes of the kids' stuff. But it was a particularly busy year for me at the firm—old Ambry had suffered a heart attack and was forced to drastically reduce his workload, transferring many of his clients' matters to me. The dual burdens of an immensely increased workload and the organizational toll Ambry's illness took on the firm often left me exhausted and preoccupied.

When Jane suddenly decided to redecorate the house, I took it as a good sign that she was busying herself with a new project. Work, I reasoned, would keep her from dwelling on the kids' absence. And so appeared leather couches where there were once upholstered ones, coffee tables made of cherry, lamps of twisted brass. New wallpaper hangs in the dining room, and the table has enough chairs to accommodate all our children and their future spouses. Though Jane did a wonderful job, I must admit that I was frequently shocked by the credit card bills when they started arriving in the mail, though I learned it was best if I didn't comment on it.

It was after she finished, however, that we both began to notice a new awkwardness in the marriage, an awkwardness that had to do not with an empty nest, but with the type of couple we'd become. Yet neither of us spoke about it. It was as if we both believed that speaking the words aloud would somehow make them permanent, and I think both of us were afraid of what might happen as a result.

This, I might add, is also the reason we've never been to counseling. Call it old-fashioned, but I've never been comfortable with the thought of discussing our problems with others, and Jane is the same way. Besides, I already know what a counselor would say. No, the children leaving didn't cause the problem, the counselor would say, nor did Jane's increased free time. They were simply catalysts that brought existing problems into sharper focus.

What, then, had led us to this point?

Though it pains me to say, I suppose our real problem has been one of innocent neglect—mostly mine, if I'm perfectly honest. In addition to frequently placing my career above the needs of my family, I've always taken the stability of our marriage for granted. As I saw it, ours was a relationship without major problems, and Lord knows I was never the type to run around doing the little things that men like Noah did for their wives. When I thought about it—which, truthfully, wasn't often—I reassured myself that Jane had always known what kind of man I was, and that would always be enough.

But love, I've come to understand, is more than three words mumbled before bedtime. Love is sustained by action, a pattern of devotion in the things we do for each other every day.

Now, as I stared at the picture, all I could think was that thirty years of innocent neglect had made my love seem like a lie, and it seemed that the bill had finally come due. We were married in name only. We hadn't made love in nearly half a year, and the few kisses we shared had little meaning for either of us. I was dying on the inside, aching for all that we'd lost, and as I stared at our wedding photograph, I hated myself for allowing it to happen.

Chapter Five

espite the heat, I spent the rest of the afternoon pulling weeds, and afterward I showered before heading off to the grocery store. It was, after all, Saturday—my day to cook—and I had decided to try my hand at a new recipe that called for side dishes of bow-tie pasta and vegetables. Though I knew this would probably be enough for both of us, I decided at the last minute to make appetizers and a Caesar salad as well.

By five o'clock, I was in the kitchen; by five-thirty, the appetizers were well under way. I had prepared mushrooms stuffed with sausage and cream cheese, and they were warming in the oven next to the bread I'd picked up at the bakery. I'd just finished setting the table and was opening a bottle of Merlot when I heard Jane come in the front door.

"Hello?" she called out.

"I'm in the dining room," I said.

When she rounded the corner, I was struck by how radiant she looked. While my thinning hair is speckled with gray, hers is still as dark and full as the day I married her. She had tucked a few strands behind her ear, and around her neck I saw the small diamond pendant I'd purchased in the first few years of our marriage. As preoccupied as I might have been at times during our marriage, I can honestly say that I have never grown inured to her beauty.

"Wow," she said. "It smells great in here. What's for dinner?"

"Veal marsala," I announced, reaching to pour her a glass of wine. I crossed the room and handed it to her. As I studied her face, I noticed that the anxiety of the night before had been replaced with a look of excitement that I hadn't seen for quite some time. I could already tell that things had gone well for her and Anna, and though I hadn't realized I'd been holding my breath, I felt myself exhale in relief.

"You're not going to believe what happened today," she gushed. "Even when I tell you, you're not going to believe it."

Taking a sip of wine, she grasped my arm to steady herself as she slid one foot and then the other out of her shoe. I felt the warmth of her touch even after she let go.

"What is it?" I asked. "What happened?"

She motioned enthusiastically with her free hand. "C'mon," she said. "Follow me into the kitchen while I tell you about it. I'm starved. We were so busy we didn't have time for lunch. By the time we realized that it was time to eat, most of the restaurants were closed and we still had a few places to visit before Anna had to get back. Thank you for making dinner, by the way. I completely forgot it was your day to cook, and I was trying to think of an excuse to order in."

She kept talking as she moved through the swinging doors into the kitchen. Trailing behind her, I admired the subtle movement of her hips as she walked.

"Anyway, I think Anna's sort of getting into it now. She seemed a lot more enthusiastic than she did last night."

Jane glanced at me over her shoulder, eyes gleaming. "But oh, just wait. You're not going to believe it."

The kitchen counters were crowded with preparations for the main course: sliced veal, assorted vegetables, a cutting board and knife. I slipped on an oven mitt to remove the appetizers and set the baking sheet on the stovetop.

"Here," I said.

She looked at me in surprise. "They're already done?"

"Lucky timing." I shrugged.

Jane reached for a mushroom and took a bite.

"So this morning, I picked her up . . . Wow, this is really good." She paused, suddenly examining the mushroom. She took another bite and let it roll around in her mouth before going on. "Anyway, the first thing we did was discuss possible photographers—someone a lot more qualified than me. I know there are a few studios downtown, but I was certain we wouldn't be able to find anyone last minute. So last night, I got to thinking that Claire's son might be able to do it. He's taking classes in photography at Carteret Community College, and that's what he wants to do when he graduates. I'd called Claire this morning and said that we might be stopping by, but Anna wasn't so sure since she'd never seen any of his work. My other idea was to use someone she knows at the newspaper, but Anna told me that the newspaper frowns on that kind of freelance work. Anyway, to make a long story short, she wanted to check the studios on the off chance that someone might be available. And you'll never guess what happened."

"Tell me," I said.

Jane popped the last of the mushroom into her mouth, letting the anticipation build. The tips of her fingers were shiny as she reached for another mushroom.

"These are really good," she enthused. "Is this a new recipe?"

"Yes," I said.

"Is it complicated?"

"Not really," I said, shrugging.

She drew a deep breath. "So anyway, just like I thought, the first two places we visited were booked. But then we went to Cayton's Studio. Have you ever seen the wedding pictures Jim Cayton does?"

"I've heard he's the best around."

"He's amazing," she said. "His work is stunning. Even Anna was impressed, and you know how she is. He did Dana Crowe's wedding, remember? He's usually booked six or seven months in advance, and even then he's hard to get. I mean, there wasn't a chance, right? But when I asked his wife—she's the one who runs the studio—she told me that he'd had a recent cancellation."

She took another bite of her appetizer, chewing slowly.

"And it just so happens," she announced with the faintest of shrugs, "that he was open for next Saturday."

I raised my eyebrows. "That's wonderful," I said.

Now that the climax had been revealed, she began to speak more quickly, filling in the rest of the blanks.

"Oh, you can't believe how happy Anna was. Jim Cayton? Even if we had a year to plan, he's the one I would have wanted. We must have spent a couple of hours flipping through some of the albums they've put together, just to get ideas. Anna would ask me whether I liked these types of shots, or I'd ask which ones she liked. I'm sure Mrs. Cayton thinks we're crazy. As soon as we'd finish an album, we'd ask for another—she was kind enough to answer every question we had. By the time we left, I think both of us were just pinching ourselves at how lucky we'd been."

"I'll bet."

"So after that," she continued breezily, "we headed out to the bakeries. Again, it took a couple of stops, but I wasn't too worried about getting a cake. It's not as if they have to prepare them months in advance, right? Anyway, we found a small place that could do it, but I didn't realize how many choices they have. There was an entire catalog devoted to wedding cakes. They have big cakes and small cakes, and every size in between. Then, of course, you have to decide what flavor you want it, what kind of frosting, the shape, what additional decorations and all those kinds of things. . . ."

"Sounds exciting," I said.

She rolled her eyes heavenward. "You don't know the half of it," she said, and I laughed at her obvious joy.

The stars weren't often in alignment, but tonight they seemed to be. Her mood was rapturous, the evening was young, and Jane and I were about to enjoy a romantic meal together. All seemed right with the world, and as I stood beside my wife of three decades, I suddenly knew that the day couldn't have gone any better had I planned it in advance.

While I finished preparing dinner, Jane continued filling me in on the rest of her day, going into detail about the cake (two layers, vanilla flavoring, sour cream frosting) and the photographs (Cayton fixes any imperfections on the computer). In the warm light of the kitchen, I could just make out the soft creases around the corners of her eyes, the feathery markings of our life together.

"I'm glad it went well," I said. "And considering it was your first day, you actually got quite a bit done."

The smell of melted butter filled the kitchen, and the veal began to sizzle slightly.

"I know. And I am happy, believe me," she said. "But we still don't know where we should have the ceremony, and until then, I don't know how to make the rest of the arrangements. I'd told Anna that we could have it here if she wanted, but she wasn't too keen on the idea."

"What does she want?"

"She isn't sure yet. She thinks she might want to have a garden wedding of some sort. Someplace not too formal."

"It shouldn't be too hard to find a place."

"You'd be surprised. The only place I could think of was the Tryon Palace, but I don't think we'll be able to do that on such short notice. I don't even know if they allow weddings there."

"Mmm . . ." I added salt, pepper, and garlic powder to the pan.

"The Orton Plantation is nice, too. Remember? That's where we went to the Brattons' wedding last year."

I remembered; it was in between Wilmington and Southport, almost two hours from New Bern. "It is sort of out of the way, isn't it?" I asked. "Considering most of the guests are from around here?"

"I know. It was just an idea. I'm sure it's booked anyway."

"How about someplace downtown? At one of the bed-and-breakfasts?"

She shook her head. "I think most of them might be too small—and I don't know how many have gardens—but I suppose I can look into it. And if that doesn't work . . . well, we'll find someplace. At least I hope we can."

Jane frowned, lost in thought. She leaned against the counter and propped her stockinged foot against the cabinet behind her, for all the world the same young girl who talked me into walking her to her car. The second time I walked her to her car, I assumed she would simply get in her car and drive away, as she had the first time. Instead she'd struck just the same pose against the driver's-side door, and we had what I consider to be our first conversation. I remember marveling at her animated features as she recounted the details of her life growing up in New Bern, and it was the first time I sensed the attributes I would always cherish: her intelligence and passion, her charm, the carefree way she seemed to view the world. Years later, she showed the same traits when raising our children, and I know it's one of the reasons they've become the kind and responsible adults they are today.

Breaking into Jane's distracted reverie, I cleared my throat. "I went to visit Noah today," I said.

At my words, Jane resurfaced. "How's he doing?"

"Okay. He looked tired, but he was in good spirits."

"Was he at the pond again?"

"Yes," I said. Anticipating her next question, I added: "The swan was there, too."

She pressed her lips together, but not wanting to ruin her mood, I quickly went on.

"I told him about the wedding," I said.

"Was he excited?"

"Very." I nodded. "He told me he's looking forward to being there."

Jane brought her hands together. "I'm bringing Anna by tomorrow. She didn't have a chance to see him last week, and I know she's going to want to tell him about it." She smiled appreciatively. "And by the way, thanks for going out to see him today. I know how much he enjoys that."

"You know I like to spend time with him, too."

"I know. But thank you anyway."

The meat was ready, and I added the rest of the ingredients: marsala wine, lemon juice, mushrooms, beef broth, minced shallot, diced green onions. I added another dab of butter for good measure, rewarding myself for the twenty pounds I'd lost in the last year.

"Have you talked to Joseph or Leslie yet?" I asked.

For a moment, Jane watched me as I stirred. Then, after retrieving a spoon from the drawer, she dipped the tip into the sauce and tasted it. "This is good," she commented, raising her eyebrows.

"You sound surprised."

"No, I'm really not. You're actually quite the chef these days. At least compared to where you started."

"What? You didn't always love my cooking?"

She brought a finger to her chin. "Let's just say burned mashed potatoes and crunchy gravy are an acquired taste."

I smiled, knowing what she said was true. My first few experiences in the kitchen had been less than an earth-shattering success.

Jane took another taste before setting the spoon on the counter.

"Wilson? About the wedding . . . ," she began.

I glanced at her. "Yes?"

"You *do* know it's going to be expensive to get a ticket for Joseph at the last minute, right?"

"Yes," I said.

"And the photographer isn't cheap, even if there was a cancellation."

I nodded. "I figured that."

"And the cake is kind of pricey, too. For a cake, I mean."

"No problem. It's for a lot of people, right?"

She looked at me curiously, clearly stumped by my answers. "Well . . . I just wanted to warn you in advance so you won't get upset."

"How could I get upset?"

"Oh, you know. Sometimes you get upset when things start getting expensive."

"I do?"

Jane cocked a brow. "Don't bother pretending. Don't you remember how you were with all the renovations? Or when the heat pump kept breaking? You even shine your own shoes. . . ."

I raised my hands in playful surrender. "Okay, you made your point," I said. "But don't worry. This is different." I looked up, knowing I had her attention. "Even if we spend everything we have, it'll still be worth it."

She almost choked on her wine and stared at me. Then, after a long moment, she took a sudden step forward and poked my arm with her finger.

"What's that for?" I asked.

"Just checking to see if you're really my husband, or if you've been replaced by one of the pod-people."

"Pod-people?"

"Yeah. *Invasion of the Body Snatchers*. You remember the movie, right?"

"Of course. But it's really me," I said.

"Thank goodness," she said, feigning relief. Then, wonder of wonders, she winked at me. "But I still wanted to warn you."

I smiled, feeling as if my heart had just been inflated. How long had it been, I wondered, since we'd laughed and joked in the kitchen like this? Months? Years, even? Even though I realized that it might be only temporary, it nonetheless stoked the small flame of hope I had begun to nurture in secret.

The first date that Jane and I went on didn't go exactly as I'd planned.

I'd made reservations at Harper's, which was regarded as the best restaurant in town. Also the most expensive. I had enough money to cover the cost of dinner, but I knew I would have to budget the rest of the month to pay my other bills. I'd also planned something special for afterward.

I picked her up in front of her dormitory at Meredith, and the drive to the restaurant took only a few minutes. Our conversation was typical of first dates and simply skimmed the surface of things. We spoke about school and how chilly it was, and I noted that it was a good thing we both brought jackets. I also remember mentioning that I thought her sweater was lovely, and she mentioned that she'd purchased it the day before. Though I wondered if she had done this in anticipation of our date, I knew enough not to ask her directly.

Owing to holiday shoppers, it was difficult to find a space near the restaurant, so we parked a couple of blocks away. I'd allotted plenty of time, however, and felt sure we would arrive at the restaurant in time to make our reservation. On the way to the restaurant, the tips of our noses turned red and our breath came out in little clouds. A few of the shop windows were ringed with twinkling lights, and as we passed one of the neighborhood pizza parlors, we could hear Christmas music coming from the jukebox inside.

It was as we were approaching the restaurant that we saw the dog. Cowering in an alley, he was medium size but skinny and covered in grime. He was shivering, and his coat made it plain that he had been on the run for quite a while. I moved between Jane and the dog in case he was dangerous, but Jane stepped around me and squatted down, trying to get the dog's attention.

"It's okay," she whispered. "We won't hurt you."

The dog shrank back farther into the shadows.

"He's got a collar," Jane pointed out. "I'll bet he's lost." She didn't look away from the dog, who seemed to be studying her with wary interest.

Checking my watch, I saw that we had a few minutes to spare until our reservation came up. Though I still wasn't sure whether or not the dog was dangerous, I squatted beside Jane and began speaking to him in the same soothing tones that she was using. This went on for a short while, but still the dog remained where he was. Jane took a small step toward him, but the dog whined, skittering away.

"He's scared," she said, looking worried. "What should we do? I don't want to leave him out here. It's supposed to fall below freezing tonight. And if he's lost, I'm sure all he wants is to get back home."

I suppose I could have said just about anything. I could have told her that we tried, or that we could call the pound, or even that we could come back after dinner, and if he was still around that we could try again. But Jane's expression stopped me. Her face was a mixture of worry and defiance—the first inkling I had of Jane's kindness and concern for those less fortunate. I knew then that I had no choice but to go along with what she wanted.

"Let me try," I said.

In all honesty, I wasn't quite sure what to do. Growing up, I'd never owned a dog for the simple reason that my mother had been allergic to them, but I held out my hand

and continued to whisper to him, resorting to what I had seen people do in the movies.

I let the dog get used to my voice, and when I slowly inched forward, the dog remained in place. Not wanting to startle the mutt, I stopped, let him get used to me for a moment, and inched forward again. After what seemed forever, I was close enough to the dog that when I held out my hand, he stretched his nose toward it. Then, deciding he had nothing to fear from me, he let his tongue flicker against my fingers. A moment later, I was able to stroke his head, and I glanced over my shoulder at Jane.

"He likes you," she said, looking amazed.

I shrugged. "I guess he does."

I was able to read the phone number on the collar, and Jane went into the bookstore next door to call the owner from a pay phone. While she was gone, I waited with the dog, and the more I stroked him, the more he seemed to crave the touch of my hand. When Jane returned, we waited for nearly twenty minutes until the owner arrived to claim him. He was in his mid-thirties, and he practically bounded from the car. Immediately the dog surged to the man's side, tail wagging. After taking time to acknowledge the sloppy licks, the man turned to us.

"Thank you so much for calling," he said. "He's been gone for a week, and my son's been crying himself to sleep every night. You have no idea how much this will mean to him. Getting his dog back was the only thing he put on his Christmas list."

Though he offered a reward, neither Jane nor I was willing to take it, and he thanked us both again before getting back into his car. As we watched him go, I believe we both felt we'd done something worthy. After the sounds of the engine faded away, Jane took my arm.

"Can we still make our reservation?" she asked.

I checked my watch. "We're half an hour late."

"They should still have our table, right?"

"I don't know. It was tough to get one in the first place. I had to have one of my professors call for me."

"Maybe we'll get lucky," she said.

We didn't. By the time we got to the restaurant, our table had been given away, and the next available slot was for nine forty-five. Jane looked up at me.

"At least we made a child happy," she said.

"I know." I took a deep breath. "And I'd do it again, too."

Studying me for a moment, she gave my arm a squeeze. "I'm glad we stopped, too, even if we don't get to have dinner here."

Surrounded by a streetlight halo, she looked almost ethereal.

"Is there anyplace else you'd like to go?" I asked.

She tilted her head. "Do you like music?"

Ten minutes later, we were seated at a table in the pizza parlor we'd passed earlier. Though I'd planned on candlelight and wine, we ended up ordering beer with our pizza.

Jane, however, didn't seem disappointed. She spoke easily, telling me about her classes in Greek mythology and English literature, her years at Meredith, her friends, and anything else that happened to be on her mind. For the most part, I simply nodded and asked enough questions to keep her talking for the next two hours, and I can honestly say that I'd never enjoyed someone's company more.

In the kitchen, I noticed that Jane was eyeing me curiously. Forcing the memory away, I put the finishing touches on our meal and brought the food to the table.

After taking our places, we bowed our heads and I said grace, thanking God for all that we had been given.

"You okay? You seemed preoccupied a couple of minutes ago," Jane commented as she forked some salad into her bowl.

I poured a glass of wine for each of us. "Actually, I was remembering our first date," I said.

"You were?" Her fork stopped in midair. "Why?"

"I don't know," I said. I slid her glass toward her. "Do you even remember it?"

"Of course I remember," she chided me. "It was right before we went home for Christmas break. We were supposed to go to dinner at Harper's, but we found a stray, and we missed our reservation. So we had dinner at this little pizza place down the street instead. And after that . . ."

She squinted, trying to recall the exact order of events.

"We got in the car and drove out to see the decorations along Havermill Road, right? You insisted that I get out of the car so we could walk around, even though it was freezing. One of the houses had set up Santa's village, and when you walked me over, the man dressed as Santa handed me the gift that you'd picked out for me for Christmas. I remember being amazed that you'd gone through all that trouble on a first date."

"Do you remember what I got you?"

"How could I forget?" She grinned. "An umbrella."

"If I recall correctly, you didn't seem too thrilled about it."

"Well," she said, throwing up her hands, "how was I supposed to meet any guys after that? Having someone walk me to my car was my modus operandi back then. You have to remember that at Meredith, the only men around were teachers or janitors."

"That's why I picked it out," I said. "I knew exactly how you operated."

"You didn't have a clue," she said with a smirk. "I was the first girl you ever dated."

"No, you weren't. I'd dated before."

Her eyes were playful. "Okay, the first girl you'd ever kissed, then."

This was true, though I've come to regret that I ever told her this, since she's never forgotten this fact and it tends to come up in moments like this. In my defense, however, I said: "I was too busy preparing for my future. I didn't have time for such a thing."

"You were shy."

"I was studious. There's a difference."

"Don't you remember our dinner? Or the drive over? You barely said anything to me at all, except about your classes."

"I talked about more than that," I said. "I told you that I liked your sweater, remember?"

"That doesn't count." She winked. "You were just lucky I was so patient with you."

"Yes," I agreed, "I was."

I said it the way I would have wanted to hear it from her, and I think she caught the tone in my voice. She smiled briefly.

"Do you know what I remember most from that night?" I went on.

"My sweater?"

My wife, I should add, has always had a quick wit. I laughed but was clearly in a more reflective mood and went on. "I liked the way you stopped for the dog, and were unwilling to leave until you made sure he was safe. It told me your heart was in the right place."

I could have sworn she blushed at my comment, but she quickly picked up her wineglass, so I couldn't be sure. Before she could say anything, I changed the subject.

"So is Anna getting nervous yet?" I asked.

Jane shook her head. "Not at all. She doesn't seem worried in the slightest. I guess she believes that it's all going to work out, like it did today with the pictures and the cake. This morning, when I showed her the list of all we had to do, all she said was, 'I guess we'd better get started, then, huh?'"

I nodded. I could imagine Anna saying those words.

"What about her friend, the pastor?" I asked.

"She said she called him last night, and he said he'd be happy to do it."

"That's good. One less thing," I offered.

"Mmm." Jane fell silent. I knew her mind was beginning to turn to the activities of the coming week.

"I think I'm going to need your help," she said at last.

"What did you have in mind?"

"Well, you'll need a tux for you, Keith, and Joseph, of course. And Daddy, too. . . ."

"No problem."

She shifted in her seat. "And Anna is supposed to be getting the names of some of the people she'd like to invite. We don't have time to send any invitations, so someone's going to have to call. And since I'm out and about with Anna, and you're on vacation . . ."

I held up my hands. "I'd be glad to take care of it," I said. "I'll start tomorrow."

"Do you know where the address book is?"

This is the type of question with which I've become quite familiar over the years. Jane has long believed that I have a natural inability to find certain items within our home. She also believes that while I misplace objects occasionally, I have assigned her the responsibility of knowing exactly where it is I might have misplaced them. Neither of these things, I might add, is completely my fault. While it's true that I don't know where every item in the house is located, this has more to do with different filing systems than any ineptitude on my part. My wife, for instance, believes the flashlight logically belongs in one of the kitchen drawers, while my reasoning tells me it should be in the pantry where we keep the washer and dryer. As a result, it shifts from one location to the next, and because I work outside the home, it's impossible for me to keep up with such things. If I set my car keys on the counter, for instance, my instincts tell me they will still be there when I go to look for them, while Jane automatically believes that I will look for them on the bulletin board near the door. As to the location of the address book, it was plain to me that it was in the drawer by the phone. That's where I put it the last time I used it, and I was just about to say this when Jane spoke up.

"It's on the shelf next to the cookbooks."

I looked at her.

"Of course it is," I agreed.

The easy mood between us lasted until we finished dinner and began to clear the table.

Then, slowly, almost imperceptibly at first, the quick banter between us gave way to more stilted conversation, punctuated by longer pauses. By the time we'd started to clean the kitchen, we had retreated into a familiar dialogue, in which the most animated sound came not from either of us, but from the scraping of plates in the kitchen.

I can't explain why this happened, other than to say that we'd run out of things to say to each other. She asked about Noah a second time, and I repeated what I'd said previously. A minute later, she started speaking of the photographer again, but halfway through her story, she stopped herself, knowing she'd already recounted that as well. Because neither of us had spoken to Joseph or Leslie, there was no news on those fronts, either. And as for work, because I was out of the office, I had nothing whatsoever to add, even in an offhanded way. I could feel the earlier mood of the evening beginning to slip away and wanted to prevent the inevitable from happening. My mind began to search for something, anything, and I finally cleared my throat.

"Did you hear about the shark attack down in Wilmington?" I asked.

"You mean the one last week? With the girl?"

"Yes," I said, "that's the one."

"You told me about it."

"I did?"

"Last week. You read me the article."

I washed her wineglass by hand, then rinsed the colander. I could hear her sorting through the cupboards for the Tupperware.

"What a horrible way to start a vacation," she remarked. "Her family hadn't even finished unpacking the car yet."

The plates came next, and I scraped the remains into the sink. I turned on the garbage disposal, and the rumbling seemed to echo against the walls, underscoring the silence between us. When it stopped, I put the plates into the dishwasher.

"I pulled some weeds in the garden," I said.

"I thought you just did that a few days ago."

∽∞∾

"I did."

I loaded the utensils and rinsed the salad tongs. I turned the water on and off, slid the dishwasher rack in and out.

"I hope you didn't stay in the sun too long," she said.

She mentioned this because my father had died of a heart attack while washing the car when he was sixty-one years old. Heart disease ran in my family, and I knew it was something that worried Jane. Though we were less like lovers than friends these days, I knew that Jane would always care for me. Caring was part of her nature and always would be.

Her siblings are the same way, and I attribute that to Noah and Allie. Hugs and laughter were a staple in their home, a place where practical jokes were relished, because no one ever suspected meanness. I've often wondered about the person I would have become had I been born into that family.

"It's supposed to be hot again tomorrow," Jane said, breaking into my thoughts.

"I heard on the news it's supposed to hit ninety-five degrees," I concurred. "And the humidity is supposed to be high, too."

"Ninety-five?"

"That's what they said."

"That's too hot."

Jane put the leftovers into the refrigerator as I wiped the counters. After our earlier intimacy, the lack of meaningful conversation seemed deafening. From the expression on Jane's face, I knew she too was disappointed by this return to our normal state of affairs. She patted her dress, as if looking for words in her pockets. Finally, she drew a deep breath and forced a smile.

"I think I'll give Leslie a call," she said.

A moment later, I was standing in the kitchen alone, wishing again that I were someone else and wondering whether it was even possible for us to start over.

In the two weeks following our first date, Jane and I saw each other five more times before she returned to New Bern for the Christmas holidays. We studied together twice, went to a movie once, and spent two afternoons walking through the campus of Duke University.

But there was one particular walk that will always stand out in my mind. It was a gloomy day, having rained all morning, and gray clouds stretched across the sky, making it look almost like dusk. It was Sunday, two days after we'd saved the stray, and Jane and I were strolling among the various buildings on campus.

"What are your parents like?" she asked.

I took a few steps before answering. "They're good people," I finally said.

She waited for more, but when I didn't answer, she nudged my shoulder with her own.

"That's all you can say?"

I knew this was her attempt to get me to open up, and though it wasn't something I'd ever been comfortable doing, I knew that Jane would keep prodding me—gently and persistently—until I did. She was smart in a way that few others were, not only academically, but about people as well. Especially me.

"I don't know what else to tell you," I said. "They're just typical parents. They work for the government and they've lived in a town house in Dupont Circle for almost twenty years. That's in D.C., where I grew up. I think they thought about buying a house in the suburbs some years back, but neither one of them wanted to deal with the commute, so we stayed where we were."

"Did you have a backyard?"

"No. There was a nice courtyard, though, and sometimes weeds would sprout between the bricks."

She laughed. "Where did your parents meet?"

"Washington. They both grew up there, and they met when they both worked for the Department of Transportation. I guess they were in the same office for a while, but that's all I know for sure. They never said much more than that."

"Do they have any hobbies?"

I considered her question as I pictured both my parents. "My mom likes to write letters to the editor of *The Washington Post,*" I said. "I think she wants to change the world. She's always taking the side of the downtrodden, and of course, she's never short of ideas to make the world a better place. She must write at least a letter a week. Not all of them get printed, but she cuts out the ones that do and posts them in a scrapbook. And my dad . . . he's on the quiet side. He likes to build ships in bottles. He must have made hundreds over the years, and when we ran out of space on the shelves, he started donating them to schools to display in the libraries. Kids love them."

"Do you do that, too?"

"No. That's my dad's escape. He wasn't all that interested in teaching me how to do it, since he thought I should have my own hobby. But I could watch him work, as long as I didn't touch anything."

"That's sad."

"It didn't bother me," I countered. "I never knew any

different, and it was interesting. Quiet, but interesting. He didn't talk much as he worked, but it was nice spending time with him."

"Did he play catch with you? Or go bike riding?"

"No. He wasn't much of an outdoor guy. Just the ships. It taught me a lot about patience."

She lowered her gaze, watching her steps as she walked, and I knew she was comparing it to her own upbringing.

"And you're an only child?" she continued.

Though I'd never told anyone else, I found myself wanting to tell her why. Even then, I wanted her to know me, to know everything about me. "My mom couldn't have any more kids. She had some sort of hemorrhage when I was born, and it was just too risky after that."

She frowned. "I'm sorry."

"I think she was, too."

By that point, we'd reached the main chapel on campus, and Jane and I paused for a moment to admire the architecture.

"That's the most you've ever told me about yourself in one stretch," she remarked.

"It's probably more than I've told anyone."

From the corner of my eye, I saw her tuck a strand of hair behind her ear. "I think I understand you a little better now," she said.

I hesitated. "Is that a good thing?"

Instead of answering, Jane turned toward me and I suddenly realized that I already knew the answer.

I suppose I should remember exactly how it happened, but to be honest, the following moments are lost to me. In one instant, I reached for her hand, and in the next, I found myself pulling her gently toward me. She looked faintly startled, but when she saw my face moving toward hers, she closed her eyes, accepting what I was about to do. She leaned in, and as her lips touched mine, I knew that I would remember our first kiss forever.

Listening to Jane as she spoke on the phone with Leslie, I thought she sounded a lot like the girl who'd walked by my side on campus that day. Her voice was animated and the words flowed freely; I heard her laughing as if Leslie were in the room.

I sat on the couch half a room away, listening with half an ear. Jane and I used to walk and talk for hours, but now there were others who seemed to have taken my place. With the children, Jane was never at a loss as to what to say, nor did she struggle when she visited her father. Her circle of friends is quite large, and she visited easily with them as well. I wondered what they would think if they spent a typical evening with us.

Were we the only couple with this problem? Or was it common in all long marriages, an inevitable function of time? Logic seemed to infer it was the latter, yet it nonetheless pained me to realize that her levity would be gone the moment she hung up the phone. Instead of easy banter, we'd speak in platitudes and the magic would be gone, and I couldn't bear another discussion of the weather.

What to do, though? That was the question that plagued me. In the span of an hour, I'd viewed both our marriages, and I knew which one I preferred, which one I thought we deserved.

In the background, I heard Jane beginning to wind down with Leslie. There's a pattern when a call is nearing an end, and I knew Jane's as well as my own. Soon I would hear her tell our daughter that she loved her, pause as Leslie said it back to her, then say good-bye. Knowing it was coming—and suddenly deciding to take a chance—I rose from the couch and turned to face her.

I was going to walk across the room, I told myself, and reach for her hand, just as I had outside the chapel at Duke. She would wonder what was happening—just as she wondered then—but I'd pull her body next to mine. I'd touch her face, then slowly close my eyes, and as soon as my lips touched hers, she'd know that it was unlike any kiss she'd ever received from me. It would be new but familiar; appreciative but filled with longing; and its very inspiration would evoke the same feelings in her. It would be, I thought, a new beginning to our lives, just as our first kiss had been so long ago.

I could imagine it clearly, and a moment later, I heard her say her final words and hit the button to hang up the call. It was time, and gathering my courage, I started toward her.

Jane's back was to me, her hand still on the phone. She paused for a moment, staring out the living room window, watching the gray sky as it slowly darkened in color. She was the greatest person I've ever known, and I would tell her this in the moments following our kiss.

I kept moving. She was close now, close enough for me to catch the familiar scent of her perfume. I could feel my heart speed up. Almost there, I realized, but when I was close enough to touch her hand, she suddenly raised the phone again. Her movements were quick and efficient; she merely pressed two buttons. The number is on speed dial, and I knew exactly what she'd done.

A moment later, when Joseph answered the phone, I lost my resolve, and it was all I could do to make my way back to the couch.

For the next hour or so, I sat beneath the lamp, the biography of Roosevelt open in my lap.

Though she'd asked me to call the guests, after hanging up with Joseph, Jane made a few calls to those who were closest to the family. I understood her eagerness, but it left us in separate worlds until after nine, and I came to the conclusion that unrealized hopes, even small ones, were always wrenching.

When Jane finished, I tried to catch her eye. Instead of joining me on the couch, she retrieved a bag from the table by the front door, one I hadn't noticed she'd brought in.

"I picked these up for Anna on the way home," she said, waving a couple of bridal magazines, "but before I give them to her, I want to have a chance to look through them first."

I forced a smile, knowing the rest of the evening would be lost. "Good idea," I said.

As we settled into silence—me on the couch, Jane in the recliner—I found my gaze drawn surreptitiously toward her. Her eyes flickered as she looked from one gown to the next; I saw her crease the corners of various pages. Her eyes, like mine, are not as strong as they once were, and I noticed that she had to crane her neck back, as if looking down her nose to see more clearly. Every now and then, I heard her whisper something, an understated exclamation, and I knew she was picturing Anna wearing whatever was on the page.

Watching her expressive face, I marveled at the fact that at one time or another, I'd kissed every part of it. *I've never loved anyone but you*, I wanted to say, but common sense prevailed, reminding me that it would be better to save those words for another time, when I had her full attention and the words might be reciprocated.

As the evening wore on, I continued to watch her while pretending to read my book. I could do this all night, I thought, but weariness set in, and I was certain that Jane would stay awake for at least another hour. The creased pages would call to her if she didn't look at them a second time, and she had yet to make her way through both magazines.

"Jane?" I said.

"Mmm?" she answered automatically.

"I have an idea."

"About what?" She continued staring at the page.

"Where we should hold the wedding."

My words finally registered and she looked up.

"It might not be perfect, but I'm sure it would be available," I said. "It's outside and there's plenty of parking. And there're flowers, too. Thousands of flowers."

"Where?"

I hesitated.

"At Noah's house," I said. "Under the trellis by the roses."

Jane's mouth opened and closed; she blinked rapidly, as if clearing her sight. But then, ever so slowly, she began to smile.

Chapter Six

$\mathcal{I}$n the morning, I made arrangements for the tuxedos and began making calls to friends and neighbors on Anna's guest list, receiving mostly the answers I expected.

Of course we'll be there, one couple said. We wouldn't miss it for the world, said another. Though the calls were friendly, I didn't linger on the phone and was finished well before noon.

Jane and Anna had gone in search of flowers for the bouquets; later in the afternoon, they planned to swing by Noah's house. With hours to go until we were supposed to meet, I decided to drive to Creekside. On the way, I picked up three loaves of Wonder Bread from the grocery store.

As I drove, my thoughts drifted to Noah's house and my first visit there a long time ago.

Jane and I had been dating for six months before she brought me home to visit. She'd graduated from Meredith in June, and after the ceremony, she rode in my car as we followed her parents back to New Bern. Jane was the oldest of her siblings—only seven years separated the four of them—and I could tell from their faces when we arrived that they were still evaluating me. While I'd stood with Jane's family at her graduation and Allie had even looped her hand through my arm at one point, I couldn't help feeling self-conscious about the impression I'd made on them.

Sensing my anxiety, Jane immediately suggested that we take a walk when we reached the house. The seductive beauty of the low country had a soothing effect on my nerves; the sky was the color of robin's eggs, and the air held neither the briskness of spring nor the heat and humidity of summer. Noah had planted thousands of bulbs over the years, and lilies bloomed along the fence line in clusters of riotous color. A thousand shades of green graced the trees, and the air was filled with the trills of songbirds. But it was the rose garden, even from a distance, that caught my gaze. The five concentric hearts—the highest bushes in the middle, the lowest on the outside—were bursting in reds, pinks, oranges, whites, and yellows. There was an orchestrated randomness to the blooms, one that suggested a stalemate between man and nature that seemed almost out of place amid the wild beauty of the landscape.

In time, we ended up under the trellis adjacent to the garden. Obviously, I'd become quite fond of Jane by then, yet I still wasn't certain whether we would have a future together. As I've mentioned, I considered it a necessity to be gainfully employed before I became involved in a serious relationship. I was still a year away from my own graduation from law school, and it seemed unfair to ask her to wait for me. I didn't know then, of course, that I would eventually work in New Bern. Indeed, in the coming year, interviews were already set up with firms in Atlanta and

Washington, D.C., while she had made plans to move back home.

Jane, however, had been making my plans difficult to keep. She seemed to enjoy my company. She listened with interest, teased me playfully, and always reached for my hand whenever we were together. The first time she did this, I remember thinking how right it felt. Though it sounds ridiculous, when a couple holds hands, it either feels right or it doesn't. I suppose this has to do with the intertwining of fingers and the proper placement of the thumb, though when I tried to explain my reasoning to her, Jane laughed and asked me why it was so important to analyze.

On that day, the day of her graduation, she took my hand again and for the first time told me the story of Allie and Noah. They'd met when they were teenagers and had fallen in love, but Allie had moved away and they didn't speak for the next fourteen years. While they were separated, Noah worked in New Jersey, headed off to war, and finally returned to New Bern. Allie, meanwhile, became engaged to someone else. On the verge of her wedding, however, she returned to visit Noah and realized it was he whom she'd always loved. In the end, Allie broke off her engagement and stayed in New Bern.

Though we'd talked about many things, she'd never told me this. At the time, the story was not as touching to me as it is now, but I suppose this was a function of my age and gender. Yet I could tell the story meant a lot to her, and I was touched by how much she cared for her parents. Soon after she began, her dark eyes were brimming with tears that spilled onto her cheeks. At first she dabbed at them, but then she stopped, as if deciding it didn't matter whether or not I saw her cry. This implied comfort affected me deeply, for I knew that she was entrusting me with something that she'd shared with few others. I myself have seldom cried at anything, and when she finished, she seemed to understand this about me.

"I'm sorry about getting so emotional," she said quietly. "But I've been waiting to tell you that story for a long time. I wanted it to be just the right moment, in just the right place."

Then she squeezed my hand as though she wanted to hold on to it forever.

I glanced away, feeling a tightness in my chest that I'd never before experienced. The scene around me was intensely vivid, every petal and blade of grass standing out in sharp relief. Behind her, I saw her family gathering on the porch. Prisms of sunlight cut patterns on the ground.

"Thank you for sharing this with me," I whispered, and when I turned to face her, I knew what it meant to finally fall in love.

I went to Creekside and found Noah seated at the pond.

"Hello, Noah," I said.

"Hello, Wilson." He continued staring out over the water. "Thanks for dropping by."

I set the bag of bread on the ground. "You doing okay?"

"Could be better. Could be worse, though, too."

I sat beside him on the bench. The swan in the pond had no fear of me and stayed in the shallows near us.

"Did you tell her," he asked, "about having the wedding at the house?"

I nodded. This had been the idea that I mentioned to Noah the day before.

"I think she was surprised she hadn't thought of it first."

"She's got a lot on her mind."

"Yes, she does. She and Anna left right after breakfast."

"Rarin' to go?"

"You could say that. Jane practically dragged Anna out the door. I haven't heard from her since."

"Allie was the same way with Kate's wedding."

He was speaking of Jane's younger sister. Like the wedding this weekend, Kate's had been held at Noah's house. Jane had been the matron of honor.

"I suppose she's already been looking at wedding gowns."

I glanced at him, surprised.

"That was the best part for Allie, I think," he went on. "She and Kate spent two days in Raleigh searching for the perfect dress. Kate tried on over a hundred of them, and when Allie got home, she described every one of them to me. Lace here, sleeves there, silk and taffeta, cinched waistlines . . . she must have rambled on for hours, but she was so beautiful when she was excited that I barely heard what she was saying."

I brought my hands to my lap. "I don't think she and Anna will have the time for something like that."

"No, I don't suppose they will." He turned to me. "But she'll be beautiful no matter what she wears, you know."

I nodded.

These days, the children share in the upkeep of Noah's house.

We own it jointly; Noah and Allie had made those arrangements before they moved to Creekside. Because the house had meant so much to them, and to the children, they simply couldn't part with it. Nor could they have given it to only one of their children, since it is the site of countless shared memories for all of them.

As I said, I visited the house frequently, and as I walked the property after leaving Creekside, I made mental notes of all that had to be done. A caretaker kept the grass mowed and the fence in good condition, but a lot of work would be needed to get the property ready for visitors, and there was no way I could do it alone. The white house was coated with the gray dust of a thousand rainstorms, but it was nothing that a good power washing couldn't spruce up. Despite the caretaker's efforts, however, the grounds were in bad shape. Weeds were sprouting along the fence posts, hedges needed to be trimmed, and only dried stalks remained of the early-blooming lilies. Hibiscus, hydrangea, and geraniums added splashes of color but needed reshaping as well.

While all that could be taken care of relatively quickly, the rose garden worried me. It had grown wild in the years the house had been empty; each concentric heart was roughly the same height, and every bush seemed to grow into the last. Countless stems poked out at odd angles, and the leaves obscured much of the color. I had no idea whether the floodlights still worked. From where I stood, it seemed there was no way it could be salvaged except by pruning everything back and waiting another year for the blooms to return.

I hoped my landscaper would be able to work a miracle. If anyone could handle the project, he could. A quiet man with a passion for perfection, Nathan Little had worked on some of the most famous gardens in North Carolina—the Biltmore Estate, the Tryon Place, the Duke Botanical Gardens—and he knew more about plants than anyone I'd ever met.

My passion for our own garden at home—small, but nonetheless stunning—had led us to become friends over the years, and Nathan often made a point of coming by in the hours after work. We had long conversations about acid in the soil and the role of shade for azaleas, differences in fertilizers, and even the watering requirements of pansies. It was something completely removed from the work I did at the office, which is perhaps the reason it gave me such joy.

As I surveyed the property, I visualized how I wanted it to look. In the midst of my earlier calls, I'd also contacted Nathan, and though it was Sunday, he'd agreed to swing by. He had three crews, most of whom spoke only Spanish, and the amount of work a single crew could accomplish in a day was staggering. Still, this was a large project, and I prayed they would be able to finish in time.

It was as I was making my mental notes that I saw Harvey Wellington, the pastor, in the distance. He was on his front porch, leaning against the post with his arms crossed. He didn't move when I spotted him. We seemed to be watching each other, and a moment later, I saw him grin. I thought it was an invitation to go see him, but when I glanced away and then back again, he'd vanished inside his home. Even though we'd spoken, even though I'd shaken his hand, I suddenly realized that I'd never set foot beyond his front door.

Nathan dropped by after lunch, and we spent an hour together. He nodded continuously as I spoke but kept his questions to a minimum. When I was finished, he shaded his eyes with his hand.

Only the rose garden will be troublesome, he finally said. It will be much work to make it look the way it should.

But it's possible?

He studied the rose garden for a long moment before nodding. Wednesday and Thursday, he finally said. The entire crew will come, he added. Thirty people.

Only two days? I asked. Even with the garden? He knew his business as I know my own, but this statement amazed me nonetheless.

He smiled and put a hand on my shoulder. "Do not worry, my friend," he said. "It will be magnificent."

By midafternoon, heat was rising from the ground in shimmering waves. The humidity had thickened the air, making the horizon seem out of focus. Feeling the perspiration beading on my brow, I removed a handkerchief from my pocket. After wiping my face, I sat on the porch to wait for Jane and Anna.

Though the home was boarded up, this hadn't been done for safety reasons. Rather, the boards were placed over the windows to prevent random vandalism and to keep people from exploring the rooms within. Noah had designed them himself before leaving for Creekside—while his sons had actually done most of the work—and they were attached to the house with hinges and internal hooks so they could be opened easily from the inside. The caretaker did that twice a year to air out the house. The electricity had been turned off, but there was a generator in the rear that the caretaker sometimes turned on to check that the outlets and switches were still in working order. The water had never been turned off because of the sprinkler system, and the caretaker had told me that he sometimes ran the faucets in the kitchen and baths to clean the pipes of any dust that had accumulated.

One day, I'm sure that someone will move back in. It won't be Jane and me, nor could I imagine any of the other siblings here, but it seemed inevitable. It was also inevitable that this would happen only long after Noah was gone.

A few minutes later, Anna and Jane arrived, dust billowing behind the car as they pulled up the drive. I met them in the shade of a giant oak tree. Both were looking around, and I could see the anxiety mounting on Jane's face. Anna was chewing gum, and she offered a brief smile.

"Hi, Daddy," she said.

"Hi, sweetheart. How did it go today?" I asked.

"It was fun. Mom was in a panic, but we finally got it worked out. The bouquet is ordered. and so are the corsages and boutonnieres."

Jane didn't seem to hear her; she was still glancing around frantically. I knew she was thinking there was no way the property would be ready in time. Because she visits less frequently than I, I think she had retained the image of how this place used to look, not how it looked today.

I brought a hand to her shoulder. "Do not worry, it will be magnificent," I reassured her, echoing the promise of the landscaper.

Later, Jane and I strolled the grounds together. Anna had wandered off to talk to Keith on her cell phone. As we walked, I related the ideas I had discussed with Nathan, but I could tell her mind was elsewhere.

When pressed, Jane shook her head. "It's Anna," she confessed with a sigh. "One minute she's into the plans, and the next minute she isn't. And she can't seem to make any decisions on her own. Even with the flowers. She didn't know what colors she wanted for the bouquets, she didn't know which varieties. But as soon as I say that I like something, she says that she does, too. It's driving me crazy. I mean, I know this whole thing is my idea, but still, it's her wedding."

"She's always been like that," I said. "Don't you remember when she was little? You used to tell me the same thing when the two of you went shopping for school clothes."

"I know," she said, but her tone suggested something else was bothering her.

"What is it?" I asked.

"I just wish we had more time." Jane sighed. "I know we've gotten a few things done, but if we had more time, I could arrange for a reception of some sort. As lovely as the ceremony will be, what about afterward? She'll never have another chance to experience something like this."

My wife, the hopeless romantic.

"Why don't we have a reception, then?"

"What are you talking about?"

"Why don't we have one here? We'll just open up the house."

She looked at me as if I'd lost my senses. "For what? We don't have a caterer, we don't have tables, we won't have any music. Those things take time to arrange. It's not as if you can snap your fingers and have everyone you need come running."

"That's what you said about the photographer, too."

"Receptions are different," she explained with an air of finality.

"Then we'll do it differently," I persisted. "Maybe we'll have some of the guests bring food."

She blinked. "Pot luck?" She didn't try to hide her dismay. "You want to have a *pot luck* dinner for the reception?"

I felt myself shrink a bit. "It was just an idea," I mumbled.

She shook her head and looked off into the distance. "It's okay," she said. "It's not a big deal, anyway. It's the ceremony that matters."

"Let me make some calls," I offered. "Maybe I can arrange something."

"There's not enough time," she repeated.

"I *do* know people who do things like this."

This was true. As one of only three estate lawyers in town—and for the early part of my career the only one— it seemed that I knew most of the business owners in the county.

She hesitated. "I know you do," she said, but the words sounded like an apology. Surprising myself, I reached for her hand.

"I'll make some calls," I said. "Trust me."

It might have been the seriousness with which I spoke, or the earnestness of my gaze, but as we stood together, she looked up and seemed to study me. Then, ever so slowly, she squeezed my hand to profess her confidence in me.

"Thank you," she said, and with her hand clutching mine, I felt a strange sensation of déjà vu, as if our years together had suddenly been reversed. And for the briefest moment, I could see Jane standing under the trellis again—I'd just heard the story of her parents, and we were our youthful selves, the future bright and promising before us. Everything was new, as it was so long ago, and when I watched her leave with Anna a minute later, I was suddenly certain that this wedding was the most blessed thing to have happened to us in years.

Chapter Seven

Dinner was nearly ready when Jane walked in the door later that evening.

I set the oven on low—tonight was chicken cordon bleu—and I wiped my hands as I left the kitchen.

"Hey there," I said.

"Hey. How'd it go with the calls?" she asked, setting her purse on the end table. "I forgot to ask you earlier."

"So far, so good," I said. "Everyone on the list said they could make it. At least the ones that I've heard from, anyway."

"Everyone? That's . . . amazing. People are usually on vacation this time of year."

"Like us?"

She gave a carefree laugh, and I was pleased to see that she seemed in a better mood. "Oh, sure," she said with a wave, "we're just sitting around and relaxing, aren't we?"

"It's not so bad."

She caught the aroma from the kitchen, and her face took on a puzzled expression. "Are you making dinner again?"

"I didn't think you'd be in the mood to cook tonight."

She smiled. "That was sweet." Her eyes met mine and seemed to linger a bit longer than usual. "Would you mind if I shower before we eat? I'm kind of sweaty. We were in and out of the car all day."

"Not at all," I said, waving a hand.

A few minutes later, I heard water moving through the pipes. I sautéed the vegetables, reheated the bread from the night before, and was setting the table when Jane entered the kitchen.

Like her, I had showered after returning from Noah's house. Afterward I'd slipped into a new pair of chinos, since most of my older ones no longer fit.

"Are those the pants I bought for you?" Jane asked, pausing in the doorway.

"Yeah. How do they look?"

She gave an appraising look.

"They fit well," she remarked. "From this angle, you can really tell you've lost a lot of weight."

"That's good," I said. "I'd hate to think I suffered this past year for nothing."

"You haven't suffered. Walked, maybe, but not suffered."

"You try getting up before the sun, especially when it's raining."

"Oh, poor baby," she teased. "Must be tough being you."

"You have no idea."

She giggled. While upstairs, she too had slipped into a pair of comfortable pants, but her painted toenails peeked out beneath the hems. Her hair was wet, and there were a couple of water spots on her blouse. Even when she wasn't trying, she was one of the most sensual women I've ever seen.

"So get this," Jane said. "Anna says Keith is thrilled with our plans. He sounds more excited than Anna."

"Anna's excited. She's just nervous about how it'll all turn out."

"No, she's not. Anna never gets nervous about anything. She's like you."

"I get nervous," I protested.

"No, you don't."

"Of course I do."

"Name one time."

I thought about it. "All right," I said. "I was nervous when I went back for my final year of law school."

She considered this before shaking her head. "You weren't nervous about law school. You were a star. You were on the *Law Review*."

"I wasn't nervous about my studies, I was scared about losing you. You started teaching in New Bern, remember? I just knew some dashing young gentleman was going to swoop in and steal you away. That would have broken my heart."

She stared at me curiously, trying to make sense of what I'd just said. Instead of responding to my comment, however, she put her hands on her hips and tilted her head. "You know, I think you're getting caught up in all this, too."

"What do you mean?"

"The wedding. I mean, making dinner two nights in a row, helping me out with all the plans, waxing nostalgic like this. I think all the excitement's getting to you."

I heard a ding as the oven timer went off.

"You know," I agreed, "I think you might be right."

I wasn't lying when I told Jane that I was nervous about losing her when I went back to Duke for my final year, and I'll admit I didn't handle these challenging circumstances as well as I might have. I knew going into my last year that it would be impossible for Jane and me to maintain the kind of relationship we'd developed over the past nine months, and I found myself wondering how she would react to this change. As the summer wore on, we discussed this a few times, but Jane never seemed worried. She seemed almost cavalier in her confidence that we'd manage somehow, and though I suppose I could have taken this as a reassuring sign, I was sometimes struck by the thought that I cared for her more than she cared for me.

Granted, I knew I had good qualities, but I don't regard my good qualities as extraordinarily rare. Nor are my bad qualities extraordinarily dire. In fact, I consider myself average in most respects, and even thirty years ago, I knew I was destined for neither fame nor obscurity.

Jane, on the other hand, could have become anyone she chose. I've long since decided that Jane would be equally at home in either poverty or wealth, in a cosmopolitan setting or a rural one. Her ability to adapt has always impressed me. When looked at together—her intelligence and passion, her kindness and charm—it seemed obvious that Jane would have made a wonderful wife to just about anyone.

Why, then, had she chosen me?

It was a question that plagued me constantly in the early days of our relationship, and I could come up with no answer that made sense. I worried that Jane would wake up one morning and realize that there was nothing special about me and move on to a more charismatic guy. Feeling so insecure, I stopped short of telling her how I felt about her. There were times I'd wanted to, but the moments would pass before I could summon the courage.

This is not to say that I kept the fact that I was seeing

her a secret. Indeed, while I was working at the law firm over the summer, my relationship with Jane was one of the topics that came up regularly over lunch with the other summer associates, and I made a point of describing it as close to ideal. I never divulged anything that I later regretted, but I do remember thinking that some of my fellow co-workers seemed jealous that I was successfully forging ahead not only professionally, but personally as well. One of them, Harold Larson—who, like me, was also a member of the *Law Review* at Duke—was particularly attentive whenever I mentioned Jane's name, and I suspected that this was because he too had a girlfriend. He'd been dating Gail for over a year and had always spoken easily about their relationship. Like Jane, Gail was no longer living in the area, having moved to be near her parents in Fredericksburg, Virginia. Harold had mentioned more than once that he planned to marry Gail as soon as he graduated.

Toward the end of the summer, we were sitting together when someone asked us whether we planned to bring our girlfriends to the cocktail party that the firm was throwing in our honor as a send-off. The question seemed to upset Harold, and when pressed, he frowned.

"Gail and I broke up last week," he admitted. Though it was clearly a painful topic, he seemed to feel the need to explain. "I thought things were great between us, even though I haven't gotten back to see her much. I guess the distance was too much for her, and she didn't want to wait until I graduated. She met someone else."

I suppose it was my memory of this conversation that colored our last afternoon of the summer together. It was Sunday, two days after I'd brought Jane to the cocktail party, and she and I were sitting in the rockers on the porch at Noah's house. I was leaving for Durham that evening, and I remember staring out over the river and wondering whether we would be able to make it work or whether Jane, like Gail, would find someone to re-place me.

"Hey, stranger," she finally said, "why so quiet today?"

"I'm just thinking about heading back to school."

She smiled. "Are you dreading it or looking forward to it?"

"Both, I guess."

"Look at it this way. It's only nine months until you graduate, and then you're done."

I nodded but said nothing.

She studied me. "Are you sure that's all that's bothering you? You've had a glum face all day."

I shifted in my seat. "Do you remember Harold Larson?" I asked. "I introduced you to him at the cocktail party."

She squinted, trying to place him. "The one who was on *Law Review* with you? Tall, with brown hair?"

I nodded.

"What about him?" she asked.

"Did you happen to notice that he was alone?"

"Not really. Why?"

"His girlfriend just broke up with him."

"Oh," she said, though I could tell she had no idea how this related to her or why I was thinking about it.

"It's going to be a tough year," I began. "I'm sure I'll practically live in the library."

She put a friendly hand on my knee. "You did great the first two years. I'm sure you'll do just fine."

"I hope so," I continued. "It's just that with everything going on, I'm probably not going to be able to make it down every weekend to see you like I did this summer."

"I figured that. But we'll still see each other. It's not like you won't have any time at all. And I can always drive up to see you, too, remember."

In the distance, I watched as a flock of starlings broke from the trees. "You might want to check before you come. To see if I'm free, I mean. The last year is supposed to be the busiest."

She tilted her head, trying to decipher my meaning. "What's going on, Wilson?"

"What do you mean?"

"This. What you just said. You sound like you've already been thinking up excuses not to see me."

"It's not an excuse. I just want to make sure you understand how busy my schedule is going to be."

Jane leaned back in her chair, her mouth settling into a straight line. "And?" she asked.

"And what?"

"And what exactly does that mean? That you don't want to see me anymore?"

"No," I protested, "of course not. But the fact is that you'll be here, and I'm going to be there. You know how hard long-distance relationships can be."

She crossed her arms. "So?"

"Well, it's just that they can ruin the best of intentions, and to be honest, I don't want either of us to get hurt."

"Get hurt?"

"That's what happened to Harold and Gail," I explained. "They didn't see each other much because he was so busy, and they broke up because of it."

She hesitated. "And you think the same thing's going to happen to us," she said carefully.

"You have to admit the odds aren't in our favor."

"The *odds*?" She blinked. "You're trying to put what we have into numbers?"

"I'm just trying to be honest. . . ."

"About what? *Odds*? What does that have to do with us? And what does Harold have to do with anything?"

"Jane, I . . ."

She turned away, unable to look at me. "If you don't want to see me anymore, just say it. Don't use a busy schedule as an excuse. Just tell me the truth. I'm an adult. I can take it."

"I am telling you the truth," I said quickly. "I do want to see you. I didn't mean for it to come out the way it did." I swallowed. "I mean . . . well . . . you're a very special person, and you mean a great deal to me."

She said nothing. In the silence that followed, I watched in surprise as a single tear spilled down her cheek. She swiped at it before crossing her arms. Her gaze was focused on the trees near the river.

"Why do you always have to do that?" Her voice was raw.

"Do what?"

"This . . . what you're doing now. Talking about odds, using statistics to explain things . . . to explain us. The world doesn't always work that way. And neither do people. We're not Harold and Gail."

"I know that. . . ."

She faced me, and for the first time, I saw the anger and pain I'd caused her. "Then why did you say it?" she demanded. "I know it's not going to be easy, but so what? My mom and dad didn't see each other for fourteen *years*, and they still got married. And you're talking about nine months? When you're only a couple of hours away? We can call, we can write. . . ." She shook her head.

"I'm sorry," I said. "I guess I'm just scared about losing you. I didn't mean to upset you. . . ."

"Why?" she asked. "Because I'm a *special person*? Because I mean a *great deal to you*?"

I nodded. "Yes, of course you do. And you are special."

She took a deep breath. "Well, I'm glad to know you, too."

With that, understanding finally dawned on me. While I meant my own words as a compliment, Jane had interpreted them differently, and the thought that I had hurt her made my throat suddenly go dry.

"I'm sorry," I said again, "I didn't mean for it to come out the way it sounded. You are very special to me, but . . . you see, the thing is . . ."

My tongue felt as if it were twisted, and my stammering finally elicited a sigh from Jane. Knowing I was running out of time, I cleared my throat and tried to tell her what was in my heart.

"What I meant to say was that I think I love you," I whispered.

She was quiet, but I knew she'd heard me when her mouth finally began to curl into a slight smile.

"Well," she said, "do you or don't you?"

I swallowed. "I do," I said. Then, wanting to be perfectly clear, I added, "Love you, I mean."

For the first time in our conversation, she laughed, amused by how hard I'd made it. Then, raising her eyebrows, she finally smiled. "Why, Wilson," she said, drawing out the words in exaggerated southern fashion, "I think that's the sweetest thing you've ever said to me."

Surprising me, she suddenly got up from her chair and sat in my lap. She slipped an arm around me and kissed me gently. Beyond her, the rest of the world was out of focus, and in the waning light, as if disembodied, I heard my own words coming back to me.

"I do, too," she said. "Love you, I mean."

I was remembering this story when Jane's voice broke in.

"Why are you smiling?" she asked.

She stared at me from across the table. Dinner was casual tonight; we had filled our plates in the kitchen, and I hadn't bothered to light a candle.

"Do you ever think about the night you came to visit me at Duke?" I asked. "When we finally got to go to Harper's?"

"That was after you got the job in New Bern, right? And you said you wanted to celebrate?"

I nodded. "You wore a strapless black dress. . . ."

"You remember that?"

"Like it was yesterday," I said. "We hadn't seen each other in about a month, and I remember watching from my window as you got out of the car."

Jane looked faintly pleased. I went on. "I can even remember what I was thinking when I saw you."

"You can?"

"I was thinking that the year we'd been dating was the happiest year I'd ever had."

Her gaze dropped to her plate, then met mine again, almost shyly. Buoyed by the memory, I plunged on.

"Do you remember what I got you? For Christmas?"

It was a moment before she answered. "Earrings," she said, her hands traveling absently to her earlobes. "You bought me diamond earrings. I knew they were expensive, and I remember being shocked that you'd splurged that way."

"How do you know they were expensive?"

"You told me."

"I did?" This I didn't remember.

"Once or twice," she said, smirking. For a moment we ate in silence. Between mouthfuls, I studied the curve of her jawline and the way the late evening sunlight played across her face.

"It doesn't seem like thirty years have passed, does it?" I said.

A shadow of that old familiar sadness flitted across her face.

"No," she said, "I can't believe Anna's actually old enough to get married. I don't know where the time goes."

"What would you have changed?" I asked. "If you could?"

"In my life, you mean?" She looked away. "I don't know. I guess I would have tried to enjoy it more while it was happening."

"I feel the same way."

"Do you really?" Jane looked genuinely surprised.

I nodded. "Of course."

Jane seemed to recover. "It's just—please don't take this the wrong way, Wilson, but you usually don't wallow in the past. I mean, you're so practical about things. You have so few regrets. . . ." She trailed off.

"And you do?" I asked softly.

She studied her hands for a moment. "No, not really."

I almost reached for her hand then, but she changed the subject, saying brightly, "We went to see Noah today. After we left the house."

"Oh?"

"He mentioned that you'd stopped by earlier."

"I did. I wanted to make sure it was okay if we used the house."

"That's what he said." She moved some vegetables around with her fork. "He and Anna looked so cute together. She held his hand the whole time she was telling him about the wedding. I wish you could have seen it. It reminded me of the way he and Mom used to sit together." For a moment, she seemed lost in thought. Then she looked up. "I wish Mom were still around," she said. "She always loved weddings."

"I think it runs in the family," I murmured.

She smiled wistfully. "You're probably right. You can't imagine how much fun this is, even on such short notice. I can't wait until Leslie gets married and we have time to really concentrate on it."

"She doesn't even have a serious boyfriend, let alone someone who wants to propose to her."

"Details, details," she said, tossing her head. "It doesn't mean we can't start planning it, does it?"

Who was I to argue? "Well, when it does happen," I commented, "I hope that whoever proposes gets my permission in advance."

"Did Keith do that?"

"No, but this wedding's such a rush, I wouldn't have expected him to. Still, it's one of those character-building experiences I think every young man should go through."

"Like when you asked Daddy?"

"Oh, I built a lot of character that day."

"Oh?" She gazed at me curiously.

"I think I could have handled it a little better."

"Daddy never told me that."

"That's probably because he took pity on me. It wasn't exactly the most opportune of moments."

"Why didn't you ever tell me?"

"Because I never wanted you to know."

"Well, now you *have* to tell me."

I reached for my glass of wine, trying not to make a

big deal out of it. "All right," I said, "here's the story. I'd come by right after work, but I was supposed to meet with the partners again later that same night, so I didn't have much time. I found Noah working in his shop. This was right before we all went to stay at the beach. Anyway, he was building a birdhouse for some cardinals that had nested on the porch, and he was right in the middle of tacking the roof on. He was pretty intent on finishing the work before the weekend, and I kept trying to figure out a way to work the subject of you and me into the conversation, but the opportunity wasn't there. Finally, I just blurted it out. He asked me if I'd get him another nail, and when I handed it to him, I said, 'Here you go. And oh, by the way, that reminds me—would you mind if I married Jane?' "

She giggled. "You always were a smooth one," she remarked. "I guess I shouldn't be surprised, given the way you proposed. It was so . . ."

"Memorable?"

"Malcolm and Linda never get tired of that story," she said, referring to a couple we'd been friends with for years. "Especially Linda. Every time we're with other people, she begs me to tell the story."

"And of course, you're willing to oblige."

She raised her hands innocently. "If my friends enjoy my stories, who am I to withhold them?"

As the easy banter continued through dinner, I was conscious of everything about her. I watched as she cut the chicken into small bites before eating it, and the way her hair caught the light; I smelled the faintest trace of the jasmine gel she'd used earlier. There was no explanation for this longer-lasting newfound ease between us, and I didn't try to understand it. I wondered if Jane even noticed. If so, she gave no indication, but then neither did

I, and we lingered over dinner until the remains grew cold on the table.

The story of my proposal is indeed memorable, and it never fails to provoke gales of laughter among those who hear it.

This sharing of history is fairly common in our social circle, and when we socialize, my wife and I cease to be individuals. We are a couple, a team, and I've often enjoyed this interplay. We can each hop into the middle of a story that the other has begun and continue the other's train of thought without hesitation. She might begin the story in which Leslie was leading a cheer at a football game when one of the running backs slipped near the sideline and began careening toward her. If Jane pauses, I know it is my signal to inform them that Jane was the first to leap out of her seat to make sure she was okay, because I was paralyzed with fear. But once I finally summoned the will to move, I bounded through the crowd, pushing and shoving and knocking people off balance, much like the running back a moment before. Then, in the moment I take a breath to pause, Jane easily picks up where I left off. I am amazed that neither of us seems to find this out of the ordinary, or even difficult. This give-and-take has become natural for us, and I often wonder what it is like for those who don't know their partners quite so well. Leslie, I might add, was not injured that day. By the time we reached her, she was already reaching for her pom-poms.

But I never join in the story of my proposal. Instead I sit in silence, knowing that Jane finds it much more humorous than I. After all, I didn't intend for it to be a humorous event. I was sure it would be a day she would always remember and hoped that she would find it romantic.

Somehow, Jane and I had made it through the year with our love intact. By late spring we were talking about getting engaged, and the only surprise was when we would make it official. I knew she wanted something special— her parents' romance had set a high bar. When Noah and Allie were together, it seemed as if everything turned out perfectly. If it rained while they were out together—a miserable experience, most would admit—Allie and Noah would use it as an excuse to build a fire and lie beside each other, falling ever more deeply in love. If Allie was in the mood for poetry, Noah could recite a series of verses from memory. If Noah was the example, I knew I must follow his lead, and for this reason, I planned to propose to her on the beach at Ocracoke, where her family was vacationing in July.

My plan, I thought, was inspired. Quite simply, after picking out an engagement ring, I planned to hide it in the conch I had picked up the year before, with the intention that she would find it later, when we were out scouring the beach for sand dollars. When she did, I planned to drop to one knee, take her hand, and tell her that she would make me the happiest man in the world if she would consent to be my wife.

Unfortunately, things didn't go exactly as planned. A storm was in full swing that weekend, with heavy rain and winds strong enough to make the trees bend almost horizontal. All day Saturday, I waited for the storm to abate, but nature seemed to have other ideas, and it wasn't until midmorning Sunday that the sky began to clear.

I was more nervous than I'd imagined I would be, and I found myself mentally rehearsing exactly what I wanted to say. This sort of rote preparation had always served me well in law school, but I didn't realize that my preparation would keep me from speaking to Jane as we made our way along the beach. I don't know how long we continued to walk in silence, but it was long enough for the sound of Jane's voice to startle me when she finally spoke up.

"The tide's really coming in, isn't it?"

I hadn't realized that the tide would be so affected even after the storm had passed, and though I was fairly certain that the shell was safe, I didn't want to take any chances. Concerned, I started to walk even more quickly, though I tried my best not to arouse her suspicion.

"Why the rush?" she asked me.

"Am I rushing?" I answered.

She didn't seem satisfied with my response and finally slowed down. For a little while, until I spotted the conch, at least, I walked by myself, a few steps ahead of her. When I saw the high-water marks in the sand near the shell, I knew we had time. Not a lot, but I felt myself relax a bit.

I turned to say something to Jane, unaware that she had already stopped a little ways back. She was bending toward the sand, one arm extended, and I knew exactly what she was doing. Whenever she was at the beach, Jane had a habit of looking for tiny sand dollars. The best ones, the ones she kept, were paper-thin and translucent, no larger than a fingernail.

"Come quick!" she called out without looking up. "There's a whole bunch right here."

The conch with the ring was twenty yards ahead of me, Jane was twenty yards behind. Finally realizing that we'd barely said more than a few words to each other since we'd been on the beach, I decided to go to Jane. When I reached her, she held up a sand dollar before me, balancing it like a contact lens on the tip of her finger.

"Look at this one."

It was the smallest one we'd found. After handing it to me, she bent over again to start looking for more.

I joined her in the search with the intention of gradually leading her to the conch, but Jane continued to hover in the same spot no matter how far I moved away. I had to keep glancing up every few seconds to make sure the shell was still safe.

"What are you looking at?" Jane finally asked me.

"Nothing," I said. Still, I felt compelled to look again a few moments later, and when Jane caught me, she raised an eyebrow uncertainly.

As the tide continued to rise, I realized we were running out of time. Still, Jane hovered in the same spot. She had found two more sand dollars that were even smaller than the first and she seemed to have no intention of moving. At last, not knowing what else to do, I pretended to notice the shell in the distance.

"Is that a conch?"

She looked up.

"Why don't you go grab it?" she said. "It looks like a nice one."

I didn't know quite what to say. After all, I wanted her to be the one to find it. By now the waves were breaking precariously close.

"Yes, it does," I said.

"Are you going to go get it?"

"No."

"Why not?"

"Maybe you should go get it."

"Me?" She looked puzzled.

"If you want it."

She seemed to debate a moment before shaking her head. "We've got lots of them at the house. No big deal."

"You sure?"

"Yeah."

This was not going well. While trying to figure out what to do next, I suddenly noticed a large swell approaching the shore. Desperate—and without a word to her—I suddenly bolted from her side, surging toward the conch.

I've never been noted for my quickness, but on that day I moved like an athlete. Sprinting as hard as I could, I grabbed the shell like an outfielder retrieving a baseball, moments before the wave swept over the spot. Unfortunately, the act of reaching for it left me off balance, and I tumbled to the sand, the air escaping my lungs in a loud *whumph*. When I stood, I did my best to look dignified as I shook the sand and water from my soaked clothing. In the distance, I could see Jane staring wide-eyed at me.

I brought the shell back and offered it to her.

"Here," I said, breathing hard.

She was still eyeing me with a curious expression. "Thank you," she said.

I expected her to turn it over, I suppose, or move the shell in such a way as to hear the movement of the ring inside, but she didn't. Instead, we simply stared at each other.

"You really wanted this shell, didn't you?" she finally said.

"Yes."

"It's nice."

"Yes."

"Thank you again."

"You're welcome."

Still, she hadn't moved it. Growing a bit anxious, I said: "Shake it."

She seemed to study my words.

"Shake it," she repeated.

"Yes."

"Are you feeling okay, Wilson?"

"Yes." I nodded in encouragement toward the shell.

"Okay," she said slowly.

When she did, the ring fell to the sand. I immediately dropped to one knee and began looking for it. Forgetting all of what I had intended to say, I went straight to the proposal, without even the presence of mind to look up at her.

"Will you marry me?"

When we finished cleaning the kitchen, Jane went outside to stand on the deck, leaving the door cracked open as if inviting me to join her. When I went out, I saw her leaning against the rail as she had the night that Anna had broken the news of her wedding.

The sun had set, and an orange moon was rising just over the trees like a jack-o'-lantern in the sky. I saw Jane staring at it. The heat had finally broken and a breeze had picked up.

"Do you really think you'll be able to find a caterer?" she asked.

I leaned in beside her. "I'll do my best."

"Oh," she said suddenly. "Remind me to make the reservations for Joseph tomorrow. I know we can get him into Raleigh, but hopefully we can get a connection straight to New Bern."

"I can do that," I volunteered. "I'll be on the phone anyway."

"You sure?"

"It's no big deal," I said. On the river, I could see a boat moving past us, a black shadow with a glowing light out front.

"So what else do you and Anna have to do?" I asked.

"More than you can imagine."

"Still?"

"Well, there's the dress, of course. Leslie wants to go with us, and it's probably going to take at least a couple of days."

"For a dress?"

"She has to find the right one, and then we have to get it fitted. We talked to a seamstress this morning, and she says that she can work it in if we can get it to her by Thursday. And then, of course, there's the reception. If there is one, I mean. A caterer is one thing, but if you can pull that off, we still need music of some kind. And we'll need to decorate, so you'll have to call the rental company. . . ."

As she spoke, I let out a quiet sigh. I knew I shouldn't have been surprised, but still . . .

"So while I'm making calls tomorrow, I take it you'll be off dress shopping, right?"

"I can't wait." She shivered. "Watching her try them on, seeing what she likes. I've been waiting for this moment ever since she was a little girl. It's exciting."

"I'm sure," I said.

She held up her thumb and forefinger in a pinching motion. "And to think that Anna was this close to not letting me do it."

"It's amazing how ungrateful children can be, isn't it."

She laughed, turning her gaze toward the water again. In the background, I could hear crickets and frogs beginning their evening song, a sound that never seems to change.

"Would you like to take a walk?" I asked suddenly.

She hesitated. "Now?"

"Why not?"

"Where do you want to go?"

"Does it matter?"

Though she seemed surprised, she answered. "Not really."

A few minutes later, we were making our way around the block. The streets were empty. From the homes on either side of us, I could see lights blazing behind curtains and shadows moving around inside. Jane and I walked on the shoulder of the road, rocks and gravel crunching beneath our feet. Above us, stratus clouds stretched across the sky, making a silver band.

"Is it this quiet in the mornings?" Jane asked. "When you walk?"

I usually leave the house before six, long before she wakes.

"Sometimes. Usually there are a few joggers out. And dogs. They like to sneak up behind you and bark suddenly."

"Good for the heart, I'll bet."

"It's like an extra workout," I agreed. "But it keeps me on my toes."

"I should start walking again. I used to love to walk."

"You can always join me."

"At five-thirty? I don't think so."

Her tone was a mixture of playfulness and incredulity. Though my wife was once an early riser, she hadn't been since Leslie moved out.

"This was a good idea," she said. "It's beautiful tonight."

"Yes, it is," I said, looking at her. We walked in silence for a few moments before I saw Jane glance toward a house near the corner.

"Did you hear about Glenda's stroke?"

Glenda and her husband were our neighbors, and though we didn't move in the same social circles, we were friendly nonetheless. In New Bern, everyone seemed to know everything about everyone.

"Yes. It's sad."

"She's not much older than I am."

"I know," I said. "I hear she's doing better, though."

We fell back into silence for a while, until Jane suddenly asked, "Do you ever think about your mother?"

I wasn't sure how to respond. My mother had died in an automobile accident during our second year of marriage. Though I wasn't as close to my parents as Jane was to hers, her death came as a terrible shock. To this day, I can't recall making the six-hour drive to Washington to be with my father.

"Sometimes."

"When you do, what do you remember?"

"Do you remember the last time we went to visit them?" I said. "When we first walked in the door, and Mom came out of the kitchen? She was wearing a blouse with purple flowers on it, and she looked so happy to see us. She opened her arms to give us both a hug. That's how I always remember her. It's an image that's never changed, kind of like a picture. She always looks the same."

Jane nodded. "I always remember my mom in her studio, with paint on her fingers. She was painting a portrait of our family, something she'd never done, and I remember how excited she was because she was going to give it to Dad for his birthday." She paused. "I don't really remember the way she looked after she started getting sick. Mom had always been so expressive. I mean, she used to wave her hands when she talked, and her face was always so animated when she told a story . . . but after the Alzheimer's set in, she changed." She glanced over at me. "It just wasn't the same."

"I know," I said.

"I worry about that sometimes," she said in a low voice. "Getting Alzheimer's, I mean."

Though I too had thought about this, I said nothing.

"I can't imagine what it would be like," Jane went on. "To not recognize Anna or Joseph or Leslie? To have to ask their names when they came to visit like Mom used to do with me? It breaks my heart to even think about it."

I watched her silently, in the dim glow of the house-lights.

"I wonder if Mom knew how bad it was going to get," she mused. "I mean, she said she did, but I wonder if she really knew deep down that she wouldn't recognize her children. Or even Daddy."

"I think she knew," I said. "That's why they moved to Creekside."

I thought I saw her close her eyes momentarily. When she spoke again, her voice was full of frustration. "I hate it that Daddy didn't want to come live with us after Mom died. We have plenty of room."

I said nothing. Though I could have explained Noah's reasons for staying at Creekside, she didn't want to hear them. She knew them as well as I did, but unlike me, she didn't accept them, and I knew that trying to defend Noah would only trigger an argument.

"I hate that swan," she added.

There is a story behind the swan, but again, I said nothing.

We circled one block, then another. Some of our neighbors had already turned out their lights, and still Jane and I moved on, neither rushing nor lagging. In time I saw our house, and knowing our walk was coming to an end, I paused and looked up at the stars.

"What is it?" she asked, following my gaze.

"Are you happy, Jane?"

Her gaze focused on me. "What brought that up?"

"I was just curious."

As I waited for her response, I wondered if she guessed the reason behind my question. It wasn't so much that I wondered whether she was happy in general as happy with me in particular.

She stared at me for a long moment, as if trying to read my mind.

"Well, there is one thing . . ."

"Yes?"

"It's kind of important."

I waited as Jane drew a long breath.

"I'll be really happy if you can find a caterer," she confessed.

At her words, I had to laugh.

Though I offered to make a pot of decaf, Jane shook her head wearily. The two long days had caught up to her, and after yawning a second time, she told me that she was going up to bed.

I suppose I could have followed her up, but I didn't. Instead, I watched her head up the steps, reliving our evening.

Later, when I did at last crawl into bed, I slipped under the covers and turned to face my wife. Her breathing was steady and deep, and I could see her eyelids fluttering, letting me know that she was dreaming. Of what, I wasn't sure, but her face was peaceful, like that of a child. I stared at her, wanting and not wanting to wake her, loving her more than life itself. Despite the darkness, I could see a lock of hair lying across her cheek, and I stretched my fingers toward it. Her skin was as soft as powder, timeless in its beauty. Tucking the strand of hair behind her ear, I blinked back the tears that had mysteriously sprung to my eyes.

Chapter Eight

Jane stared at me openmouthed the following evening, purse dangling on her arm.

"You did it?"

"So it would seem," I said nonchalantly, doing my best to make it seem as though finding a caterer had been a simple feat. Meanwhile, I'd been pacing excitedly, waiting for her to come home.

"Who'd you get?"

"The Chelsea," I said. Located in downtown New Bern across the street from my office, the restaurant is housed in the building where Caleb Bradham once had his offices when he formulated a drink now known as Pepsi-Cola. Remodeled into a restaurant ten years ago, it was one of Jane's favorite dinner spots. The menu was extensive, and the chef specialized in exotic original sauces and marinades to accompany typically southern meals. On Friday and Saturday evenings, it was impossible to be seated without a reservation, and guests made a game out of trying to guess what ingredients had been used to create such distinctive flavors.

The Chelsea was also known for its entertainment. In the corner stood a grand piano, and John Peterson—who gave Anna lessons for years—would sometimes play and sing for the patrons. With an ear for contemporary melodies and a voice reminiscent of Nat King Cole's, Peterson could perform any song requested and did well enough to perform in restaurants as far-flung as Atlanta, Charlotte, and Washington, D.C. Jane could spend hours listening to him, and I know Peterson was touched by her almost motherly pride in him. Jane, after all, had been the first in town to take a chance on him as a teacher.

Jane was too stunned to respond. In the silence, I could hear the ticking of the clock on the wall as she debated whether or not she understood me correctly. She blinked. "But . . . how?"

"I talked to Henry, explained the situation and what we needed, and he said he'd take care of it."

"I don't understand. How can Henry handle something like this at the last minute? Didn't he have something else scheduled?"

"I have no idea."

"So you just picked up the phone and called and that was it?"

"Well, it wasn't quite that easy, but in the end, he agreed."

"What about the menu? Didn't he need to know how many people were coming?"

"I told him about a hundred in total—that seemed about right. And as for the menu, we talked it over, and he said he'd come up with something special. I suppose I can call him and request something in particular."

"No, no," she said quickly, regaining her equilibrium. "That's fine. You know I like everything they cook. I just can't believe it." She stared at me with wonder. "You did it."

"Yes." I nodded.

She broke into a smile, then suddenly looked from me to the phone. "I have to call Anna," she cried. "She's not going to believe this."

Henry MacDonald, the owner of the restaurant, is an old friend of mine. Though New Bern is a place where privacy seems all but impossible, it nonetheless has its advantages. Because a person tends to run into the same people with regularity—while shopping, driving, attending church, going to parties—an underlying courtesy has taken root in this town, and it is often possible to do things that may seem impossible elsewhere. People do favors for one another because they never know when they might need one in return, and it's one of the reasons New Bern is so different from other places.

This isn't to say that I wasn't pleased with what I'd done. As I headed into the kitchen, I could hear Jane's voice on the phone.

"Your dad did it!" I heard her exclaim. "I have no idea how, but he did!" My heart surged at the pride in her voice.

At the kitchen table, I started sorting through the mail I'd brought in earlier. Bills, catalogs, *Time* magazine. Because Jane was talking to Anna, I reached for the magazine. I imagined that she would be on the phone for quite a while, but, surprising me, she hung up before I began the first article.

"Wait," she said, "before you start, I want to hear all about it." She drew near. "Okay," she began, "I know

Henry's going to be there and he'll have food for every-one. And he'll have people there to help, right?"

"I'm sure," I said. "He can't serve it all himself."

"What else? Is it a buffet?"

"I thought that was the best way to do it, considering the size of the kitchen at Noah's."

"Me too," she agreed. "How about tables and linens? Will he bring all that?"

"I assume so. To be honest, I didn't ask, but I don't think it's that big of a deal even if he doesn't. We can prob-ably rent what we need if we have to."

She nodded quickly. Making plans, updating her list. "Okay," she said, but before she could speak again, I held up my hands.

"Don't worry. I'll call him first thing in the morning to make sure everything is just the way it should be." Then, with a wink, I added, "Trust me."

She recognized my words from the day before at Noah's house, and she smiled up at me almost coyly. I expected the moment to pass quickly, but it didn't. Instead, we gazed at each other until—almost hesitantly—she leaned toward me and kissed me on the cheek.

"Thank you for finding the caterer," she said.

I swallowed with difficulty.

"You're welcome."

Four weeks after my proposal to Jane, we were married; five days after we were married, when I came in from work, Jane was waiting for me in the living room of the small apartment we'd rented.

"We have to talk," she said, patting the couch.

I set my briefcase aside and sat beside her. She reached for my hand.

"Is everything okay?" I asked.

"Everything's fine."

"Then what is it?"

"Do you love me?"

"Yes," I said. "Of course I love you."

"Then will you do something for me?"

"If I can. You know I'd do anything for you."

"Even if it's hard? Even if you don't want to?"

"Of course," I repeated. I paused. "Jane—what's going on?"

She took a long breath before answering. "I want you to come to church with me this Sunday."

Her words caught me off guard, and before I could speak, she went on. "I know you've told me that you have no desire to go and that you were raised an atheist, but I want you to do this for me. It's very important to me, even if you feel like you don't belong there."

"Jane . . . I—" I started.

"I need you there," she said.

"We've talked about this," I protested, but again Jane cut me off, this time with a shake of her head.

"I know we have. And I understand that you weren't brought up the way I was. But there's nothing you could ever do that would mean more to me than this simple thing."

"Even if I don't believe?"

"Even if you don't believe," she said.

"But—"

"There are no buts," she said. "Not about this. Not with me. I love you, Wilson, and I know that you love me. And if we're going to make it work between us, we're both going to have to give a little. I'm not asking you to believe. I'm asking you to come with me to church. Marriage is about compromise; it's about doing something for the other person, even when you don't want to. Like I did with the wedding."

I brought my lips together, knowing already how she'd felt about our wedding at the courthouse.

"Okay," I said. "I'll go." And at my words, Jane kissed me, a kiss as ethereal as heaven itself.

When Jane kissed me in the kitchen, the memories of that early kiss came flooding back. I suppose it was because it reminded me of the tender rapprochements that had worked so well to heal our differences in the past: if not burning passion, then at least a truce with a commitment to working things out.

In my mind, this commitment to each other is the reason we've been married as long as we have. It was this element of our marriage, I suddenly realized, that had worried me so during the past year. Not only had I begun to wonder whether Jane still loved me, I wondered whether she *wanted* to love me.

There must have been so many disappointments, after all—the years when I returned home long after the kids were in bed; the evenings in which I could speak of nothing but work; the missed games, parties, family vacations; the weekends spent with partners and clients on the golf course. Upon reflection, I think I must have been something of an absent spouse, a shadow of the eager young man she had married. Yet she seemed to be saying with her kiss, I'm still willing to try if you are.

"Wilson? Are you okay?"

I forced a smile. "I'm fine." I took a deep breath, anxious to change the subject. "So how did your day go? Did you and Anna find a dress?"

"No. We went to a couple of stores, but Anna didn't see anything in her size that she liked. I didn't realize how long it takes—I mean, Anna's so thin they have to pin everything just so we can get an idea of what she'll look like. But we're going to try a few different places tomorrow and we'll see how it goes. On the plus side, she said that Keith would handle everything with his side of the family, so that we don't have to. Which reminds me—did you remember to book Joseph's flight?"

"Yes," I said. "He'll be in Friday evening."

"New Bern or Raleigh?"

"New Bern. He's supposed to arrive at eight thirty. Was Leslie able to join you today?"

"No, not today. She called while we were driving. She had to do some additional research for her lab project, but she'll be able to make it tomorrow. She said there were some shops in Greensboro, too, if we wanted to go there."

"Are you going to?"

"It's three and a half hours away," she groaned. "I really don't want to be in the car for seven hours."

"Why don't you just stay overnight?" I suggested. "That way, you'll be able to visit both places."

She sighed. "That's what Anna suggested. She said we should go to Raleigh again, then Greensboro on Wednesday. But I don't want to leave you stranded. There's still a lot to do here."

"Go ahead," I urged. "Now that we have the caterer, everything's coming together. I can handle whatever else needs to be done on this end. But we can't have a wedding unless she gets a dress."

She eyed me skeptically. "Are you sure?"

"Absolutely. In fact, I was thinking that I might even have time to squeeze in a couple of rounds of golf."

She snorted. "You wish."

"But what about my handicap?" I said in feigned protest.

"After thirty years, my feeling is that if you haven't improved yet, it's probably not in the cards."

"Is that an insult?"

"No. Just a fact. I've seen you play, remember?"

I nodded, conceding her point. Despite the years I've spent working on my swing, I'm far from a scratch golfer. I glanced at the clock.

"Do you want to head out to get a bite to eat?"

"What? No cooking tonight?"

"Not unless you want leftovers. I didn't have a chance to run to the store."

"I was kidding," she said with a wave. "I don't expect you to do all the cooking now, though I have to admit, it's been nice." She smiled. "Sure, I'd love to go. I'm getting kind of hungry. Just give me a minute to get ready."

"You look fine," I protested.

"It'll only take a minute," she called out as she headed for the stairs.

It would not take a minute. I knew Jane, and over the years, I'd come to understand that these "minutes" it took to get ready actually averaged closer to twenty. I'd learned to occupy my time while waiting with activities that I enjoyed but required little thought. For instance, I might head to my office and straighten the items on my desk or adjust the amplifier on the stereo after the children had used it.

I discovered that these innocuous things made time slip by unnoticed. Often, I would finish whatever it was I was doing, only to find my wife standing behind me with her hands on her hips.

"Are you ready?" I might ask.

"I've been ready," she would say in a huff. "I've been waiting ten minutes for you to finish whatever it is you're doing."

"Oh," I'd reply, "sorry. Let me make sure I have the keys and we can go."

"Don't tell me you lost them."

"No, of course not," I'd say, patting my pockets, puzzled that I couldn't find them. Then, looking around, I'd quickly add: "I'm sure they're close. I just had them a minute ago."

At that, my wife would roll her eyes.

Tonight, however, I grabbed *Time* magazine and headed for the couch. I finished a few articles as I heard Jane padding around upstairs and set the magazine aside. I was wondering what she was in the mood to eat when the phone rang.

Listening to the shaky voice on the other end of the receiver, I felt my sense of anticipation evaporate, replaced by a deep sense of dread. Jane came downstairs as I was hanging up.

Seeing my expression, she froze.

"What happened?" she asked. "Who was it?"

"That was Kate," I said quietly. "She's going to the hospital now."

Jane's hand flew to her mouth.

"It's Noah," I said.

$$\multimap\!\!\Longleftrightarrow\!\!\multimap$$

Chapter Nine

*T*ears brimmed in Jane's eyes as we drove to the hospital. Though I'm usually a cautious driver, I changed lanes frequently and bore down on the accelerator when the lights turned yellow, feeling the weight of every passing minute.

When we arrived, the scene in the emergency room was reminiscent of this spring, after Noah had his stroke, as if nothing had changed in the previous four months. The air smelled of ammonia and antiseptic, the fluorescent lights cast a flat glare over the crowded waiting room.

Metal-and-vinyl chairs lined the walls and marched in rows through the middle of the room. Most of the seats were occupied by groups of twos or threes, speaking in hushed tones, and a line of people waiting to fill out forms snaked past the intake counter.

Jane's family was clustered near the door. Kate stood pale and nervous beside Grayson, her husband, who looked every bit the cotton farmer he was in his overalls and dusty boots. His angular face was weathered with creases. David, Jane's youngest brother, stood beside them with his arm around his wife, Lynn.

At the sight of us, Kate ran forward, tears already beginning to spill down her cheeks. She and Jane immediately fell into each other's arms.

"What happened?" Jane asked, her face taut with fear. "How is he?"

Kate's voice cracked. "He fell near the pond. No one saw it happen, but he was barely conscious when the nurse found him. She said he hit his head. The ambulance brought him in about twenty minutes ago, and Dr. Barnwell is with him now," Kate said. "That's all we know."

Jane seemed to sag in her sister's arms. Neither David nor Grayson could look at them; both of their mouths were set into straight lines. Lynn stood with her arms crossed, rocking back and forth on her heels.

"When can we see him?"

Kate shook her head. "I don't know. The nurses out here keep telling us to wait for Dr. Barnwell or one of the other nurses. I guess they'll let us know."

"But he's going to be okay, right?"

When Kate didn't answer immediately, Jane inhaled sharply.

"He's going to be okay," Jane said.

"Oh, Jane . . ." Kate squeezed her eyes shut. "I don't know. Nobody knows anything."

For a moment, they simply clung to each other.

"Where's Jeff?" Jane asked, referring to their missing sibling. "He's coming, right?"

"I finally got hold of him," David informed her. "He's stopping by the house to pick up Debbie, then he's coming straight here."

David joined his sisters, the three of them huddling together as if trying to pool the strength they knew they might need.

A moment later, Jeff and Debbie arrived. Jeff joined his siblings and was quickly updated on the situation, his drawn face expressing the same dread reflected on their faces.

As the minutes dragged by, we separated into two groups: the progeny of Noah and Allie and their spouses. Though I love Noah and Jane was my wife, I've come to learn that there are times when Jane needed her siblings more than me. Jane would need me later, but now was not the time.

Lynn, Grayson, Debbie, and I had been through this before—in the spring when Noah had his stroke, and when Allie died, and when Noah had a heart attack six years ago. While their group had its rituals, including hugs and prayer circles and anxious questions repeated over and over, ours was more stoic. Grayson, like me, has always been quiet. When nervous, he pushes his hands into his pocket and jingles his keys. Lynn and Debbie—while they accepted that David and Jeff needed their sisters at times like these—seemed lost when crises arose, unsure what to do other than stay out of the way and keep their voices down. I, on the other hand, always found myself searching for practical ways to help—an effective means of keeping my emotions in check.

Noticing that the line at the intake desk had cleared, I headed over. A moment later, the nurse looked up from behind a tall stack of forms. Her expression was frazzled.

"Can I help you?"

"Yes," I said. "I was wondering if you had any more information about Noah Calhoun. He was brought in about half an hour ago."

"Has the doctor come out to see you yet?"

"No. But the whole family is here now, and they're pretty upset."

I nodded toward them and saw the nurse's gaze follow mine.

"I'm sure the doctor or one of the nurses will be out shortly."

"I know. But is there any way you could find out when we might be able to see our father? Or whether he's going to be okay?"

For a moment, I wasn't sure she would help me, but when her gaze turned toward the family again, I heard her exhale.

"Just give me a few minutes to process some of these forms. Then I'll see what I can find out, okay?"

Grayson joined me at the desk, hands in his pockets. "You holdin' up okay?"

"Trying," I said.

He nodded again, keys jingling.

"I'm going to sit," he said after a few seconds. "Who knows how long we're going to be here."

We both took a seat in the chairs behind the siblings. A few minutes later, Anna and Keith arrived. Anna joined the huddle, while Keith sat next to me. Dressed in black, Anna already looked as though she'd come from a funeral.

Waiting is always the worst part of a crisis like this, and I've come to despise hospitals for this very reason. Nothing is happening, yet the mind whirls with ever darkening images, subconsciously preparing for the worst. In the tense silence, I could hear my own heart beating, and my throat was strangely dry.

I noticed that the intake nurse was no longer at her desk, and I hoped she'd gone to check on Noah. From the corner of my eye, I saw Jane approaching. Standing from my seat, I raised my arm, letting her lean into me.

"I hate this," she said.

"I know you do. I hate it, too."

Behind us, a young couple with three crying children entered the emergency room. We moved over to make room for them to pass, and when they reached the desk, I saw the nurse emerge from the back. She held up a finger signaling the couple to wait and headed toward us.

"He's conscious now," she announced, "but he's still a little woozy. His vital signs are good. We'll probably be moving him to a room in an hour or so."

"So he's going to be okay?"

"They're not planning to move him to intensive care, if that's what you're asking," she hedged. "He'll probably have to stay in the hospital for a few days of observation."

There was a collective murmur of relief at her words.

"Can we see him now?" Jane pressed.

"We can't have all of you back there at once. There's not enough room for everyone, and the doctor thinks it would be best if you let him rest a bit. The doctor said that one of you could go back there now, as long as you don't visit too long."

It seemed obvious that either Kate or Jane would go, but before any of us could speak, the nurse continued.

"Which one of you is Wilson Lewis?" she asked.

"I am," I said.

"Why don't you come with me? They're getting ready to hook up an IV, and you should probably see him before he starts getting sleepy."

I felt my family's eyes drift to me. I thought I knew why he wanted to see me, but I held up my hands to ward off the possibility.

"I know I'm the one who talked to you, but maybe Jane or Kate should go," I suggested. "They're his daughters. Or maybe David or Jeff."

The nurse shook her head.

"He asked to see you. He made it very clear that you should be the one to see him first."

Though Jane smiled briefly, I saw in her smile what I felt from the others. Curiosity, of course. And surprise as well. But from Jane, what I suppose I sensed most of all was a sort of subtle betrayal, as if she knew exactly why he'd chosen me.

Noah was lying in bed with two tubes in his arms and hooked up to a machine that broadcast the steady rhythm of his heart. His eyes were half-closed, but he rotated his head on the pillow when the nurse pulled the curtain closed behind us. I heard the nurse's steps fade away, leaving us alone.

He looked too small for the bed, and his face was paper white. I took a seat in the chair beside him.

"Hello, Noah."

"Hello, Wilson," he said shakily. "Thanks for dropping by."

"You doing okay?"

"Could be better," he said. He offered a ghost of a smile. "Could be worse, though, too."

I reached for his hand. "What happened?"

"A root," he said. "Been by it a thousand times, but it jumped up and grabbed my foot this time."

"And you hit your head?"

"My head, my body. Everything. Landed like a potato sack, but nothing's broke, thank goodness. I'm just a little dizzy. The doctor said I should be up and around in a couple of days. I said good, because I've got a wedding this weekend I have to go to."

"Don't worry about that. You just worry about getting healthy."

"I'll be fine. I've still got some time left in me. "

"You better."

"So how are Kate and Jane? Worried sick, I'll bet."

"We're all worried. Me included."

"Yeah, but you don't look at me with those sorrowful eyes and practically cry every time I mumble something."

"I do that when you're not looking."

He smiled. "Not like they do. Odds are one of them will be with me around the clock for the next couple of days, tucking in my blankets and adjusting my bed and fluffing my pillows. They're like mother hens. I know they mean well, but all that hovering is enough to drive me crazy. The last time I was in the hospital, I don't think I was alone for more than a minute. I couldn't even go to the bathroom without one of them leading the way, and then waiting outside the door for me to finish."

"You needed help. You couldn't walk on your own, remember?"

"A man still needs his dignity."

I squeezed his hand. "You'll always be the most digni-fied man I've ever known."

Noah held my gaze, his expression softening. "They're going to be all over me as soon as they see me, you know. Hovering and fussing, just like always." His smiled mis-chievously. "I might have a little fun with 'em."

"Go easy, Noah. They're just doing it because they love you."

"I know. But they don't have to treat me like a child."

"They won't."

"They will. So when the time comes, why don't you tell them that you think I might need some rest, okay? If I say I'm getting tired, they'll just start worrying again."

I smiled. "Will do."

For a moment, we sat without speaking. The heart machine beeped steadily, soothing in its monotony.

"Do you know why I asked for you to come back here instead of one of the kids?" he asked.

Despite myself, I nodded. "You want me to go to Creekside, right? To feed the swan like I did last spring?"

"Would you mind?"

"Not at all. I'd be glad to help."

He paused, his tired expression imploring me. "You know I couldn't have asked you if the others were in the room. They get upset at the very mention of it. They think it means I'm losing my mind."

"I know."

"But you know better, don't you, Wilson?"

"Yes."

"Because you believe it, too. She was there when I woke up, you know. She was standing over me, making sure that I was okay, and the nurse had to shoo her away. She stayed with me the whole time."

I knew what he wanted me to say, but I couldn't seem to find the words he wanted to hear. Instead I smiled. "Wonder Bread," I said. "Four pieces in the morning and three pieces in the afternoon, right?"

Noah squeezed my hand, forcing me to look at him again.

"You do believe me, don't you, Wilson?"

I was silent. Since Noah understood me better than anyone, I knew I couldn't hide the truth. "I don't know," I said at last.

At my answer, I could see the disappointment in his eyes.

An hour later, Noah was moved to a room on the second floor, where the family joined him at last.

Jane and Kate entered the room, mumbling, "Oh, Daddy," in chorus. Lynn and Debbie followed next, while David and Jeff moved to the far side of the bed. Grayson stood at the foot of the bed, while I remained in the background.

As Noah predicted, they hovered over him. They reached for his hand, adjusted the covers, raised the head of the bed. Scrutinized him, touched him, fawned over him, hugged and kissed him. All of them, fussing and peppering him with questions.

Jeff spoke up first. "Are you sure you're okay? The doctor said you took a nasty fall."

"I'm fine. I've got a bump on my head, but other than that, I'm just a little tired."

"I was scared to death," Jane declared. "But I'm so glad you're okay."

"Me too," David joined in.

"You shouldn't have been out there alone if you were feeling dizzy," Kate scolded. "Next time, just wait there until someone comes to get you. They'll come and find you."

"They did anyway," Noah said.

Jane reached behind his head and fluffed his pillows.

"You weren't out there that long, were you? I can't bear to think that no one found you right away."

Noah shook his head. "No more than a couple of hours, I'd guess."

"A couple of hours!" Jane and Kate exclaimed. They froze, exchanging horrified looks.

"Maybe a little longer. Hard to tell because the clouds were blocking the sun."

"Longer?" Jane asked. Her hands were clenched into fists.

"And I was wet, too. I guess it must have rained on me. Or maybe the sprinklers came on."

"You could have died out there!" Kate cried.

"Oh, it wasn't so bad. A little water never hurt anyone. The worst part was the raccoon when I finally came to. With the way he kept staring at me, I thought he might be rabid. Then he came at me."

"You were attacked by a raccoon?" Jane looked as though she might faint.

"Not really attacked. I fought him off before he could bite me."

"It tried to bite you!" Kate cried.

"Oh, it's no big deal. I've fought off raccoons before."

Kate and Jane stared at each other with shell-shocked expressions, then turned toward their siblings. Appalled silence reigned before Noah finally smiled. He pointed his finger at them and winked. "Gotcha."

I brought a hand to my mouth, trying to stifle a chuckle. Off to the side, I could see Anna doing her best to keep a straight face.

"Don't tease us like that!" Kate snapped, tapping the side of the bed.

"Yeah, Daddy, that's not nice," Jane added.

Noah's eyes creased with amusement. "Had to. You set yourselves up for it. But just to let you know, they found me within a couple of minutes. And I'm fine. I offered to drive to the hospital, but they made me take the ambulance."

"You can't drive. You don't even have a valid license anymore."

"It doesn't mean that I've forgotten how. And the car's still in the lot."

Though they said nothing, I could see Jane and Kate mentally planning to remove his keys.

Jeff cleared his throat. "I was thinking that maybe we should get you one of those wrist alarms. So if it happens again, you can get help right away."

"Don't need one. I just tripped over a root. Wouldn't have had time to press the button on the way down. And when I came to, the nurse was already there."

"I'll have a talk with the director," David said. "And if he doesn't take care of that root, I will. I'll chop it out myself."

"I'll give you a hand," Grayson chimed in.

"It not his fault I'm getting clumsy in my old age. I'll be up and around in a day or so, and good as new by the weekend."

"Don't worry about that," Anna said. "Just get better, okay?"

"And take it easy," Kate urged. "We're worried about you."

"Scared to death," Jane repeated.

Cluck, cluck, cluck. I smiled inwardly. Noah was right—they were all mother hens.

"I'll be fine," Noah insisted. "And don't you go canceling that wedding on my account. I'm looking forward to going, and I don't want you to think a bump on my head is enough to keep me from being there."

"That's not important right now," Jeff said.

"He's right, Grampa," Anna said.

"And don't postpone it, either," Noah added.

"Don't talk like that, Daddy," Kate said. "You're going to stay here as long as it takes for you to get better."

"I'll be fine. I just want you to promise that it's still on. I've been looking forward to this."

"Don't be stubborn," Jane pleaded.

"How many times do I have to tell you? This is important to me. It's not every day that a wedding happens around here." Recognizing that he was getting nowhere with his daughters, he sought out Anna. "You understand what I mean, don't you, Anna?"

Anna hesitated. In the silence, her eyes flicked toward me before returning to Noah. "Of course I do, Grampa."

"Then you'll go ahead with it, won't you?"

Instinctively she reached for Keith's hand.

"If that's what you want," she said simply.

Noah smiled, visibly relieved. "Thank you," he whispered.

Jane adjusted his blanket. "Well then, you're going to have to take care of yourself this week," she said. "And be more careful in the future."

"Don't worry, Dad," David promised, "I'll have that root gone by the time you get back."

The discussion returned to how Noah had fallen, and I suddenly realized what had been left out of the conversation thus far. Not one of them, I noticed, was willing to mention the reason he'd been at the pond in the first place.

But then again, none of them ever wanted to talk about the swan.

Noah told me about the swan a little less than five years ago. Allie had been gone for a month, and Noah had seemed to be aging at an accelerated rate. He seldom left his room, even to read poetry to others. Instead, he sat at his desk, reading the letters that he and Allie had written to each other over the years or thumbing through his copy of *Leaves of Grass*.

We did our best to get him out of his room, of course, and I suppose it's ironic that I was the one who brought him to the bench by the pond. That morning was the first time we saw the swan.

I can't say I knew what Noah was thinking, and he certainly gave no indication at the time that he read anything significant into it at all. I do remember that the swan floated toward us, as if looking for something to eat.

"Should have brought some bread," Noah remarked.

"Next time we will," I agreed in a perfunctory way.

When I visited two days later, I was surprised not to find Noah in his room. The nurse told me where he was. At the pond, I found him seated on the bench. Beside him was a single piece of Wonder Bread. When I approached, the swan seemed to watch me, but even then it showed no fear.

"It looks like you've made yourself a friend," I commented.

"Looks that way," he said.

"Wonder Bread?" I asked.

"She seems to like it the best."

"How do you know it's a she?"

Noah smiled. "I just know," he said, and that was how it began.

Since then he has fed the swan regularly, visiting the pond in all kinds of weather. He has sat in the rain and the sweltering heat, and as the years passed, he began spending more and more time on the bench, watching and whispering to the swan. Now, full days can pass when he never leaves the bench at all.

A few months after his first encounter with the swan, I asked him why he spent so much time at the pond. I assumed he found it peaceful or that he enjoyed talking to someone—or something—without expecting a response.

"I come here because she wants me to."

"The swan?" I asked.

"No," he said. "Allie."

My insides tightened at the sound of her name, but I didn't know what he meant. "Allie wants you feed the swan?"

"Yes."

"How do you know?"

With a sigh, he looked up at me. "It's her," he said.

"Who?"

"The swan," he said.

I shook my head uncertainly. "I'm not sure what you're trying to say."

"Allie," he repeated. "She found a way to come back to me, just like she promised she would. All I had to do was find her."

This is what the doctors mean when they say Noah is delusional.

We stayed at the hospital another thirty minutes. Dr. Barnwell promised to call us with an update after he made his rounds the following morning. He was close to our family, looking after Noah as he would his own father. We trusted him completely. As I'd promised, I suggested to the family that Noah seemed to be getting tired and that it might be best for him to rest. On our way out, we arranged to visit him in shifts, then hugged and kissed in the parking lot. A moment later, Jane and I were alone, watching the others leave.

I could see the weariness in Jane's unfocused gaze and sagging posture and felt it myself.

"You doing okay?" I asked.

"I think so." She sighed. "I know he seems to be fine, but he doesn't seem to understand that he's almost ninety. He's not going to be up and around as fast as he thinks he will." She closed her eyes for a moment, and I guessed that she was worrying about the wedding plans as well.

"You're not thinking of asking Anna to postpone the wedding, are you? After what Noah said?"

Jane shook her head. "I would have tried, but he was so adamant. I just hope that he's not insisting on it because he knows . . ."

She trailed off. I knew exactly what she was going to say.

"Because he knows he doesn't have much longer," she went on. "And that this is going to be his last big event, you know?"

"He doesn't believe that. He still has more than a few years left."

"You sound so sure of that."

"I am sure. For his age, he's actually doing well. Especially compared to the others his age at Creekside. They barely leave their rooms, and all they do is watch television."

"Yeah, and all he does is go to the pond to see that stupid swan. Like that's any better."

"It makes him happy," I pointed out.

"But it's wrong," she said fiercely. "Can't you see that? Mom's gone. That swan has nothing to do with her."

I didn't know how to respond, so I stayed quiet.

"I mean, it's crazy," she continued. "Feeding it is one thing. But thinking that Mom's spirit has somehow come back doesn't make any sense." She crossed her arms. "I've heard him talking to it, you know. When I go to see him. He's having a regular conversation, as if he honestly believes the swan can understand him. Kate and David have caught him doing it, too. And I know you've heard him."

She leveled an accusing stare.

"Yes," I admitted, "I've heard him, too."

"And it doesn't bother you?"

I shifted my weight from one foot to the other. "I think," I said carefully, "that right now, Noah needs to believe that it's possible."

"But why?"

"Because he loves her. He misses her."

At my words, I saw her jaw quiver. "I do, too," she said.

Even as she said the words, we both knew it wasn't the same.

Despite our weariness, neither of us could face the prospect of going straight home after the ordeal at the hospital. When Jane declared suddenly that she was "starving," we decided to stop at the Chelsea for a late dinner.

Even before we entered, I could hear the sounds of John Peterson at the piano inside. Back in town for a few weeks, he played each weekend; on weekdays, however, John sometimes showed up unexpectedly. Tonight was such a night, the tables surrounding the piano crowded, the bar packed with people.

We were seated upstairs, away from the music and the crowd, where only a few other tables were occupied. Jane surprised me by ordering a second glass of wine with her entrée, and it seemed to ease some of the tension of the past several hours.

"What did Daddy say to you when you two were alone?" Jane asked, carefully picking a bone out of her fish.

"Not much," I answered. "I asked him how he was doing, what happened. For the most part, it wasn't any different from what you heard later."

She raised an eyebrow. "For the most part? What else did he say?"

"Do you really want to know?"

She laid her silverware down. "He asked you to feed the swan again, didn't he."

"Yes."

"Are you going to?"

"Yes," I said, but seeing her expression, I went on quickly, "but before you get upset, remember that I'm not doing it because I think it's Allie. I'm doing it because he asked, and because I don't want the swan to starve to death. It's probably forgotten how to forage on its own."

She looked at me skeptically.

"Mom hated Wonder Bread, you know. She would never have eaten it. She liked to make her own."

Luckily, the approach of our waiter saved me from further discussion of this topic. When he asked how we were enjoying our entrées, Jane suddenly asked if these dishes were on the catering menu.

At her question, a look of recognition crossed his features.

"Are you the folks throwing the wedding?" he asked. "At the old Calhoun place this weekend?"

"Yes, we are," Jane said, beaming.

"I thought so. I think half the crew is working that event." The waiter grinned. "Well, it's great to meet you. Let me refill your drinks, and I'll bring the full catering menu when I come back."

As soon as he'd left, Jane leaned across the table.

"I guess that answers one of my questions. About the service, I mean."

"I told you not to worry."

She drained the last of her wine. "So are they going to set up a tent? Since we're eating outside?"

"Why don't we use the house?" I volunteered. "I'm going to be out there anyway when the landscapers come, so why don't I try to get a cleaning crew out there to get it ready? We've got a few days—I'm sure I can find someone."

"We'll give it a try, I guess," she said slowly, and I knew she was thinking of the last time she'd been inside. "You know it'll be pretty dusty, though. I don't think anyone's cleaned it in years."

"True, but it's only cleaning. I'll make some calls. Let me see what I can do," I urged.

"You keep saying that."

"I keep having to do things," I countered, and she laughed good-naturedly. Through the window over her shoulder, I could see my office and noticed that the light in Saxon's window was on. No doubt he was there on urgent business, for Saxon seldom stayed late. Jane caught me staring.

⟨∽⟩

"Missing work already?" she asked.

"No," I said. "It's nice to be away from it for a while."

She eyed me carefully. "Do you really mean that?"

"Of course." I tugged at my polo shirt. "It's nice not to always have to put on a suit during the week."

"I'll bet you've forgotten what that's like, haven't you. You haven't taken a long vacation in . . . what? Eight years?"

"It hasn't been that long."

After a moment, she nodded. "You've taken a few days here and there, but the last time you actually took a week off was in 1995. Don't you remember? When we took all the kids to Florida? It was right after Joseph graduated from high school."

She was right, I realized, but what I once regarded as a virtue, I now considered a fault.

"I'm sorry," I said.

"For what?"

"For not taking more vacations. That wasn't fair to you or the family. I should have tried to do more with you and the kids than I did."

"It's fine," she said with a wave of her fork, "no big deal."

"Yes, it is," I said. Though she had long since grown used to my dedication at the office and now accepted it as part of my character, I knew it had always been a sore spot with her. Knowing that I had her attention, I went on.

"It's always been a big deal," I continued. "But I'm not sorry only about that. I'm sorry about all of it. I'm sorry for letting work interfere with all the other events I missed when the kids were growing up. Like some of their birthday parties. I can't even remember how many I missed because I had late meetings that I refused to reschedule.

And everything else I missed—the volleyball games and track meets, piano concerts, school plays . . . It's a wonder that the kids have forgiven me, let alone seem to like me."

She nodded in acknowledgment but said nothing. Then again, there was nothing she could say. I took a deep breath and plunged on.

"I know I haven't always been the best husband, either," I said quietly. "Sometimes I wonder why you've put up with me for as long as you have."

At that, her eyebrows rose.

"I know you spent too many evenings and weekends alone, and I put all the responsibility for child rearing on you. That wasn't fair to you. And even when you told me that what you wanted more than anything was to spend time with me, I didn't listen. Like for your thirtieth birthday." I paused, letting my words sink in. Across the table, I watched Jane's eyes flash with the memory. It was one of the many mistakes I'd made in the past that I'd tried to forget.

What she'd asked for back then had been quite simple: Overwhelmed with the new burdens of motherhood, she'd wanted to feel like a woman again, at least for an evening, and had dropped various hints in advance about what such a romantic evening might entail—clothes laid out on the bed for her, flowers, a limousine to whisk us to a quiet restaurant, a table with a lovely view, quiet conversation without worrying that she had to rush home. Even back then, I knew it was important to her, and I remember making a note to do everything she wanted. However, I got so embroiled in some messy proceedings relating to a large estate that her birthday arrived before I could make the arrangements. Instead, at the last minute I had my secretary pick out a stylish tennis bracelet, and on the way home, I convinced myself that because it had been expensive, she would regard it as equally special. When she unwrapped it, I promised that I'd make the necessary plans for a wonderful evening together, an evening even better than the one she'd described. In the end, it was another in a long line of promises that I ended up breaking, and in hindsight, I think Jane realized it as soon as I said it.

Feeling the weight of lost opportunity, I didn't continue. I rubbed my forehead in the silence. I pushed my plate aside, and as the past sped by in a series of disheartening memories, I felt Jane's eyes on me. Surprising me, however, she reached across the table and touched my hand.

"Wilson? Are you okay?" There was a note of tender concern in her voice that I didn't quite recognize.

I nodded. "Yes."

"Can I ask you a question?"

"Of course."

"Why all the regrets tonight? Was it something that Daddy said?"

"No."

"Then what made you bring it up?"

"I don't know . . . maybe it's the wedding." I gave a halfhearted smile. "But I've been thinking about those things a lot these days."

"It doesn't sound like something you'd do."

"No, it doesn't," I admitted. "But it's still true."

Jane cocked her head. "I haven't been perfect, either, you know."

"You've been a lot closer than I've been."

"That's true," she said with a shrug.

I laughed despite myself, feeling the tension ease a little.

"And yes, you have worked a lot," she went on. "Probably too much. But I always knew you were doing it because you wanted to provide for our family. There's a lot to be said for that, and I was able to stay home and raise the kids because of it. That was always important to me."

I smiled, thinking about her words and the forgiveness I heard in them. I was a lucky man, I thought, and I leaned across the table.

"You know what else I've been thinking about?" I asked.

"Is there more?"

"I was trying to figure out why you married me in the first place."

Her expression softened. "Don't be so hard on yourself. I wouldn't have married you unless I wanted to."

"Why did you marry me?"

"Because I loved you."

"But why?"

"There were a lot of reasons."

"Like what?"

"You want specifics?"

"Humor me. I just told you all my secrets."

She smiled at my insistence.

"All right. Why I married you . . . Well, you were honest and hardworking and kind. You were polite and patient, and more mature than any guy I'd dated before. And when we were together, you listened in a way that made me feel like I was the only woman in the world. You made me feel complete, and spending time with you just seemed *right*."

She hesitated for a moment. "But it wasn't just about my feelings. The more I got to know you, the more I was certain that you'd do whatever it took to provide for your family. That was important to me. You have to understand that back then, a lot of people our age wanted to change the world. Even though it's a noble idea, I knew I wanted something more traditional. I wanted a family like my parents had, and I wanted to concentrate on my little corner of the world. I wanted someone who wanted to marry a wife and mother, and someone who would respect my choice."

"And have I?"

"For the most part."

I laughed. "I notice you didn't mention my dashing good looks or dazzling personality."

"You wanted the truth, right?" she teased.

I laughed again, and she squeezed my hand. "I'm just kidding. Back then, I used to love how you looked in the mornings, right after you put on your suit. You were tall and trim, a young go-getter out to make a good life for us. You were very attractive."

Her words warmed me. For the next hour—while we perused the catering menu over coffee and listened to the music floating up from downstairs—I noticed her eyes occasionally on my face in a way that felt almost unfamiliar. The effect was quietly dizzying. Perhaps she was remembering the reasons she'd married me, just as she'd related them to me. And though I couldn't be absolutely certain, her expression as she gazed at me made me believe that every now and then, she was still glad that she had.

Chapter Ten

On Tuesday morning, I woke before dawn and slid out of bed, doing my best not to wake Jane. After dressing, I slipped through the front door. The sky was black; even the birds hadn't begun to stir, but the temperature was mild, and the asphalt was slick from a shower that had passed through the night before. Already I could feel the first hint of the day's coming humidity, and I was glad to be out early.

I settled into an easy pace at first, then gradually quickened my stride as my body began to warm up. Over the past year, I'd come to enjoy these walks more than I thought I would. Originally, I figured that once I'd lost the weight that I wanted, I'd cut back, but instead I added a bit of distance to my walks and made a point of noting the times of both my departure and my return.

I had come to crave the quiet of the mornings. There were few cars out at this hour, and my senses seemed heightened. I could hear my breath, feel the pressure as my feet moved over the asphalt, watch the dawn as it unfolded—at first a faint light on the horizon, an orange glow over the treetops, then the steady displacement of black by gray. Even on dreary mornings, I found myself looking forward to my walks and wondering why I'd never exercised like this before.

My walk usually took forty-five minutes, and toward the end, I slowed my pace to catch my breath. There was a thin sheen of sweat on my forehead, but it felt good. Noticing the kitchen light at my house was already on, I turned into our driveway with an eager smile.

As soon as I pushed through the front door, I caught the aroma of bacon wafting from the kitchen, a scent that reminded me of our earlier life. When there were children in the house, Jane usually prepared a family breakfast, but our differing schedules in recent years had brought them to an end. It was yet another change that had somehow overtaken our relationship.

Jane poked her head around the corner as I padded through the living room. She was already dressed and wearing an apron.

"How'd your walk go?" she asked.

"I felt pretty good," I said, "for an old guy, that is." I joined her in the kitchen. "You're up early."

"I heard you leave the bedroom," she said, "and since I knew there was no way I'd fall asleep again, I decided to get up. Want a cup of coffee?"

"I think I need some water first," I said. "What's for breakfast?"

"Bacon and eggs," she said, reaching for a glass. "I hope you're hungry. Even though we ate so late last night, I was still hungry when I got up." She filled the glass from the tap and handed it to me. "Must be nerves," she said with a grin.

As I took the glass, I felt her fingers brush mine. Perhaps it was just my imagination, but her gaze seemed to linger on me a little longer than usual. "Let me go shower and throw on some clean clothes," I said. "How much longer till breakfast is ready?"

"You've got a few minutes," she said. "I'll get the toast going."

By the time I came back downstairs, Jane was already serving up at the table. I sat next to her.

"I've been thinking about whether or not to stay overnight," she said.

"And?"

"It'll depend on what Dr. Barnwell says when he calls. If he thinks Daddy's doing well, I might as well head on to Greensboro. If we don't find a dress, that is. Otherwise I'll just have to make the drive tomorrow anyway. But I'll have my cell phone in case anything happens."

I crunched on a piece of bacon. "I don't think you'll need it. Had he taken a turn for the worse, Dr. Barnwell would have called already. You know how much he cares for Noah."

"I'm still going to wait until I talk to him, though."

"Of course. And as soon as visiting hours start, I'll head in to see Noah."

"He'll be grouchy, you know. He hates hospitals."

"Who doesn't? Unless you're having a baby, I can't imagine anyone liking them."

She buttered her toast. "What are you thinking about doing with the house? Do you really think there'll be enough room for everyone?"

I nodded. "If we get the furniture out, there should be plenty of room. I figured we'd just store it in the barn for a few days."

"And you'll hire someone to move it all?"

"If I have to. But I don't think I'll need to. The land-scaper has a fairly large crew coming. I'm sure he won't mind if they take a few minutes to help me."

"It'll be kind of empty, won't it?"

"Not once we have the tables inside. I was thinking of setting up the buffet line next to the windows, and we can leave an area open for dancing right in front of the fireplace."

"What dancing? We don't have any music arranged."

"Actually, that was on my agenda for today. Along with getting the cleaners set up and dropping off the menu at the Chelsea, of course."

She tilted her head, scrutinizing me. "You sound like you've put a lot of thought into this."

"What do you think I was doing this morning while I was walking?"

"Panting. Wheezing. The usual."

I laughed. "Hey, I'm actually getting in fairly good shape. I passed someone today."

"The old man in the walker again?"

"Ha, ha," I said, but I was enjoying her high spirits. I wondered if it had anything to do with the way she'd looked at me the night before. Whatever the reason, I knew I wasn't imagining it. "Thanks for making breakfast, by the way."

"It's the least I could do. Considering the fact that you've been such a big help this week. And you've made dinner *twice*."

"Yes," I agreed, "I have been quite the saint."

She laughed. "I wouldn't go that far."

"No?"

"No. But without your help, I would have been insane by now."

"And hungry."

She smiled. "I need your opinion," she said. "What do

you think about something sleeveless for this weekend? With a cinched waist and a medium train?"

I brought my hand to my chin and considered this. "Sounds okay," I said. "But I think I'd look better in a tuxedo."

She tossed me a look of exasperation, and I raised my hands in mock innocence.

"Oh, for *Anna*," I said. Then, mimicking what Noah had said, I went on, "I'm sure she'll be beautiful no matter what she wears."

"But don't you have an opinion?"

"I don't even know what a cinched waist is."

She sighed. "Men."

"I know," I said, imitating her sigh. "It's a wonder how we function in society at all."

Dr. Barnwell called the house a little after eight. Noah was fine, and they expected to release him later that day or, at the latest, the next. I breathed a sigh of relief and put Jane on the phone. She listened as he went over the same information. After hanging up, she called the hospital and spoke to Noah, who prodded her to go with Anna.

"Looks like I might as well pack," she said as she hung up.

"Might as well."

"Hopefully, we'll find something today."

"But if not, just enjoy your time with the girls. This only happens once."

"We've still got two more kids to go," she said happily. "This is only the beginning!"

I smiled. "I hope so."

An hour later, Keith dropped Anna off at the house, small suitcase in hand. Jane was still upstairs gathering her things, and I opened the front door as Anna was coming up the walk. Surprise of surprises, she was dressed in black.

"Hi, Daddy," she said.

I stepped onto the porch. "Hey, sweetheart. How are you?"

Putting down her suitcase, she leaned in and gave me a hug.

"I'm fine," she said. "This is actually a lot of fun. I wasn't so sure about it in the beginning, but it's been great so far. And Mom's been having a blast. You should see her. I haven't seen her this excited in a long time."

"I'm glad," I said.

When she smiled, I was struck anew by how grown-up she looked. Moments ago, it seemed, she'd been a little girl. Where had the time gone?

"I can't wait for this weekend," she whispered.

"Neither can I."

"Will you have everything ready at the house?"

I nodded.

She peeked around. Seeing her expression, I already knew what she was going to ask.

"How are you and Mom doing?"

She'd first asked me this a few months after Leslie had moved out; in the past year, she'd done so more frequently, though never when Jane was around. At first I'd been puzzled; lately I'd come to expect it.

"Good," I said.

This was, by the way, the answer I always gave, though I knew that Anna didn't always believe me.

This time, however, she searched my face, and then, surprising me, she leaned in and hugged me again. Her arms were tight around my back. "I love you, Daddy," she whispered. "I think you're great."

"I love you, too, sweetheart."

"Mom's a lucky lady," she said. "Don't ever forget that."

"Okay," Jane said as we stood in the drive. "I guess that's it."

Anna was waiting in the car.

"You'll call, right? I mean, if *anything* comes up."

"I promise," I said. "And say hey to Leslie for me."

As I opened the car door for her, I could already feel the heat of the day bearing down on me. The air was thick and heavy, making the homes up the street look hazy. Another scorcher, I thought.

"Have a good time today," I said, missing her already.

Jane nodded and took a step toward the open door. Watching her, I knew she could still turn the head of any man. How had I become middle-aged while the ravages of time ignored her? I didn't know and didn't care, and before I could stop them, the words were already out.

"You're beautiful," I murmured.

Jane turned back with a look of faint surprise. By her expression, I knew she was trying to figure out whether she'd heard me correctly. I suppose I could have waited for her to respond, but instead I did what was once as natural to me as breathing. Moving close before she could turn away, I kissed her gently, her lips soft against my own.

This wasn't like any of the other kisses we'd shared recently, quick and perfunctory, like acquaintances greeting each other. I didn't pull back and neither did she, and the kiss took on a life of its own. And when we finally drew apart and I saw her expression, I knew with certainty that I'd done exactly the right thing.

Chapter Eleven

was still reliving the kiss in the driveway when I got
in the car to start my day. After swinging by the grocery
store, I drove to Creekside. Instead of heading straight to
the pond, however, I entered the building and walked to
Noah's room.

As always, the smell of antiseptic filled the air. Multi-
colored tiles and wide corridors reminded me of the hospital, and as I passed the entertainment room, I noticed
that only a few of the tables and chairs were occupied.
Two men were playing checkers in the corner, another few
were watching a television that had been mounted on the
wall. A nurse sat behind the main desk, her head bent,
impervious to my presence.

The sounds of television followed me as I made my
way down the hall, and it was a relief to enter Noah's room.
Unlike so many of the guests here, whose rooms seemed
largely devoid of anything personal, Noah had made his
room into something he could call his own. A painting by
Allie—a flowering pond and garden scene reminiscent of
Monet—hung on the wall above his rocking chair. On the

shelves stood dozens of pictures of the children and of Allie; others had been tacked to the wall. His cardigan sweater was draped over the edge of the bed, and in the corner sat the battered rolltop desk that had once occupied the far wall of the family room in their home. The desk had originally been Noah's father's, and its age was reflected in the notches and grooves and ink stains from the fountain pens that Noah had always favored.

I knew that Noah sat here frequently in the evenings, for in the drawers were the possessions he treasured above all else: the hand-scripted notebook in which he'd memorialized his love affair with Allie, his leather-bound diaries whose pages were turning yellow with age, the hundreds of letters he'd written to Allie over the years, and the last letter she ever wrote to him. There were other items, too—dried flowers and newspaper clippings about Allie's shows, special gifts from the children, the edition of *Leaves of Grass* by Walt Whitman that had been his companion throughout World War II.

Perhaps I was exhibiting my instincts as an estate lawyer, but I wondered what would become of the items when Noah was finally gone. How would it be possible to distribute these things among the children? The easiest solution would be to give everything to the children equally, but that posed its own problems. Who, for instance, would keep the notebook in their home? Whose drawer would house the letters or his diaries? It was one thing to divide the major assets, but how was it possible to divide the heart?

The drawers were unlocked. Although Noah would be back in his room in a day or two, I searched them for the items he would want with him at the hospital, tucking them under my arm.

Compared to the air-conditioned building, the air out-side was stifling, and I started to perspire immediately. The courtyard was empty, as always. Walking along the gravel path, I looked for the root that had caused Noah's fall. It took a moment for me to find it, at the base of a towering magnolia tree; it protruded across the path like a small snake stretching in the sun.

The brackish pond reflected the sky like a mirror, and for a moment I watched the clouds drifting slowly across the water. There was a faint odor of brine as I took my seat. The swan appeared from the shallows at the far end of the pond and drifted toward me.

I opened the loaf of Wonder Bread and tore the first piece into small bits, the way Noah always did. Tossing the first piece into the water, I wondered whether he'd been telling the truth in the hospital. Had the swan stayed with him throughout his ordeal? I had no doubt he saw the swan when he regained consciousness—the nurse who found him could vouch for that—but had the swan watched over him the whole time? Impossible to know for sure, but in my heart I believed it.

I wasn't willing, however, to make the leap that Noah had. The swan, I told myself, had stayed because Noah fed and cared for it; it was more like a pet than a creature of the wild. It had nothing to do with Allie or her spirit. I simply couldn't bring myself to believe that such things could happen.

The swan ignored the piece of bread I'd thrown to it; instead it simply watched me. Strange. When I tossed another piece, the swan glanced at it before swinging its head back in my direction.

"Eat," I said, "I've got things to do."

Beneath the surface, I could see the swan's feet moving slowly, just enough to keep it in place.

"C'mon," I urged under my breath, "you ate for me before."

I threw a third piece into the water, less than a few inches from where the swan floated. I heard the gentle tap as it hit the water. Again, the swan made no move toward it.

"Aren't you hungry?" I asked.

Behind me, I heard the sprinklers come on, spurting air and water in a steady rhythm. I glanced over my shoulder toward Noah's room, but the window only reflected the sun's glare. Wondering what else to do, I threw a fourth piece of bread without luck.

"He asked me to come here," I said.

The swan straightened its neck and ruffled its wings. I suddenly realized that I was doing the same thing that provoked concern about Noah: talking to the swan and pretending it could understand me.

Pretending it was Allie?

Of course not, I thought, pushing the voice away. People talked to dogs and cats, they talked to plants, they sometimes screamed at sporting events on the television. Jane and Kate shouldn't be so concerned, I decided. Noah spent hours here every day; if anything, they should worry if he didn't talk to the swan.

Then again, talking was one thing. Believing it was Allie was another. And Noah truly believed it.

The pieces of bread that I'd thrown were gone now. Waterlogged, they'd dissolved and sunk beneath the surface, but still the swan continued to watch me. I threw yet another piece, and when the swan made no move toward it, I glanced around to make sure that no one else was watching. Why not? I finally decided, and with that, I leaned forward.

"He's doing fine," I said. "I saw him yesterday and talked to the doctor this morning. He'll be here tomorrow."

The swan seemed to contemplate my words, and a moment later, I felt the hairs on the back of my neck rise as the swan began to eat.

At the hospital, I thought I'd entered the wrong room.

In all my years with Noah, I'd never seen him watch television. Though he had one in his home, it had been primarily for the children when they were young, and by the time I came into their lives, it was seldom turned on. Instead, most evenings were spent on the porch, where stories were told. Sometimes the family sang as Noah played guitar; other times they simply talked over the hum of crickets and cicadas. On cooler evenings, Noah would light a fire and the family would do the same things in the living room. On other nights, each of them would simply curl up on the couch or in the rocking chairs to read. For hours, the only sounds were of pages turning as all escaped into a different world, albeit in proximity to one another.

It was a throwback to an earlier era, one that cherished family time above all, and I looked forward to those evenings. They reminded me of those nights with my father as he worked on his ships and made me realize that while television was regarded as a form of escape, there was nothing calming or peaceful about it. Noah had always managed to avoid it. Until this morning.

Pushing open the door, I was assaulted by the noise of the television. Noah was propped up in bed and staring at the screen. In my hand were the items I'd brought with me from his desk.

"Hello, Noah," I said, but instead of responding with his usual greeting, he turned toward me with a look of incredulity.

"C'mere," he said, motioning toward me, "you won't believe what they're showing right now."

I moved into the room. "What are you watching?"

"I don't know," he said, still focused on the screen. "Some kind of talk show. I thought it would be like Johnny Carson, but it's not. You can't imagine what they're talking about."

My mind immediately conjured up a series of vulgar programs, the kind that always made me wonder how their producers could sleep at night. Sure enough, the station was tuned to one of them. I didn't need to know the topic to know what he'd seen; for the most part, they all featured the same disgusting topics, told as luridly as possible by guests whose single goal, it seemed, was to be on television, no matter how degraded they were made to look.

"Why would you choose a show like that?"

"I didn't even know it was on," he explained. "I was looking for the news, then there was a commercial, and this came on. And when I saw what was going on, I couldn't help but watch. It was like staring at an accident on the side of the highway."

I sat on the bed beside him. "That bad?"

"Let's just say I wouldn't want to be young these days. Society's going downhill fast, and I'm glad that I won't be around to see it crash."

I smiled. "You're sounding your age, Noah."

"Maybe, but that doesn't mean I'm wrong." He shook his head and picked up the remote. A moment later, the room was quiet.

I set down the items I'd brought from his room.

"I thought you might like these to help you pass the time. Unless you'd rather watch television, of course."

His face softened as he saw the stack of letters and Whitman's *Leaves of Grass.* The pages of the book, thumbed through a thousand times, looked almost swollen. He ran his finger over the tattered cover. "You're a good man, Wilson," he said. "I take it you just went to the pond."

"Four pieces in the morning," I informed him.

"How was she today?"

I shifted on the bed, wondering how to answer.

"I think she missed you," I offered at last.

He nodded, pleased. Shifting up straighter in the bed, he asked, "So Jane's off with Anna?"

"They're probably still driving. They left an hour ago."

"And Leslie?"

"She's meeting them in Raleigh."

"This is really going to be something," he said. "The weekend, I mean. How's everything from your end? With the house?"

"So far, so good," I started. "My hope is that it'll be ready by Thursday, and I'm pretty sure it will be."

"What's on your agenda today?"

I told him what I planned, and when I finished, he whistled appreciatively. "Sounds like you've got quite a bit on your plate," he said.

"I suppose," I said. "But so far, I've been lucky."

"I'll say," he said. "Except for me, of course. My stumble could have ruined everything."

"I told you I've been lucky."

He raised his chin slightly. "What about your anniversary?" he asked.

My mind flashed to the many hours I'd spent preparing for the anniversary—all the phone calls, all the trips to the post office box and various stores. I'd worked on the gift during spare moments in the office and at lunchtime and had thought long and hard about the best way to present it. Everyone in the office knew what I'd planned, although they'd been sworn to secrecy. More than that, they'd been incredibly supportive; the gift was not something I could have put together alone.

"Thursday night," I said. "It seems like it'll be the only chance we get. She's gone tonight, tomorrow she'll probably want to see you, and on Friday, Joseph and Leslie will be here. Of course, Saturday's out for obvious reasons." I paused. "I just hope she likes it."

He smiled. "I wouldn't worry about it, Wilson. You couldn't have picked a better gift if you had all the money in the world."

"I hope you're right."

"I am. And I can't imagine a better start to the weekend."

The sincerity in his voice warmed me, and I was touched that he seemed so fond of me, despite how different we were.

"You're the one who gave me the idea," I reminded him.

Noah shook his head. "No," he said, "it was all you. Gifts of the heart can't be claimed by anyone except the giver." He patted his chest to emphasize the point. "Allie would love what you've done," he remarked. "She was always a softie when it came to things like this."

I folded my hands in my lap. "I wish she could be there this weekend."

Noah glanced at the stack of letters. I knew he was imagining Allie, and for a brief moment, he looked strangely younger.

"So do I," he said.

Heat seemed to scald the soles of my feet as I walked through the parking lot. In the distance, buildings looked as if they were made of liquid, and I could feel my shirt tacking itself to my back.

Once in the car, I headed for the winding country roads that were as familiar as the streets of my own neighborhood. There was an austere beauty to the coastal lowlands, and I wove past farms and tobacco barns that looked almost abandoned. Strands of loblolly pines separated one farm from the next, and I caught sight of a tractor moving in the distance, a cloud of dirt and dust rising behind it.

From certain points in the road, it was possible to see the Trent River, the slow waters rippling in the sunlight. Oaks and cypress trees lined the banks, their white trunks and knotted roots casting gnarled shadows. Spanish moss hung from the branches, and as the farms gradually gave way to forest, I imagined that the sprawling trees I saw from behind my windshield were the same trees that both Union and Confederate soldiers had seen when they marched through the area.

In the distance, I saw a tin roof reflecting the sun; next came the house itself; and a few moments later I was at Noah's.

As I surveyed the house from the tree-lined drive, I thought it looked abandoned. Off to the side was the faded red barn where Noah stored lumber and equipment; numerous holes now dotted the sides, and the tin roof was caked with rust. His workshop, where he had spent most of his hours during the day, was directly behind the house. The swinging doors hung crookedly, and the windows were coated with dirt. Just beyond that was the rose garden that had become as overgrown as the banks along the river. The caretaker, I noticed, hadn't mowed recently, and the once grassy lawn resembled a wild meadow.

I parked next to the house, pausing for a moment to study it. Finally, I fished the key from my pocket, and after unlocking the door, I pushed it open. Sunlight immediately crossed the floor.

With the windows boarded, it was otherwise dark, and I made a note to turn on the generator before I left. After my eyes adjusted to the dim light, I could make out the features of the house. Directly in front of me were the stairs that led to the bedrooms; on my left was a long, wide family room that stretched from the front of the house to the back porch. It was here, I thought, that we would put the tables for the reception, for the room could easily accommodate everyone.

The house smelled of dust, and I could see traces of it on the sheets that draped the furniture. I knew I'd have to remind the movers that each piece was an antique dating from the original construction of the house. The fireplace was inlaid with hand-painted ceramic tile; I remembered Noah telling me that when he'd replaced the ones that had cracked, he'd been relieved to discover that the original manufacturer was still in business. In the corner was a piano—also covered by a sheet—that had been played not only by Noah's children, but by the grandchildren as well.

On either side of the fireplace were three windows. I tried to imagine what the room would look like when it was ready, but standing in the darkened house, I couldn't. Though I had pictured how I wanted it to look—and even described my ideas to Jane—being inside the house evoked memories that made changing its appearance seem impossible.

How many evenings had Jane and I spent here with Noah and Allie? Too many to count, and if I concentrated,

I could almost hear the sounds of laughter and the rise and fall of easy conversation.

I'd come here, I suppose, because the events of the morning had only deepened my nagging sense of nostalgia and longing. Even now, I could feel the softness of Jane's lips against my own and taste the lipstick she'd been wearing. Were things really changing between us? I desperately wanted to think so, but I wondered whether I was simply projecting my own feelings onto Jane. All I knew for certain was that for the first time in a long time, there was a moment, just a moment, when Jane seemed as happy with me as I was with her.

Chapter Twelve

The rest of the day was spent on the phone in my den. I spoke to the cleaning company that worked in our home, and we finalized arrangements to have Noah's house cleaned on Thursday; I spoke to the man who pressure-washed our deck, and he would be there around noon to brighten the grand home. An electrician was coming to make sure that the generator, the outlets inside the house, and the floodlights in the rose garden were still in working order. I called the company that had repainted our law offices last year, and they promised to send a crew to begin freshening the walls inside, as well as the fence that surrounded the rose garden. A rental company would provide tents and tables, chairs for the ceremony, linens, glasses, and silverware, and all would be delivered on Thursday morning. A few employees of the restaurant would be there later to set things up, well in advance of the event on Saturday. Nathan Little was looking forward to starting his project, and when I called he informed me that the plants I'd ordered earlier that week from the nursery were already loaded on his truck. He also agreed to have his employees cart the excess furniture from the home. Finally, I made the necessary music arrangements for both the wedding and the reception; the piano would be tuned on Thursday.

The arrangements to have everything accomplished quickly weren't as difficult as one might imagine. Not only was I acquainted with most of the people I called, but it was something I had done once before. In many ways, this burst of frenzied activity was like the work we'd done on the first home Jane and I had purchased after we got married. An old row house that had fallen on hard times, it needed a thorough remodeling job . . . which was why we'd been able to afford it. We did much of the initial gutting ourselves but soon reached the point where the skills of carpenters, plumbers, and electricians were needed.

Meanwhile, we had wasted no time trying to start a family.

We were both virgins when we said our vows; I was twenty-six, Jane was twenty-three. We taught each other how to make love in a way that was both innocent and filled with passion, gradually learning how to please each other. It seemed that no matter how tired we were, most evenings were spent entwined in each other's arms.

We never took precautions to prevent a pregnancy. I remember believing that Jane would become pregnant right away, and I even started adding to my savings account in anticipation of the event. She didn't, however, get pregnant in the first month of our marriage, nor did she in the second or third months.

Sometime around the sixth month, she consulted with Allie, and later that night, when I got home from work, she informed me that we had to talk. Again, I sat beside her on the couch as she told me there was something that she wanted me to do. This time, instead of asking me to go to church, she asked me to pray with her, and I did. Somehow I knew that it was the right thing to do. We began praying together as a couple regularly after that night, and the more we did, the more I came to look forward to it. Yet more months passed, and Jane still didn't become pregnant. I don't know if she was ever truly worried about her ability to conceive, but I do know it was always on her mind, and even I'd started to wonder about it. By then, we were a month away from our first anniversary.

Though I'd originally planned to have contractors submit bids and conduct a series of interviews to finish the work on our home, I knew that the process had begun to wear on Jane. Our tiny apartment was cramped, and the excitement of remodeling had lost its luster. I made a secret goal to move Jane into our home before our first anniversary.

With that in mind, I did the same thing that, ironically, I would do again some three decades later: I worked the phones, called in favors, and did whatever was necessary to guarantee the work would be completed in time. I hired crews, dropped by the house at lunch and after work to monitor its progress, and ended up paying far more than I originally budgeted. Nonetheless, I found myself marveling at the speed with which the house began to take form. Workers came and went; floors were laid, cabinets, sinks, and appliances were installed. Light fixtures were replaced and wallpaper hung, as day by day I watched the calendar inch closer to our anniversary.

In the final week before our anniversary, I invented excuses to keep Jane from the house, for it is in the last week of a renovation that a house ceases to be a shell and becomes a home. I wanted it to be a surprise that she would remember forever.

"No reason to go to the house tonight," I'd say. "When

I went by earlier, the contractor wasn't even there." Or, "I've got a lot of work to do later, and I'd rather relax with you around here."

I don't know whether she believed my excuses—and looking back, I'm sure she must have suspected something—but she didn't press me to bring her there. And on our anniversary, after we'd shared a romantic dinner downtown, I drove her to the house instead of our apartment.

It was late. The moon was full and cratered; cicadas had begun their evening song, their trill notes filling the air. From the outside, the house looked unchanged. Piles of scrap still lay heaped in the yard, paint cans were stacked near the door, and the porch looked gray with dust. Jane gazed toward the house, then glanced at me quizzically.

"I just want to check on what they've been doing," I explained.

"Tonight?" she asked.

"Why not?"

"Well, for one thing, it's dark inside. We won't be able to see anything."

"C'mon," I said, reaching for a flashlight I'd stashed under my seat. "We don't have to stay long if you don't want to."

I got out of the car and opened her door for her. After guiding her gingerly through the debris and up onto the porch, I unlocked the door.

In the darkness, it was impossible not to notice the smell of new carpet, and a moment later, when I turned on the flashlight and swept it through the living room and the kitchen, I saw Jane's eyes widen. It wasn't completely finished, of course, but even from where we stood in the doorway, it was plain that it was close enough for us to move in.

Jane stood frozen in place. I reached for her hand.

"Welcome home," I said.

"Oh, Wilson," she breathed.

"Happy anniversary," I whispered.

When she turned toward me, her expression was a mixture of hope and confusion.

"But how . . . I mean, last week, it wasn't even close . . ."

"I wanted it to be a surprise. But come—there's one more thing I have to show you."

I led her up the stairs, turning toward the master bedroom. As I pushed open the door, I aimed the flashlight and then stepped aside so Jane could see.

In the room was the only piece of furniture that I've ever bought on my own: an antique canopy bed. It resembled the one at the inn in Beaufort where we'd made love on our honeymoon.

Jane was silent, and I was suddenly struck by the thought that I'd somehow done something wrong.

"I can't believe you did this," she finally said. "Was this your idea?"

"Don't you like it?"

She smiled. "I love it," she said softly. "But I can't believe that you thought of this. This is almost . . . *romantic*."

To be honest, I hadn't thought of it in that way. The simple fact was that we needed a decent bed, and this was the one style I was certain that she liked. Knowing she meant it as a compliment, however, I raised an eyebrow, as if asking, What else would you expect?

She approached the bed and ran a finger along the canopy. A moment later, she sat on the edge and patted the mattress beside her in invitation. "We have to talk," she said.

As I moved to join her, I couldn't help but remember the previous times she'd made this announcement. I expected that she was about to ask me to do something else for her, but when I sat down, she leaned in to kiss me.

"I have a surprise, too," she said. "And I've been waiting for the right moment to tell you."

"What is it?" I asked.

She hesitated for the barest second. "I'm pregnant."

At first, her words didn't register, but when they did, I knew with certainty that I'd been given a surprise even better than my own.

In early evening, when the sun was getting low and the brunt of the heat was breaking, Jane called. After asking about Noah, she informed me that Anna still couldn't make up her mind about the dress and that she wouldn't make it home that night. Though I assured her that I had expected as much, I could hear a trace of frustration in her voice. She wasn't as angry as she was exasperated, and I smiled, wondering how on earth Jane could still be surprised by our daughter's behavior.

After hanging up, I drove to Creekside to feed the swan three pieces of Wonder Bread, then swung by the office on the way back home.

Parking in my usual spot out front, I could see the Chelsea Restaurant just up the street; opposite was a small grass park, where Santa's village was set up every winter. Despite the thirty years I've worked in this building, it still amazed me to realize that the early history of North Carolina could be found in any direction I looked. The past has always held special meaning for me, and I loved the fact that within blocks, I could walk through the first Catholic church built in the state, or tour the first public school and learn how the settlers were educated, or stroll the grounds of Tryon Palace, the former home of the colonial governor that now boasts one of the finest formal gardens in the South. I'm not alone in this pride in my town; the New Bern Historical Society is one of the most active in the country, and on nearly every corner, signs document the important role New Bern played in the early years of our country.

My partners and I own the building where we keep our law offices, and though I wish there was an interesting anecdote concerning its past, there really isn't one. Erected in the late 1950s, when functionality was the single criterion architects valued in design, it's really quite drab. In this single-story, rectangular brick structure, there are offices for the four partners and four associates, three conference rooms, a file room, and a reception area for clients.

I unlocked the front door, heard the warning that the alarm would sound in less than a minute, then punched in the code to shut it off. Switching on the lamp in the reception area, I headed toward my office.

Like my partners' offices, my office has a certain air of formality that clients seem to expect: dark cherry desk topped with a brass lamp, law books shelved along the wall, a set of comfortable leather chairs facing the desk.

As an estate lawyer, I sometimes feel as if I've seen every type of couple in the world. Though most strike me as perfectly normal, I've watched some couples begin to brawl like street fighters, and I once witnessed a woman pour hot coffee onto her husband's lap. More often than I would ever have believed possible, I've been pulled aside by a husband asking whether he was legally obligated to leave something to his wife or whether he could omit her entirely in favor of his mistress. These couples, I should add, often dress well and look perfectly ordinary as they sit before me, but when at last they leave my office, I find myself wondering what goes on behind the closed doors of their homes.

Standing behind my desk, I found the appropriate key on my chain and unlocked the drawer. I put Jane's gift on my desk and gazed at it, wondering how she would respond when I gave it to her. I thought she would like it, but more than that, I wanted her to recognize it as a heart-felt—if belated—attempt to apologize for the man I'd been for most of our marriage.

Yet because I've failed her in ways too frequent to count, I couldn't help but wonder about her expression as we'd stood in the driveway this morning. Hadn't it been almost . . . well, dreamy? Or had I simply been imagining it?

As I glanced toward the window, it was a moment before the answer came, and all at once, I knew I hadn't been imagining it. No, somehow, even accidentally, I'd stumbled onto the key to my success in courting her so long ago. Though I'd been the same man I'd been for the past year—a man deeply in love with his wife and trying his best to keep her—I'd made one small but significant adjustment.

This week, I hadn't been focusing on my problems and doing my best to correct them. This week, I'd been think-ing of *her;* I'd committed myself to helping her with family responsibilities, I'd listened with interest whenever she spoke, and everything we discussed seemed new. I'd laughed at her jokes and held her as she'd cried, apolo-gized for my faults, and showed her the affection she both needed and deserved. In other words, I'd been the man she'd always wanted, the man I once had been, and—like an old habit rediscovered—I now understood that it was all I ever needed to do for us to begin enjoying each other's company again.

Chapter Thirteen

When I arrived at Noah's house the following morning, my eyebrows rose at the sight of the nursery trucks already parked in the drive. There were three large flatbeds crowded with small trees and bushes, while another was loaded with bales of pine straw to spread atop the flower beds, around the trees, and along the fence line. A truck and trailer held various tools and equipment, and three pickups were packed with flats of low flowering plants.

In front of the trucks, workers congregated in groups of five or six. A quick count showed that closer to forty people had come—not the thirty that Little had promised—and all were wearing jeans and baseball caps despite the heat. When I got out of the car, Little approached me with a smile.

"Good—you're here," he said, putting his hand on my shoulder. "We've been waiting for you. We can get started, then, yes?"

Within minutes, mowers and tools were unloaded, and the air was soon filled with the sound of engines rising and falling as they crisscrossed the property. Some of the workers began to unload the plants, bushes, and trees, stacking them into wheelbarrows and rolling them to their appropriate spots.

But it was the rose garden that attracted the most attention, and I followed Little as he grabbed a set of pruning shears and headed that way, joining the dozen workers who were already waiting for him. Beautifying the garden struck me as the type of job where it is impossible even to know where to begin, but Little simply started pruning the first bush while describing what he was doing. The workers clustered around him, whispering to one another in Spanish as they watched, then finally dispersed when they understood what he wanted. Hour by hour, the natural colors of the roses were artfully exposed as each bush was thinned and trimmed. Little was adamant that few blooms be lost, necessitating quite a bit of twine as stems were pulled and tied, bent and rotated, into their proper place.

Next came the trellis. Once Little was comfortable, he began to shape the roses that draped it. As he worked, I pointed out where the chairs for the guests would go, and my friend winked.

"You wanted impatiens to line the aisle, yes?"

When I nodded, he brought two fingers to his mouth and whistled. A moment later, flower-filled wheelbarrows were rolled to the spot. Two hours later, I marveled at an aisle gorgeous enough to be photographed by a magazine.

Throughout the morning, the rest of the property began to take shape. Once the yard was mowed, bushes were pruned, and workers started edging around the fence posts, walkways, and the house itself. The electrician arrived to turn on the generator, check the outlets, and the floodlights in the garden. An hour later, the painters arrived; six men in splattered overalls emerged from a run-down van, and they helped the landscaping crew store the furniture in the barn. The man who'd come to pressure-wash the house rolled up the drive and parked next to my car. Within minutes of unloading his equipment, the first intense blast of water hit the wall, and slowly but steadily, each plank turned from gray to white.

With all the individual crews busily at work, I made my way to the workshop and grabbed a ladder. The boards from the windows had to be removed, so I set myself to the task. With something to do, the afternoon passed quickly.

By four, the landscapers were loading their trucks and getting ready to head back; the pressure washer and painters were finishing up as well. I had been able to take off most of the boards; a few remained on the second floor, but I knew I could do those in the morning.

By the time I finished storing the boards under the house, the property seemed strangely silent, and I found myself surveying all that had been done.

Like all half-completed projects, it looked worse than it had when we'd begun that morning. Pieces of land-scaping equipment dotted the property; empty pots had been piled haphazardly. Both inside and out, only half the walls had been touched up and reminded me of detergent commercials where one brand promises to clean a white T-shirt better than the next. A mound of yard scrap was piled near the fence, and while the outer hearts of the rose garden had been completed, the inner hearts looked for-lorn and wild.

Nonetheless, I felt strangely relieved. It had been a good day's work, one that left no doubt that everything would be finished in time. Jane would be amazed, and knowing she was on her way home, I was starting for my car when I saw Harvey Wellington, the minister, leaning on the fence that separated Noah's property from his. Slowing my pace, I hesitated only briefly before crossing the yard to join him. His forehead glistened like polished mahogany, and his spectacles perched low on his nose. Like me, he was dressed as if he'd spent most of the day working outside. As I drew near, he nodded toward the house.

"Getting it all ready for the weekend, I see," he said.

"Trying," I said.

"You've got enough people working on it, that's for sure. It looked like a parking lot out there today. What did you have? Fifty people total?"

"Something like that."

He whistled under his breath as we shook hands. "That'll take a bite out of the old wallet, won't it?"

"I'm almost afraid to find out," I said.

He laughed. "So how many you expecting this weekend?"

"I'd guess about a hundred or so."

"It's going to be some party, that's for sure," he said. "I know Alma's been looking forward to it. This wedding's been all she can talk about lately. We both think it's wonderful that you're making such a big deal about it."

"It's the least I could do."

For a long moment, he held my gaze without responding. As he watched me, I had the strange impression that despite our limited acquaintance, he understood me quite well. It was a little unnerving, but I suppose I shouldn't have been surprised. As a pastor, he was frequently sought for counsel and advice, and I sensed the kindness of someone who'd learned to listen well and sympathize with another's plight. He was, I thought, a man whom hundreds probably regarded as one of their closest friends.

As if knowing what I was thinking, he smiled. "So, eight o'clock?"

"Any earlier, and I think it would be too hot."

"It'll be hot anyway. But I don't think anyone would care one way or the other." He motioned toward the house. "I'm glad you're finally doing something about it. That's a wonderful place. Always has been."

"I know."

He removed his spectacles and began wiping the lenses with his shirttail. "Yeah, I'll tell you—it's been a shame watching what's become of it over the last few years. All it ever needed was for someone to care for it again." He put his spectacles back on, smiling softly. "It's funny, but have you ever noticed that the more special something is, the more people seem to take it for granted? It's like they think it won't ever change. Just like this house here. All it ever needed was a little attention, and it would never have ended up like this in the first place."

There were two messages on the answering machine when I arrived home: one from Dr. Barnwell informing me that Noah was back at Creekside and another from Jane saying that she would meet me there around seven.

By the time I arrived at Creekside, most of the family had come and gone. Only Kate remained by Noah's side when I reached his room, and she brought a finger to her lips as I entered. She rose from her chair and we hugged.

"He just fell asleep," she whispered. "He must have been exhausted."

I glanced at him, surprised. In all the years I'd known him, he'd never napped during the day. "Is he doing okay?"

"He was a little cranky while we were trying to get him settled in again, but other than that, he seemed fine." She tugged at my sleeve. "So tell me—how did it go at the house today? I want to hear all about it."

I filled her in on the progress, watching her rapt expression as she tried to imagine it. "Jane'll love it," she said. "Oh, that reminds me—I talked to her a little while ago. She called to see how Daddy was doing."

"Did they have any luck with the dresses?"

"I'll let her tell you about it. But she sounded pretty excited on the phone." She reached for the purse that was slung over the chair. "Listen, I should probably go. I've been here all afternoon, and I know Grayson is waiting for me." She kissed me on the cheek. "Take care of Daddy, but try not to wake him, okay? He needs his sleep."

"I'll be quiet," I promised.

I moved to the chair next to the window and was just about to sit down when I heard a ragged whisper.

"Hello, Wilson. Thanks for dropping by."

When I turned toward him, he winked.

"I thought you were sleeping."

"Nah," he said. He began to sit up in the bed. "I had to fake it. She's been fussing over me all day like a baby. She even followed me into the bathroom again."

I laughed. "Just what you wanted, right? A little pampering from your daughter?"

"Oh, yeah, that's just what I need. I didn't have half that fussing when I was in the hospital. By the way she was acting, you'd think I had one foot in the grave and another on a banana peel."

"Well, you're in rare form today. I take it you're feeling like new?"

"Could be better," he said with a shrug. "Could be

worse, though, too. But my head's fine, if that's what you're asking."

"No dizziness? Or headaches? Maybe you should rest a bit anyway. If you need me to feed you some yogurt, just let me know."

He waggled a finger at me. "Now don't you start with me. I'm a patient man, but I'm not a saint. And I'm not in the mood. I've been cooped up for days and haven't so much as smelled a breath of fresh air." He motioned toward the closet. "Would you mind getting me my sweater?"

I already knew where he wanted to go.

"It's still pretty warm out there," I offered.

"Just get me the sweater," he said. "And if you offer to help me put it on, I should warn you that I just might punch you in the nose."

A few minutes later, we left the room, Wonder Bread in hand. As he shuffled along, I could see him beginning to relax. Though Creekside would always be a foreign place to us, it had become home to Noah, and he was obviously comfortable here. It was clear how much others had missed him, too—at each open door, he waved a greeting and said a few words to his friends, promising most of them that he'd be back later to read.

He refused to let me take his arm, so I walked close to his side. He seemed slightly more unsteady than usual, and it wasn't until we were out of the building that I was confident he could make it on his own. Still, at the pace we walked, it took a while to reach the pond, and I had plenty of time to observe that the root had been taken out. I wondered if Kate had reminded one of her brothers to take care of it or whether they'd remembered on their own.

We sat in our usual places and gazed out over the water, though I couldn't see the swan. Figuring it was hiding in the shallows off to either side of us, I leaned back in my seat. Noah began to tear the bread into small pieces.

"I heard what you told Kate about the house," he said. "How are my roses doing?"

"They're not finished, but you'll like what the crew has done so far."

He piled the pieces of bread in his lap. "That garden means a lot to me. It's almost as old as you are."

"Is it?"

"The first bushes went in the ground in April 1951," he said, nodding. "Of course, I've had to replace most of them over the years, but that's when I came up with the design and started working on it."

"Jane told me you surprised Allie with it . . . to show how much you loved her."

He snorted. "That's only half the story," he said. "But I'm not surprised she thinks that. Sometimes I think Jane and Kate believe I spent every waking moment doting on Allie."

"You mean you didn't?" I asked, feigning shock.

He laughed. "Hardly. We had rows now and then, just like everyone else. We were just good at making up. But as for the garden, I suppose they're partly right. At least in the beginning." He set the pieces of bread off to one side. "I planted it when Allie was pregnant with Jane. She wasn't more than a few months along, and she was sick all the time. I figured it would pass after the first few weeks, but it didn't. There were days when she could barely get out of bed, and I knew that with summer coming, she was going to be even more miserable. So I wanted to give her something pretty to look at that she could see from her window." He squinted into the sun. "Did you know that at first there was only one heart, not five?"

I raised my eyebrows. "No, I didn't."

"I didn't plan on that, of course, but after Jane was born, I sort of got to thinking that the first heart looked mighty skimpy and I needed to plant some more bushes to fill it out. But I kept putting it off because it had been so much work the first time, and by the time I finally got around to the task, she was already pregnant again. When she saw what I was doing, she just assumed I'd done it because we had another child on the way, and she told me it was the sweetest thing I'd ever done for her. After that, I couldn't exactly stop. That's what I mean when I say it's only partly right. The first one might have been a romantic gesture; but by the last one, it felt more like a chore. Not just the planting, but keeping them going. Roses are tough. When they're young, they sort of sprout up like a tree, but you have to keep cutting them back so they form right. Every time they started blooming, I'd have to head out with my shears to prune them back into shape, and for a long time, the garden seemed as though it would never look right. And it hurt, too. Those thorns are sharp. I spent a lot of years with my hands bandaged up like a mummy."

I smiled. "I'll bet she appreciated what you were doing, though."

"Oh, she did. For a while, anyway. Until she asked me to plow the whole thing under."

At first, I didn't think I'd heard him correctly, but his expression let me know I had. I recalled the melancholy I sometimes felt when staring at Allie's paintings of the garden.

"Why?"

Noah squinted into the sun before sighing. "As much

as she loved the garden, she said it was too painful to look at. Whenever she looked out the window, she'd start crying, and sometimes it seemed like she'd never stop."

It took a moment before I realized why.

"Because of John," I said softly, referring to the child who'd died of meningitis when he was four. Jane, like Noah, seldom mentioned him.

"Losing him nearly killed her." He paused. "Nearly killed me, too. He was such a sweet little boy—just at that age where he was beginning to discover the world, when everything's new and exciting. As the baby, he used to try to keep up with the bigger kids. He was always chasing after them in the yard. And he was healthy, too. Never had so much as an ear infection or a serious cold before he got sick. That's why it was such a shock. One week he was playing in the yard, and the next week, we were at his funeral. After that, Allie could barely eat or sleep, and when she wasn't crying, she just sort of wandered around in a daze. I wasn't sure she'd ever get over it. That's when she told me to plow the garden under."

He drifted off. I said nothing, knowing it wasn't possible to fully imagine the pain of losing a child.

"Why didn't you?" I asked after a while.

"I thought it was just her grief talking," he said quietly, "and I wasn't sure if she really wanted me to do it, or just said it because her pain was so awful that day. So I waited. I figured if she asked me a second time, I would do it. Or I'd offer to remove just the outer heart, if she wanted to keep the rest of it. But in the end, she never did. And after that? Even though she used it in a lot of her paintings, she never felt the same way about it. When we lost John, it stopped being a happy thing for her. Even when Kate got married there, she had mixed feelings about it."

"Do the kids know why there are five rings?"

"Maybe in the back of their minds they do, but they would have had to figure it out on their own. It wasn't something Allie or I liked to talk about. After John died, it was easier to think about the garden as a single gift, rather than five. And so that's what it became. And when the kids were older and finally got around to asking about it, Allie just told them that I'd planted it for her. So to them, it's always been this romantic gesture."

From the corner of my eye, I saw the swan appear and glide toward us. It was curious that it hadn't appeared before now, and I wondered where it had been. I thought that Noah would toss a piece of bread immediately, but he didn't. Instead, he simply watched it paddle closer. When it was a few feet away, the swan seemed to hover briefly, but then, to my surprise, it approached the bank.

A moment later it waddled toward us, and Noah stretched out his hand. The swan leaned into his touch, and as Noah spoke quietly to it, I was suddenly struck by the thought that the swan had actually missed Noah, too.

Noah fed the swan, and afterward I watched in wonder as—just as he'd once confided—the swan settled down at his feet.

An hour later, the clouds began to roll in. Dense and full bellied, they portended the type of summer storm common in the South—intense rain for twenty minutes, then slowly clearing skies. The swan was back-paddling in the pond, and I was about to suggest that we go back inside when I heard Anna's voice behind us.

"Hey, Grampa! Hey, Daddy!" she called out. "When you weren't in the room, we thought we might find you out here."

I turned to see a cheerful Anna approaching. Jane trailed wearily a few steps behind. Her smile seemed strained—this, I knew, was the one place she dreaded finding her father.

"Hey, sweetheart," I said, rising. Anna hugged me fiercely, her arms tight around my back.

"How'd it go today?" I asked. "Did you find the dress?"

When she released me, she couldn't hide the excitement. "You're going to love it," she promised, squeezing my arms. "It's perfect."

By then Jane had reached us, and letting go of Anna, I embraced Jane as if doing so had somehow become natural again. She felt soft and warm, a reassuring presence.

"C'mere," Noah said to Anna. He patted the bench. "Tell me about what you've been doing to get yourself ready for the weekend."

Anna sat down and reached for his hand. "It's been fantastic," she said. "I never imagined how much fun it would be. We must have gone into a dozen stores. And you should see Leslie! We found a dress for her too that's totally awesome."

Jane and I stood off to the side as Anna recounted the whirlwind activities of the past couple of days. As she told one story after another, she alternately bumped Noah playfully or squeezed his hand. Despite the sixty years between them, it was obvious how comfortable they were together. Though grandparents often have special relationships with their grandchildren, Noah and Anna were clearly friends, and I felt a surge of parental pride at the young woman Anna had become. I could tell by the softness in Jane's expression that she was feeling exactly the same way, and though I hadn't done such a thing in years, I slowly slipped my arm around her.

I suppose I wasn't sure what to expect—for a second she seemed almost startled—but when she relaxed beneath my arm, there was an instant where all seemed right in the world. In the past, words had always failed me at moments like this. Perhaps I'd secretly feared that speaking my feelings aloud would somehow diminish them. Yet now I realized how wrong I'd been to withhold my thoughts, and bringing my lips to her ear, I whispered the words that I should never have kept inside:

"I love you, Jane, and I'm the luckiest man in the world to have you."

Though she didn't say a word, the way she leaned further against me was all the response I needed.

The thunder began half an hour later, a deep echo that seemed to ripple across the sky. After walking Noah to his room, Jane and I left for home, parting ways with Anna in the parking lot.

Riding through downtown, I stared out the windshield at the sun cutting through thickening clouds, casting shadows and making the river shine like gold. Jane was surprisingly quiet, gazing out the window, and I found myself glancing at her from the corner of my eye. Her hair was tucked neatly behind her ear, and the pink blouse she wore made her skin glow like that of a young child. On her hand shone the ring she'd worn for almost thirty years, the diamond engagement ring coupled with the narrow gold band.

We entered our neighborhood; a moment later, we pulled into the drive and Jane roused herself with a weary smile.

"Sorry about being so quiet. I guess I'm sort of tired."

"It's okay. It's been a big week."

I brought her suitcase inside, watching as she dropped her purse on the table near the door.

"Would you like some wine?" I asked.

Jane yawned and shook her head. "No, not tonight. If I had a glass, I think I'd fall asleep. I'd love a glass of water, though."

In the kitchen, I filled two glasses with ice and water from the refrigerator. She took a long drink, then leaned against the counter and propped one leg against the cupboards behind her in her habitual pose.

"My feet are killing me. We barely stopped for a minute all day. Anna looked at a couple hundred dresses before she found the right one. And actually, Leslie was the one who pulled it off the rack. I think she was getting desperate by then—Anna's got to be one of the most indecisive people I've ever met."

"What's it like?"

"Oh, you should see her in it. It's one of those mermaid-style dresses, and it really flatters her figure. It's still got to be fitted, but Keith's going to love it."

"I'll bet she looks beautiful."

"She does." By her dreamy expression, I knew she was seeing it again. "I'd show you, but Anna doesn't want you to see it until the weekend. She wants it to be a surprise." She paused. "So how did it go on your end? Did anyone show up at the house?"

"Everyone," I said, filling her in on the details of the morning.

"Amazing," she said, refilling her glass. "Considering it's so last minute, I mean."

From the kitchen, we could see the sliding glass windows that led to the deck. The light outside had dimmed under the thickening clouds, and the first drops of rain began to hit the window, lightly at first. The river was gray and ominous; a moment later, there was a flash of light followed by the crackling of thunder, and the downpour began in earnest. Jane turned toward the windows as the storm unleashed its fury.

"Do you know if it's going to rain on Saturday?" she asked. Her voice, I thought, was surprisingly calm; I expected her to be more anxious. I thought of her peacefulness in the car, and I realized she hadn't said a word about Noah's presence at the pond. Watching her, I had the strange sense that her mood had something to do with Anna.

"It's not supposed to," I said. "They're forecasting clear skies. This is supposed to be the last of the showers passing through."

Silently we stared at the falling rain together. Aside from the gentle patter of water, all was quiet. There was a faraway look in Jane's eyes, and the ghost of a smile played on her lips.

"It's lovely, isn't it?" she asked. "Watching the rain? We used to do that at my parents' house, remember? When we'd sit on the porch?"

"I remember."

"It was nice, wasn't it?"

"Very."

"We haven't done this in a long time."

"No," I said, "we haven't."

She seemed lost in thought, and I prayed that this newfound sense of calm wouldn't give way to the familiar sadness I had come to dread. Yet her expression didn't change, and after a long moment, she glanced at me.

"Something else happened today," she said, looking down at her glass.

"Oh?"

Looking up again, she met my eyes. They seemed to be sparkling with unshed tears.

"I won't be able to sit with you at the wedding."

"You won't?"

"I can't," she said. "I'll be up front with Anna and Keith."

"Why?"

Jane brought her hand to the glass. "Because Anna asked me to be her matron of honor." Her voice cracked a little. "She said she was closer to me than to anyone, and that I'd done so much for her and the wedding. . . ." She blinked rapidly and gave a small sniff. "I know it's silly, but I was just so surprised when she asked me that I barely knew what to say. The thought hadn't even crossed my mind. She was so sweet when she asked, like it really meant something to her."

She swiped at her tears, and I felt a tightness in my throat. Asking a father to be best man was fairly typical in the South, but it was rare for a mother to act as matron of honor.

"Oh, sweetheart," I murmured. "That's wonderful. I'm so happy for you."

Lightning was followed by thunder again, though they both barely registered, and we stood in the kitchen until long after the storm had passed, sharing our silent joy.

When the rain had stopped completely, Jane slid open the glass doors and skipped out onto the deck. Water still dripped from the gutters and the porch railings, while tendrils of steam rose from the deck.

As I followed her, I felt my back and arms aching from my earlier exertions. I rolled my shoulders in an attempt to loosen them up.

"Have you eaten?" Jane asked.

"Not yet. Do you want to head out and grab a bite?"

She shook her head. "Not really. I'm pretty worn out."

"How about if we order in to celebrate? Something easy? Something . . . fun."

"Like what?"

"How about a pizza?"

She put her hands on her hips. "We haven't ordered a pizza since Leslie moved out."

"I know. But it sounds good, doesn't it?"

"It's always good. It's just that you always get indigestion afterward."

"True," I admitted. "But I'm willing to live dangerously tonight."

"Wouldn't you rather I just throw something together? I'm sure we've got something in the freezer."

"C'mon," I said. "We haven't split a pizza in years. Just the two of us, I mean. We'll kick back on the couch, eat straight from the box—you know? Just like we used to. It'll be fun."

She stared at me quizzically. "You want to do something . . . fun."

It was more of a statement than a question.

"Yes," I said.

"Do you want to order, or should I?" she finally asked.

"I'll take care of it. What do you want on it?"

She thought for a moment. "How about the works?" she said.

"Why not?" I agreed.

The pizza arrived half an hour later. By then, Jane had changed into jeans and a dark T-shirt, and we ate the pizza like a couple of college students in a dorm room. Despite her earlier refusal of a glass of wine, we ended up sharing a cold beer from the fridge.

While we ate, Jane filled in more details about her day. The morning had been spent looking for dresses for Leslie and Jane, despite Jane's protests that she could "just pick up something simple at Belk's." Anna had been adamant that Jane and Leslie each pick out something they loved— and could wear again.

"Leslie found the most elegant dress—knee-length, like a cocktail dress. It looked so good on Leslie that Anna insisted on trying it on just for kicks." Jane sighed. "The girls have really turned into such beauties."

"They got your genes," I said seriously.

Jane only laughed and waved a hand at me, her mouth full of pizza.

As the evening wore on, the sky outside turned indigo blue and the moonlit clouds were edged with silver. When we finished, we sat unmoving, listening to the sound of wind chimes in the summer breeze. Jane leaned her head back on the couch, staring at me through half-closed eyes, her gaze oddly seductive.

"That was a good idea," she said. "I was hungrier than I thought."

"You didn't eat that much."

"I have to squeeze into my dress this weekend."

"I wouldn't worry," I said. "You're as beautiful as the day I married you."

At her tense smile, I saw that my words didn't have quite the effect I'd hoped. Abruptly, she turned to face me on the couch. "Wilson? Can I ask you something?"

"Sure."

"I want you to tell me the truth."

"What is it?"

She hesitated. "It's about what happened at the pond today."

The swan, I immediately thought, but before I could explain that Noah had asked me to take him there—and would have gone with or without me—she went on.

"What did you mean when you said what you did?" she asked.

I frowned in puzzlement. "I'm not sure I know what you're asking."

"When you said you loved me and that you were the luckiest man in the world."

For a stunned moment, I simply stared at her. "I meant what I said," I repeated dumbly.

"Is that all?"

"Yes," I said, unable to hide my confusion. "Why?"

"I'm trying to figure out why you said it," she said matter-of-factly. "It isn't like you to say something like that out of the blue."

"Well . . . it just felt like the right thing to say."

At my answer, she brought her lips together, her face growing serious. She glanced up at the ceiling and seemed to be steeling herself before turning her gaze on me again. "Are you having an affair?" she demanded.

I blinked. "What?"

"You heard me."

I suddenly realized she wasn't kidding. I could see her trying to read my face, evaluating the truthfulness of what I intended to say next. I took her hand in my own and rested my other hand on top of it. "No," I said, looking directly at her. "I'm not having an affair. I've never had an affair, and I never will. Nor have I ever wanted to."

After a few moments of careful scrutiny, she nodded. "Okay," she said.

"I'm serious," I emphasized.

She smiled and gave my hand a squeeze. "I believe you. I didn't think you were, but I had to ask."

I stared at her in bewilderment. "Why would the thought have even crossed your mind?"

"You," she said. "The way you've been acting."

"I don't understand."

She gave me a frankly assessing look. "Okay, look at it from my perspective. First, you start exercising and losing weight. Then, you start cooking and asking me about my days. If that weren't enough, you've been unbelievably helpful this whole week . . . with everything, lately. And now, you've started saying these uncharacteristically sweet things. First, I thought it was a phase, then I thought it was because of the wedding. But now . . . well, it's like you're someone else all of a sudden. I mean . . . apologizing for not being around enough? Telling me you love me out of the blue? Listening to me talk for hours about shopping? Let's order pizza and have *fun*? I mean, it's great, but I just wanted to make sure you weren't doing it because you felt guilty about something. I still don't understand what's happened to you."

I shook my head. "It's not that I feel guilty. Well, except about working too much, I mean. I do feel bad about that. But the way I've been acting . . . it's just . . ."

When I trailed off, Jane leaned toward me.

"Just what?" she pressed.

"Like I said the other night, I haven't been the best husband, and I don't know . . . I guess I'm trying to change."

"Why?"

Because I want you to love me again, I thought, but I kept those words to myself.

"Because," I said after a moment, "you and the kids are the most important people in the world to me—you always have been—and I've wasted too many years acting as if you weren't. I know I can't change the past, but I can change the future. I can change, too. And I will."

She squinted at me. "You mean you'll quit working so hard?"

Her tone was sweet but skeptical, and it made me ache to think of what I'd become.

"If you asked me to retire right now, I would," I said.

Her eyes took on their seductive gleam again.

"See what I mean? You're not yourself these days."

Though she was teasing—and wasn't quite sure whether she believed me—I knew she'd liked what I said.

"Now can I ask you something?" I went on.

"Why not?" she said.

"Since Anna will be over at Keith's parents' house tomorrow night, and with Leslie and Joseph coming in on Friday, I was thinking that we might do something special tomorrow evening."

"Like what?"

"How about . . . you let me come up with something and surprise you."

She rewarded me with a coy smile. "You know I like surprises."

"Yes," I said, "I do."

"I'd love that," she said with undisguised pleasure.

Chapter Fourteen

On Thursday morning, I arrived at Noah's house early with my trunk packed. As it had been the day before, the property was already crowded with vehicles, and my friend Nathan Little waved to me from across the yard, pantomiming that he'd join me in a few minutes.

I parked in the shade and got to work right away. Using the ladder, I finished removing the boards from the windows, so that the pressure washers could have complete access.

Again, I stored the boards under the house. I was closing the cellar door when a cleaning crew of five arrived and began to lay siege to the house. Since the painters were already working downstairs, they hauled in buckets, mops, cloths, and detergents and scoured the kitchen, the staircase, the bathrooms, the windows, and the rooms upstairs, moving quickly and efficiently. New sheets and blankets that I'd brought from home were placed on the beds; meanwhile Nathan brought in fresh flowers for every room in the house.

Within the hour, the rental truck arrived and workers

began unloading white foldout chairs, setting them in rows. Holes were dug near the trellis, and pots with pre-planted wisteria were sunk; the purple blooms were wound through the trellis and tied in place. Beyond the trellis, the former wildness of the rose garden gave way to vivid color.

Despite the clear skies predicted by the weather service, I'd made arrangements for a tent to provide shade for the guests. The white tent was erected over the course of the morning; once it was up, more potted wisteria was sunk into the ground, then wrapped around the poles, intermingled with strands of white lights.

The power washer cleaned the fountain in the center of the rose garden; a little after lunch, I turned it on and listened to water cascading through the three tiers like a gentle waterfall.

The piano tuner arrived and spent three hours tuning the long unused piano. When he was done, a set of special microphones was installed to route music first to the ceremony, then to the reception. Other speakers and microphones enabled the pastor to be heard during the service and ensured that music could be heard in every corner of the house.

Tables were set throughout the main room—with the exception of the dance area in front of the fireplace—and linen tablecloths were spread on each. Fresh candles and flowering centerpieces appeared as if conjured so that when the crew from the restaurant arrived, they had only to fold linen napkins into the shape of swans to put the finishing touches on the place settings.

I also reminded everyone about the single table I wanted set up on the porch, and within moments it was done.

The final touch was potted hibiscus trees decorated with white lights and placed in each corner of the room.

By midafternoon, the work was winding down. Everyone loaded their cars and trucks, and the crew in the yard was in the final stages of cleanup. For the first time since the project began, I was alone in the house. I felt good. The work over the past two days, though frenzied, had gone smoothly, and while the furniture was gone, the house's regal appearance reminded me of the years it had been occupied.

As I watched the trucks pull out of the driveway, I knew I should be heading out as well. After having had their dresses fitted and shopping for shoes in the morning, Jane and Anna had made afternoon appointments to get their nails done.

I wondered whether Jane was thinking about the date I had planned. Given all the excitement, I thought it unlikely—and knowing me as she did, I doubted she was expecting much in the way of a surprise, despite what I had intimated last night. I'd been wonderfully adept at setting the bar rather low over the years, but I couldn't help but hope that it would make what I had planned even more special.

As I gazed at the house, I realized that the months I'd spent preparing for our anniversary would reach fruition. Keeping the secret from Jane had been anything but easy, but now that the evening was at hand, I realized that most of what I'd wanted for Jane and me had already happened. I'd originally thought my gift a token of a new beginning; now it seemed like the end of a journey I'd been on for over a year.

The property had finally emptied, and I made one final tour through the house before getting in my car. On my way home, I swung by the grocery store, then made a few other stops, gathering everything else that I needed. By the time I got home, it was nearly five o'clock. I took a few minutes to straighten up, then hopped in the shower to wash off the day's accumulated grime.

Knowing I had little time, I moved quickly over the next hour. Following the list I'd crafted at the office, I began preparations for the evening I had planned, the evening I'd thought about for months. One by one, items fell into place. I'd asked Anna to call me as soon as Jane had dropped her off, to give me a sense of when Jane would arrive. She did, alerting me to the fact that Jane was only fifteen minutes away. After making sure the house looked perfect, I completed my last task, taping a note to the locked front door, impossible for Jane to miss:

"Welcome home, darling. Your surprise awaits you inside. . . ."

Then I got into my car and drove away.

Chapter Fifteen

lmost three hours later, I gazed out the front
windows of Noah's house and saw headlights approaching. Checking my watch, I saw that she was right on time.

As I straightened my jacket, I tried to imagine Jane's
state of mind. Though I hadn't been with her when she'd
arrived at our home, I tried to picture her. Was she surprised that my car wasn't in the drive? I wondered. Surely
she would have noticed that I'd drawn the drapes before
leaving—perhaps she had paused in the car, puzzled or
even intrigued.

I guessed her hands were full when she exited the car,
if not with the dress for the wedding, then no doubt with
the new shoes she'd purchased that day. Either way, there
would be no mistaking the note as she approached the
steps, and I could just see the look of curiosity crossing her
features.

When she read it on the steps, how had she reacted to
my words? This, I didn't know. A baffled smile, perhaps?
Her uncertainty was no doubt heightened by the fact that
I wasn't home.

What, then, would she have thought when she unlocked the door to reveal a darkened living room lit only by the pale yellow glow of candles and the plaintive sound of Billie Holiday on the stereo? How long had it taken her to notice the scattered rose petals on the floor that trailed from the foyer through the living room and up the staircase? Or the second note I'd taped to the balustrade:

> *Sweetheart, this evening is for you. Yet there is a role you must play to fulfill it. Think of this as a game: I'm going to give you a list of instructions, and your role is to do as I ask.*
>
> *The first task is simple: Please blow out the candles downstairs, and follow the rose petals to the bedroom. Further instructions will await you there.*

Had she gasped in surprise? Or laughed in disbelief? I couldn't be sure, yet knowing Jane, I was certain she would want to play along. When she reached the bedroom, her curiosity must have been piqued.

Inside the bedroom, she would find candles lit on every surface and the soothing music of Chopin playing quietly. A bouquet of thirty roses lay on the bed; on either side of the flowers lay a neatly wrapped box, each with a note attached. The card on the left was labeled "Open now." The card on the right was labeled "Open at eight o'clock."

I pictured her moving slowly toward the bed and bringing the bouquet to her face, inhaling its heady scent. When she opened the card on the left, this is what she read: "You've had a busy day, so I thought you'd like to relax before our date this evening. Open the gift that accompanies this card and carry the contents with you to the bathroom. More instructions await you there."

If she glanced over her shoulder, she would have seen still more candles glowing in the bathroom—and upon opening the gift, she would have found the package of bath oils and body lotions and new silk bathrobe right away.

Knowing Jane, I'm guessing that she toyed with the card and package on the right, the one she couldn't open until eight. Had she debated whether or not to follow the instructions? Had she traced her fingers over the wrapping paper, then pulled back? I suspected as much but knew that ultimately she would have sighed and headed for the bathroom.

On the vanity was yet another note:

> *Is there anything better than a long hot bath after a busy day? Pick the bath oil you want, add plenty of bubbles, and fill the tub with hot water. Next to the tub you'll find a bottle of your favorite wine, still chilled, and already uncorked. Pour yourself a glass. Then slip out of your clothes, get in the tub, lean your head back, and relax. When you're ready to get out, towel off and use one of the new lotions I bought you. Do not dress; instead, put on the new robe and sit on the bed as you open the other gift.*

In the remaining box was a new cocktail dress and black pumps, both of which I'd purchased after determining the appropriate sizes from the clothing in her closet. The card that accompanied her clothing for the evening was simple.

> *You're almost done. Please open the box and put on the items I've bought you. If you would, wear the earrings I bought you for Christmas when we were first dating. Don't*

dally, though, my dear—you have exactly forty-five min-
utes to finish everything. Blow out all the candles, drain the
tub, and shut off the music. At eight forty-five, go down to
the front porch. Lock the door behind you. Close your eyes
and stand with your back to the street. When you turn
around again, open your eyes, for our date will then be ready
to begin. . . .

Out front, waiting for her was the limousine I'd
ordered. The driver, who was holding yet another gift,
was instructed to say, "Mrs. Lewis? I'll bring you to your
husband now. He wants you to open this gift as soon as
you get in the car. He's left you something else inside
as well."

In the box he held was a bottle of perfume, accompanied by a short note: "I picked this perfume especially for
the evening. After you get in the car, put some on and
open the other gift. The note inside will tell you what
to do."

In that box was a narrow black scarf. The card nestled
in its folds read as follows:

You're going to be driven to the place where I'll meet you,
but I want it to be a surprise. Please use the scarf as a blind-
fold—and remember, don't peek. The drive will be less than
fifteen minutes, and the driver will begin when you say, "I'm
ready." When the car stops, the driver will open your door.
Keep the blindfold on, and ask him to guide you out of the car.
I'll be waiting for you.

Chapter Sixteen

The limousine came to a stop in front of the house, and I drew a long breath. When the driver exited the car, he nodded to let me know that everything had gone smoothly, and I nodded nervously in return.

In the last couple of hours, I'd alternated between excitement and terror at the thought that Jane might have found all of this . . . well, silly. As the driver moved toward her door, I suddenly found it difficult to swallow. Still, I crossed my arms and leaned against the porch railing, doing my best to look nonchalant. The moon was glowing white, and I could hear the sounds of crickets chirping.

The driver opened the door. Jane's leg appeared first, and almost as if in slow motion, she emerged from the car, the blindfold still in place.

All I could do was stare at her. In the moonlight, I could see the faint outlines of a smile on her face, and she looked both exotic and elegant. I motioned to the driver, letting him know that he was free to leave.

As the car drove off, I approached Jane slowly, gathering the courage to speak.

"You look wonderful," I murmured into her ear.

She turned toward me, her smile broadening. "Thank you," she said. She waited for me to add something more, and when I didn't, she shifted her weight from one foot to the other. "Can I take off the blindfold yet?"

I glanced around, making sure everything looked the way I wanted.

"Yes," I whispered.

She tugged on the scarf; it immediately loosened and fell from her face. It took her eyes a moment to focus—resting first on me, then on the house, then back on me. Like Jane, I had dressed for the evening; my tuxedo was new and tailored. She blinked as if awakening from a dream.

"I thought you'd want to see how it will look this weekend," I offered.

She turned slowly from side to side. Even from a distance, the property looked enchanted. Beneath the inky sky, the tent glowed white, and the floodlights in the garden cast fingerlike shadows while illuminating the color of the rose blossoms. The water in the fountain glittered in the moonlight.

"Wilson . . . it's . . . incredible," she stammered.

I took her hand. I could smell the new perfume I'd bought her and saw the small diamonds in her ears. Dark lipstick accentuated her full lips.

Her expression was full of questions as she faced me. "But how? I mean . . . you only had a couple of days."

"I promised you it would be magnificent," I said. "Like Noah said, it's not every weekend that we have a wedding around here."

Jane seemed to notice my appearance for the first time, and she took a step back.

"You're wearing a tuxedo," she said.

"I got it for the weekend, but I figured I should break it in first."

She assessed me from top to bottom. "You look . . . great," she admitted.

"You sound surprised."

"I am," she said quickly, then caught herself. "I mean, I'm not surprised by how good you look, it's just that I didn't expect to see you this way."

"I'll take that as a compliment."

She laughed. "Come on," she said, tugging on my hand. "I want to see everything you did up close."

I had to admit, the view *was* magnificent. Set amid the oaks and cypress trees, the thin fabric of the tent glowed in the floodlights like a living force. The white chairs had been placed in curved rows like an orchestra, mirroring the curve of the garden just beyond. They were angled around a focal point, and the trellis gleamed with light and colored foliage. And everywhere we gazed, there were flowers.

Jane began to move slowly down the aisle. I knew that in her mind's eye, she was seeing the crowd and imagining Anna, what she would see from her designated vantage point near the trellis. When she turned to look at me, her expression was dazzled and uncomprehending.

"I never believed it could look like this."

I cleared my throat. "They did a good job, didn't they."

She shook her head solemnly. "No," she said. "They didn't. *You* did."

When we reached the head of the aisle, Jane released my hand and approached the trellis. I stayed in place, watching her as she ran her hands over the carvings and fingered the strand of lights. Her gaze drifted to the garden.

"It looks exactly the way it used to," she marveled.

As she circled the trellis, I stared at the dress she wore, noticing how it clung to the curves I knew so well. What was it about her that still took my breath away? The person she was? Our life together? Despite the years that had passed since I'd first seen her, the effect she had on me had only grown stronger.

We entered the rose garden and circled the outermost concentric heart; in time, the lights from the tent behind us grew dimmer. The fountain burbled like a mountain brook. Jane said nothing; instead, she simply absorbed the surroundings, occasionally looking over her shoulder to make sure I was close. On the far side, only the roof of the tent was evident. Jane stopped and scanned the rosebushes, then finally selected a red bud and broke it free. She plucked the thorns before approaching me and tucked it into my lapel. After adjusting it until she was satisfied, she patted my chest gently and looked up.

"You look more finished with a boutonniere," she said.

"Thank you."

"Did I mention how handsome you look all dressed up?"

"I think you used the word . . . great. But feel free to say it as often as you like."

She laid a hand on my arm. "Thank you for what you did here. Anna's going to be absolutely amazed."

"You're welcome."

Leaning in close, she murmured, "And thank you for tonight, too. That was . . . quite a little game I came home to."

In the past, I would have seized the opportunity to press her about it and reassure myself that I'd done well, but instead I reached for her hand.

"There's something else I want you to see," I said simply.

"Don't tell me you've got a carriage led by a team of white horses out in the barn," she teased.

I shook my head. "Not quite. But if you think that might be a good idea, I could try to arrange something."

She laughed. As she moved closer, the heat of her body was tantalizing. Her eyes were mischievous. "So what else did you want to show me?"

"Another surprise," I offered.

"I don't know if my heart's going to be able to take it."

"Come on," I said, "this way."

I drew her out of the garden and down a gravel path, toward the house. Above us, the stars were blinking in a cloudless sky, and the moon reflected in the river beyond the house. Branches dripped with Spanish moss, scraggly limbs stretched in all directions like ghostly fingers. The air carried the familiar scent of pine and salt, an odor unique to the low country. In the silence, I felt Jane's thumb moving against my own.

She seemed to feel no need to rush. We walked slowly, taking in the sounds of the evening: the crickets and cicadas, leaves rustling in the trees, the gravel crunching underfoot.

She stared toward the house. Silhouetted against the trees, it was a timeless image, the white columns along the porch lending the home an almost opulent air. The tin roof had darkened in color over the years and seemed to vanish into the evening sky, and I could see the yellow glow of candles through the windows.

As we entered the house, the candles flickered in the sudden draft. Jane stood in the doorway, staring into the living room. The piano, cleaned and dusted, gleamed in the soft light, and the wood floor in front of the fireplace where Anna would dance with Keith shone like new. The tables—with white napkins folded into the shape of swans set atop the gleaming china and crystal—resembled photographs of an exclusive restaurant. Silver goblets at each setting glittered like Christmas ornaments. The tables along the far wall that would be used for the food on the weekend seemed to vanish amid the flowers between the chafing dishes.

"Oh, Wilson . . . ," she breathed.

"It'll be different when everyone arrives on Saturday, but I wanted you to see how it looked without the crowd."

She released my hand and walked around the room, absorbing every detail.

At her nod, I went to the kitchen, opened the wine, and poured two glasses. Glancing up, I saw Jane staring at the piano, her face shadowed in profile.

"Who's going to be playing?" she asked.

I smiled. "If you could have chosen, who would you pick?"

She gave me a hopeful look. "John Peterson?"

I nodded.

"But how? Isn't he playing at the Chelsea?"

"You know he's always had a soft spot for you and Anna. The Chelsea will survive without him for a night."

She continued to stare at the room in wonder as she approached me. "I just don't see how you could have done all this so fast . . . I mean, I was just here a few days ago."

I handed her a wineglass. "Then you approve?"

"Approve?" She took a slow sip of wine. "I don't think I've ever seen the house look this beautiful."

I watched the candlelight flickering in her eyes.

"Are you hungry yet?" I asked.

She seemed almost startled. "To be honest, I haven't even thought about it. I think I'd like to enjoy my wine and look around for a while before we have to go."

"We don't have to go anywhere. I was planning on having dinner here."

"But how? There's nothing in the cupboards."

"Wait and see." I motioned over my shoulder. "Why don't you relax and look around while I get started?"

Leaving her side, I went to the kitchen, where the preparations for the elaborate meal I'd planned were already under way. The crab-stuffed sole I had made was ready to go, and I set the oven to the proper temperature. The ingredients for the hollandaise sauce were already measured and set aside; the contents simply needed to be added to the saucepan. Our salads were tossed and the dressing made.

As I worked, I glanced up from time to time and saw Jane moving slowly through the main room. Though each table was the same, she paused at each one, imagining the particular guest who would be seated there. She absently adjusted the silverware and rotated the vases of flowers, usually returning them to their original position. There was a calm, almost content satisfaction about her that I found strangely moving. Then again, almost everything about her moved me these days.

In the silence, I pondered the sequence of events that had brought us to this point. Experience had taught me that even the most precious memories fade with the passage of time, yet I didn't want to forget a single moment of the last week we'd spent together. And, of course, I wanted Jane to remember every moment as well.

"Jane?" I called out. She was out of my sight line, and I guessed she was near the piano.

She appeared from the corner of the room. Even from a distance, her face was luminous. "Yes?"

"While I'm getting dinner ready, would you do me a favor?"

"Sure. Do you need a hand in the kitchen?"

"No. I left my apron upstairs. Would you mind getting it for me? It's on the bed in your old room."

"Not at all," she said.

A moment later, I watched her disappear up the stairs. I knew she wouldn't be coming back down until dinner was nearly ready.

I hummed as I began rinsing the asparagus, anticipating her reaction when she discovered the gift awaiting her upstairs.

"Happy anniversary," I whispered.

While the water came to a boil on the stove, I slid the sole into the oven and strolled out to the back porch. There, the caterers had set up a table for the two of us. I thought about opening the champagne but decided to wait for Jane. Breathing deeply, I tried to clear my mind.

Jane had by now surely found what I'd left her on the bed upstairs. The album—hand stitched with a carved leather binding—was exquisite, but it was the contents that I hoped would truly move her. This was the gift I'd assembled with the help of so many for our thirtieth anniversary. Like the other gifts she'd received this evening, it had come with a note. It was the letter I had tried but failed to write in the past, the kind that Noah had once suggested, and though I'd once found the very idea impossible, the epiphanies of the past year, and particularly the past week, lent my words an uncharacteristic grace.

When I finished writing, I read through it once, then read it again. Even now, the words were as clear in my mind as they were on the pages Jane now held in her hand.

> *My darling,*
>
> *It's late at night, and as I sit at my desk, the house is silent except for the ticking of the grandfather clock. You're asleep upstairs, and though I long for the warmth of your body against my own, something compels me to write this letter, even though I'm not exactly sure where to begin. Nor, I realize, do I know exactly what to say, but I can't escape the conclusion that after all these years, it's something I must do, not only for you, but for myself as well. After thirty years, it's the least I can do.*
>
> *Has it really been that long? Though I know it has, the very thought is amazing to me. Some things, after all, have never changed. In the mornings, for instance, my first thoughts after waking are—and always have been—of you. Often, I'll simply lie on my side and watch you; I see your hair spread across the pillow, one arm above your head, the gentle rise and fall of your chest. Sometimes when you're dreaming, I'll move closer to you in the hope that somehow this will allow me to enter your dreams. That, after all, is how I've always felt about you. Throughout our marriage, you've been my dream, and I'll never forget how lucky I've felt ever since the first day we walked together in the rain.*
>
> *I often think back on that day. It's an image that has never left me, and I find myself experiencing a sense of déjà vu whenever lightning streaks across the sky. In those moments, it seems as if we're starting over once more, and I can feel the hammering of my young man's heart, a man who'd suddenly glimpsed his future and couldn't imagine a life without you.*
>
> *I experience this same sensation with nearly every mem-*

ory I can summon. If I think of Christmas, I see you sitting beneath the tree, joyfully handing out gifts to our children. When I think of summer nights, I feel the press of your hand against my own as we walked beneath the stars. Even at work, I frequently find myself glancing at the clock and wondering what you're doing at that exact moment. Simple things—I might imagine a smudge of dirt on your cheek as you work in the garden, or how you look as you lean against the counter, running a hand through your hair while you visit on the phone. I guess what I'm trying to say is that you are there, in everything I am, in everything I've ever done, and looking back, I know that I should have told you how much you've always meant to me.

I'm sorry for that, just as I'm sorry for all the ways I've let you down. I wish I could undo the past, but we both know that's impossible. Yet I've come to believe that while the past is unchangeable, our perceptions of it are malleable, and this is where the album comes in.

In it, you will find many, many photographs. Some are copies from our own albums, but most are not. Instead, I asked our friends and family for any photographs they had of the two of us, and over the past year, the photographs were sent to me from across the country. You'll find a photo Kate took at Leslie's christening, still another from a company picnic a quarter of a century ago, taken by Joshua Tundle. Noah contributed a picture of the two of us that he'd taken on a rainy Thanksgiving while you were pregnant with Joseph, and if you look closely, it's possible to see the place where I first realized that I'd fallen in love with you. Anna, Leslie, and Joseph each contributed pictures as well.

As each photograph came in, I tried to recall the moment in which it was taken. At first, my memory was like the snapshot itself—a brief, self-contained image—but I found *that if I closed my eyes and concentrated, time would begin to roll backward. And in each instance, I remembered what I'd been thinking.*

This, then, is the other part of the album. On the page opposite each picture, I've written what I remember about those moments or, more specifically, what I remember about you.

I call this album "The Things I Should Have Said."

I once made a vow to you on the steps outside the courthouse, and as your husband of thirty years, it's time I finally made another: From this point on, I will become the man I always should have been. I'll become a more romantic husband, and make the most of the years we have left together. And in each precious moment, my hope is that I'll do or say something that lets you know that I could never have cherished another as much as I've always cherished you.

With all my love,
Wilson

At the sound of Jane's footsteps, I looked up. She stood at the top of the steps, the hallway light behind her obscuring her features. Her hand reached for the railing as she began moving down the steps.

The light from the candles illuminated her in stages: first her legs, then her waist, then finally her face. Stopping halfway down, she met my eyes, and even from across the room, I could see her tears.

"Happy anniversary," I said, my voice echoing in the room. Continuing to gaze at me, she finished descending the steps. With a gentle smile, she crossed the room toward me and I suddenly knew exactly what to do.

Opening my arms, I drew her close. Her body was warm and soft, her cheek damp against my own. And as we stood in Noah's house two days before our thirtieth anniversary, I held her against me, wishing with all my heart for time to stop, now and forever.

We stood together for a long time, before Jane finally leaned back. With her arms still around me, she stared up at me. Her cheeks were damp and shiny in the dim light.

"Thank you," she whispered.

I gave her a gentle squeeze. "Come on. I want to show you something."

I led her through the living room, toward the rear of the house. I pushed open the back door and we stepped out onto the porch.

Despite the moonlight, I could still make out the Milky Way arcing above us like a spray of jewels; Venus had risen in the southern sky. The temperature had cooled slightly, and in the breeze, I caught a scent of Jane's perfume.

"I thought we could eat out here. And besides, I didn't want to mess up any of the tables inside."

She looped her arm through mine and surveyed the table before us. "It's wonderful, Wilson."

I pulled away reluctantly to light the candles and reached for the champagne.

"Would you like a glass?"

At first, I wasn't sure she'd heard me. She was staring out over the river, her dress fluttering slightly in the breeze.

"I'd love one."

I removed the bottle from the wine bucket, held the cork steady, and twisted. It opened with a pop. After pouring two glasses, I waited for the fizz to settle, and then topped them both off. Jane moved closer to me.

"How long have you been planning this?" she asked me.

"Since last year. It was the least I could do after forgetting the last one."

She shook her head and turned my face to hers. "I couldn't have dreamed of anything better than what you did tonight." She hesitated. "I mean, when I found the album and the letter and all those passages you wrote . . . well, that's the most remarkable thing you've ever done for me."

I started making more noises about it being the least I could do, but she interrupted me.

"I mean it," she said quietly. "I can't even put it into words how much this means to me." Then, with a sly wink, she fingered my lapel. "You look awfully handsome in that tux, stranger."

I laughed beneath my breath, feeling the tension break slightly, and put my hand on hers and squeezed it. "On that note, I hate to have to leave you . . ."

"But?"

"But I've got to check on dinner."

She nodded, looking sensual, looking beautiful. "Need any help?"

"No. It's just about done."

"Would you mind if I stayed outside, then? It's so peaceful out here."

"Not at all."

In the kitchen, I saw that the asparagus I had steamed had cooled, so I turned on the burner to reheat them. The hollandaise had congealed a bit, but after I stirred it, it seemed fine. Then I turned my attention to the sole, opening the oven to test it with a fork. It needed just another couple of minutes.

The station I'd tuned the kitchen radio to was playing music from the big band era, and I was reaching for the knob when I heard Jane's voice behind me.

"Leave it on," she said.

I looked up. "I thought you were going to enjoy the evening."

"I was, but it's not the same without you," she said. She leaned against the counter and struck her usual pose. "Did you specifically request this music for tonight, too?" she teased.

"This program has been on for the past couple of hours. I guess it's their special theme for the night."

"It sure brings back memories," she said. "Daddy used to listen to big band all the time." She ran a hand slowly through her hair, lost in reminiscence. "Did you know that he and Mom used to dance in the kitchen? One minute, they'd be washing dishes, and the next minute, they'd have their arms around each other and be swaying to the music. The first time I saw them, I guess I was around six and didn't think anything of it. When I got a little older, Kate and I used to giggle when we saw them. We'd point and snicker, but they'd just laugh and keep right on dancing, like they were the only two people in the world."

"I never knew that."

"The last time I ever saw them do it was about a week before they moved to Creekside. I was coming over to see how they were doing. I saw them through the kitchen window when I was parking, and I just started to cry. I knew it was the last time I'd ever see them do it here, and it felt like my heart broke in two." She paused, lost in thought. Then she shook her head. "Sorry. That's kind of a mood spoiler, isn't it?"

"It's okay," I said. "They're a part of our lives, and this is their house. To be honest, I'd be shocked if you didn't think about them. Besides, it's a wonderful way to remember them."

She seemed to consider my words for a moment. In the silence, I removed the sole from the oven and set it on the stove.

"Wilson?" she asked softly.

I turned.

"When you said in your letter that from this point on, you were going to try to be more romantic, did you mean that?"

"Yes."

"Does that mean I can expect more nights like tonight?"

"If that's what you want."

She brought a finger to her chin. "It'll be tougher to surprise me, though. You'll have to come up with something new."

"I don't think it'll be as hard as you think."

"No?"

"I could probably come up with something right now, if I had to."

"Like what?"

I met her appraising stare and was suddenly determined not to fail. After a brief hesitation, I reached over to shut off the burner and set the asparagus to the side. Jane's gaze followed me with interest. I adjusted my jacket before crossing the kitchen and holding out my hand.

"Would you care to dance?"

Jane blushed as she took my hand, twining her other arm around my back. Pulling her firmly to me, I felt her body press against mine. We began to turn in slow circles as music filled the room around us. I could smell the lavender shampoo she'd used and feel her legs brush against my own.

"You're beautiful," I whispered, and Jane responded by tracing her thumb against the back of my hand.

When the song ended, we continued to hold each other until the next began, dancing slowly, the subtle movement intoxicating. When Jane pulled back to look at me, her smile was tender, and she brought a hand to my face. Her touch was light, and like an old habit rediscovered, I leaned toward her, our faces drawing nearer.

Her kiss was almost breathlike, and we gave in then to everything we were feeling, everything we wanted. I wrapped my arms around her and kissed her again, sensing her desire and sensing my own. I buried my hand in her hair and she moaned slightly, the sound both familiar and electric, new and old, a miracle in the way all miracles should be.

Without a word, I pulled back and simply stared at her before leading her from the kitchen. I felt her thumb tracing the back of my hand as we moved among the tables, blowing out one candle after the next.

In the welcoming darkness, I escorted her upstairs. In her old bedroom, moonlight streamed through the window, and we held each other, bathed in milky light and shadow. We kissed again and again, and Jane ran her hands over my chest as I reached for the zipper on the back of her dress. She sighed softly when I began to slide it open.

My lips slid over her cheek and neck, and I tasted the curve of her shoulder. She tugged at my jacket and it slipped to the floor, along with the dress she was wearing. Her skin was hot to the touch as we collapsed on the bed.

We made love slowly and tenderly, and the passion we felt for each other was a dizzying rediscovery, tantalizing in its newness. I wanted it to last forever, and I kissed her again and again while whispering words of love. Afterward, we lay in each other's arms, exhausted. I traced her skin with my fingertips as she fell asleep by my side, trying to hold on to the still perfection of the moment.

Just after midnight, Jane woke and noticed me watching her. In the darkness, I could just make out her mischievous expression, as if she were simultaneously scandalized and thrilled by what had happened.

"Jane?" I asked.

"Yes?"

"I want to know something."

She smiled contentedly, waiting.

I hesitated before drawing a long breath. "If you had to do it all over—and knowing how everything would turn out with us—would you marry me again?"

She was quiet for a long time, giving the question careful thought. Then, patting my chest, she looked up, her expression softened.

"Yes," she said simply, "I would."

These were the words I'd longed to hear most of all, and I pulled her close. I kissed her hair and neck, wanting the moment to last forever.

"I love you more than you'll ever know," I said.

She kissed my chest. "I know," she said. "And I love you, too."

Chapter Seventeen

When the morning sunlight began pouring through the window, we woke in each other's arms and made love one more time before pulling apart and getting ready for the long day ahead.

After breakfast, we went through the house, getting it ready for the wedding on Saturday. The candles on the tables were replaced, the table on the porch was cleaned of its settings and stored in the barn, and with a bit of disappointment, the dinner I'd prepared was tossed into the garbage.

When we were satisfied with everything, we headed back home. Leslie was supposed to arrive around four; Joseph had been able to book an earlier flight and would be coming in around five. On the answering machine, there was a message from Anna, saying that she was going to go over the last minute preparations with Keith, which—other than making sure her dress was ready— mainly entailed checking to see that no one we'd hired had canceled at the last minute. She also promised to pick up Jane's dress and bring it with her when she came by with Keith for dinner later that night.

In the kitchen, Jane and I threw the makings of a beef stew into the Crock-Pot, where it would slow-cook the rest of the afternoon. As we worked, we discussed the logistical arrangements for the wedding, but every now and then, Jane's secret smile told me she was remembering the night before.

Knowing it would only get busier as the day wore on, we drove downtown for a quiet lunch together. We grabbed a couple of sandwiches from the Pollock Street Deli and strolled to the Episcopal church, where we ate in the shade of the magnolia trees that covered the grounds.

After lunch, we walked hand in hand to Union Point, where we gazed out over the Neuse River. The swells were mild and the water was crowded with boats of all types as kids enjoyed the last days of summer before heading back to school. For the first time in a week, Jane seemed completely relaxed, and as I put my arm around her, it felt strangely as if we were a couple just starting out in the world. It was the most perfect day we'd spent together in years, and I reveled in the feeling until we returned home and listened to the message on the answering machine.

It was Kate, calling about Noah.

"You'd better get down here," she said. "I don't know what to do."

Kate was standing in the corridor when we arrived at Creekside.

"He won't talk about it," she said anxiously. "Right now, he's just staring out at the pond. He even snapped at me when I tried to talk to him, saying that since I didn't believe in it anyway, I wouldn't understand. He kept insisting that he wanted to be alone, and he finally shooed me away."

"But physically, he's okay?" Jane asked.

"I think so. He refused to eat his lunch—even seemed angry about it—but other than that, he seems fine. But he's really upset. The last time I peeked in his room, he actually shouted at me to go away."

I glanced at the closed door. In all our years, I'd never heard Noah raise his voice.

Kate twisted her silk scarf nervously. "He wouldn't talk to Jeff or David—they just left a few minutes ago. I think they were a little hurt by the way he was acting."

"And he doesn't want to talk to me, either?" Jane asked.

"No," Kate answered. She gave a helpless shrug. "Like I said on the message, I'm not sure that he'll talk to anyone. The only one I think he might talk to is you." She looked at me skeptically.

I nodded. Though I worried that Jane would be upset—as she had been when Noah had asked to see me in the hospital—she gave my hand a squeeze of support and looked up at me.

"I guess you'd better see how he's doing."

"I suppose so."

"I'll wait out here with Kate. See if you can get him to eat something."

"I will."

I found Noah's door, knocked twice, and pushed it partly open.

"Noah? It's me, Wilson. May I come in?"

In his chair by the window, Noah made no response. I

waited a moment before stepping into his room. On the bed, I saw the uneaten tray of food, and after closing the door, I brought my hands together.

"Kate and Jane thought you might want to talk to me."

I saw his shoulders rise as he drew a long breath, then fall again. With his white hair spilling over the top of his sweater, he looked diminutive in the rocker.

"Are they out there now?"

His voice was so soft that I barely heard it.

"Yes."

Noah said nothing more. In the silence, I crossed the room and sat on the bed. I could see the lines of strain on his face, though he refused to look at me.

"I'd like to hear what happened," I said tentatively.

He dropped his chin before his gaze rose again. He stared out the window.

"She's gone," he said. "When I went out this morning, she wasn't there."

I knew immediately whom he was referring to.

"She might have been in another part of the pond. Maybe she didn't know you were there," I suggested.

"She's gone," he said, his voice flat and emotionless. "I knew it as soon as I woke up. Don't ask me how, but I knew. I could sense that she was gone, and when I started toward the pond, the feeling just got stronger and stronger. I didn't want to believe it, though, and I tried calling for her for an hour. But she never showed." Wincing, he straightened in the chair, continuing to stare through the window. "Finally, I just gave up."

Beyond the window, the pond was glistening in the sun. "Do you want to go back and check to see if she's there now?"

"She isn't."

"How do you know?"

"Because I do," he said. "The same way I knew she was gone this morning."

I opened my mouth to respond, then thought better of it. There was no use in arguing the point. Noah had already made up his mind. Besides, something inside me was sure that he was right.

"She'll come back," I said, trying to sound convincing.

"Maybe," he said. "Or maybe not. I can't tell one way or the other."

"She'll miss you too much to stay away."

"Then why did she leave in the first place?" he demanded. "It doesn't make any sense!"

He slapped his good hand on the arm of the chair before shaking his head.

"I wish they could understand."

"Who?"

"My kids. The nurses. Even Dr. Barnwell."

"You mean about Allie being the swan?"

For the first time, he looked my way. "No. About me being Noah. About me being the same man I've always been."

I wasn't sure what he meant but knew enough to stay silent while I waited for him to explain.

"You should have seen them today. All of them. So what if I didn't want to talk to them about it? No one believes me anyway, and I didn't feel like trying to convince them that I know what I'm talking about. They just would have argued with me about it like they always do. And then, when I didn't eat my lunch? Well, you would have thought that I'd tried to jump out the window. I'm upset, and I have every right to be upset. When I get upset, I don't eat. I've been that way my whole life, but now, they act like my mental abilities have slipped another notch. Kate was in here trying to spoon-feed me and pretending nothing happened. Can you believe that? And then Jeff and David showed up, and they explained it away by saying that she probably went off to forage, completely ignoring the fact that I feed her twice a day. None of them seems to care what might have happened to her."

As I struggled to understand what was going on, I suddenly realized that there was more to Noah's sudden rage than the way his children had reacted.

"What's really bothering you?" I asked gently. "That they acted as if it were just a swan?" I paused. "That's what they've always believed, and you know that. You've never let it get to you before."

"They don't care."

"If anything," I countered, "they care too much."

He turned away stubbornly.

"I just don't understand it," he said again. "Why would she leave?"

With that, it suddenly dawned on me that he wasn't angry with his kids. Nor was he simply reacting to the fact that the swan had vanished. No, it was something deeper, something I wasn't sure he would admit even to himself.

Instead of pressing it, I said nothing, and we sat together in silence. As I waited, I watched his hand fidget in his lap.

"How did it go with Jane last night?" he asked after a moment, apropos of nothing.

At his words—and despite all that we'd been discussing—I flashed on an image of him dancing with Allie in the kitchen.

"Better than I'd imagined it would," I said.

"And she liked the album?"

"She loved it."

"Good," he said. For the first time since I'd come in, he smiled, but it vanished as quickly as it came.

"I'm sure she wants to talk to you," I said. "And Kate's still out there, too."

"I know," he said, looking defeated. "They can come in."

"You sure?"

When he nodded, I reached over and put a hand on his knee. "Are you going to be okay?"

"Yes."

"Do you want me to tell them not to talk about the swan?"

He considered my words briefly before shaking his head. "It doesn't matter."

"Do I have to tell you to go easy on them?"

He gave me a long-suffering look. "I'm not much in the mood for teasing, but I promise that I won't yell again. And don't you worry—I'm not going to do anything to upset Jane. I don't want her worrying about me when she should be thinking about tomorrow."

I rose from the bed and rested a hand on his shoulder before turning to leave.

Noah, I knew, was angry with himself. He'd spent the last four years believing that the swan was Allie—he'd needed to believe that she would find a way to come back to him—but the swan's inexplicable disappearance had shaken his faith profoundly.

As I left his room, I could almost hear him asking, *What if the kids had been right all along?*

In the hallway, I kept this information to myself. I did suggest, however, that it might be best if they simply let Noah do most of the talking and react as naturally as possible.

Both Kate and Jane nodded, and Jane led the way back inside. Noah looked toward us. Jane and Kate stopped, waiting to be invited in farther, not knowing what to expect.

"Hi, Daddy," Jane said.

He forced a smile. "Hi, sweetheart."

"Are you doing okay?"

He glanced at Jane and me, then at the tray of food that had grown cold on the bed. "I'm getting a little hungry, but other than that, I'm fine. Kate—would you mind . . ."

"Sure, Daddy," Kate said, stepping forward. "I'll get you something. How about some soup? Or a ham sandwich?"

"A sandwich sounds good." He nodded. "And maybe a glass of sweet tea."

"I'll run down and get it for you," Kate said. "Do you want a piece of chocolate cake, too? I heard they made it fresh today."

"Sure," he said. "Thank you. Oh—and I'm sorry about how I acted earlier. I was upset and had no reason to take it out on you."

Kate smiled briefly. "It's okay, Daddy."

Kate shot me a relieved look, though her concern was still obvious. As soon as she'd left the room, Noah motioned toward the bed.

"C'mon in," he said, his voice quiet. "Make yourselves comfortable."

As I crossed the room, I watched Noah, wondering what was going on. Somehow, I suspected that he'd asked Kate to leave because he wanted to talk to Jane and me alone.

Jane sat on the bed. As I joined her, she took my hand. "I'm sorry about the swan, Daddy," she offered.

"Thank you," he said. By his expression, I knew he would say nothing more about it. "Wilson's been telling me about the house," he said instead. "I hear it's really something."

Jane's expression softened. "It's like a fairy tale, Daddy. It's even prettier than it was for Kate's wedding." She paused. "We were thinking that Wilson could swing by and pick you up around five. I know it's early, but it'll give you a chance to spend some time at the house. You haven't been there in a while."

"That's fine," he agreed. "It'll be good to see the old place again." He looked from Jane to me, then back to Jane again. He seemed to notice for the first time that we were holding hands, and he smiled.

"I have something for you both," he said. "And if you don't mind, I'd like to give it to you before Kate gets back. She might not understand."

"What is it?" Jane asked.

"Help me up, would you?" he asked. "It's in my desk, and it's hard for me to get up after I've been sitting for a while."

I rose and reached for his arm. He stood and gingerly crossed the room. After opening his drawer, he removed a wrapped gift, then returned to his chair. The walk seemed to have tired him, and he winced as he sat again.

"I had one of the nurses wrap it yesterday," he said, holding it out to us.

It was small and rectangular, draped in red foil, but even as he presented it, I knew what was inside. Jane, too, seemed to know, for neither of us reached for it.

"Please," he said.

Jane hesitated before finally accepting it. She ran her hand over the paper, then looked up.

"But . . . Daddy . . . ," she said.

"Open it," he urged.

Jane popped the tape and folded back the paper; without a box, the worn book was immediately recognizable. So was the small bullet hole in the upper right corner, a bullet that had been meant for him in World War II. It was *Leaves of Grass* by Walt Whitman, the book I'd brought to him in the hospital, the book that I could never imagine him without.

"Happy anniversary," he said.

Jane held the book as if she were afraid it would break. She glanced at me, then back to her father. "We can't take this," she said, her voice soft, sounding as choked up as I felt.

"Yes, you can," he said.

"But . . . why?"

He gazed at us. "Did you know I read it every day while I was waiting for your mom? After she left that summer when we were kids? In a way, it was like I was reading the poetry to her. And then, after we were married, we used to read it on the porch, just the way I imagined we would. We must have read every poem a thousand times over the years. There would be times when I'd be reading, and I'd look over and see your mom's lips moving right along with mine. She got to the point where she could recite all the poems by heart."

He stared out the window, and I suddenly knew he was thinking of the swan again.

"I can't read the pages anymore," Noah went on. "I just can't make out the words, but it troubles me to think that no one will ever read it again. I don't want it to be a relic, something that just sits on the shelf as some sort of memento to Allie and me. I know you're not as fond of Whitman as I am, but of all my kids, you're the only two who read it from cover to cover. And who knows, you might just read him again."

Jane glanced down at the book. "I will," she promised.

"So will I," I added.

"I know," he said, looking at each of us in turn. "That's why I wanted you both to have it."

After eating lunch, Noah looked as if he needed rest, so Jane and I went back home.

Anna and Keith arrived in midafternoon, Leslie pulled up in the driveway a few minutes later, and we all stood around in the kitchen together, chatting and joking, just like old times. While we mentioned the news about the swan, we didn't linger on the topic. Instead, with the weekend calling, we piled into two cars and headed out to Noah's house. Like Jane the night before, Anna, Keith, and Leslie were amazed. They spent an hour touring the garden and the house with their mouths agape, and as I stood near the stairs in the living room, Jane moved close and stood next to me, beaming. She caught my eye, nodded toward the stairs, and winked. I laughed. When Leslie asked what was so funny, Jane played innocent.

"Just something between your father and me. Private joke."

On our way home, I swung by the airport and picked up Joseph. He greeted me with his usual, "Hey, Pop," then—despite all that was going on—added only, "You've lost weight." After grabbing his luggage, he rode with me to Creekside to pick up Noah. As always, Joseph was reticent in my presence, but as soon as he saw Noah, he brightened considerably. Noah, too, was pleased to see that Joseph had come along. They sat in the backseat chatting, both of them growing more animated as we made our way back home, where they were enveloped with hugs the moment they walked in the door. Soon, Noah was seated on the couch with Leslie on one side and Joseph on the other, sharing stories back and forth, while Anna and Jane chatted in the kitchen. The sounds of the house were suddenly familiar again, and I found myself thinking that this was the way it should always be.

Dinner was punctuated with laughter as Anna and Jane recounted the details of the mad rush of the week, and as the evening wound down, Anna surprised me by tapping her glass with a fork.

When the table grew silent, this is what she said:

"I'd like to make a toast to Mom and Dad," she said, raising her glass. "Without you two, none of this would have been possible. This is going to be the most wonderful wedding anyone could ever want."

When Noah tired, I drove him back to Creekside. The corridors were empty as I walked him to his room.

"Thank you again for the book," I said, pausing at the door. "That's the most special gift you could have given us."

His eyes, going gray with cataracts, seemed to see through me. "You're welcome."

I cleared my throat. "Maybe she'll be there in the morning," I offered.

He nodded, knowing I meant well.

"Maybe," he said.

Joseph, Leslie, and Anna were still sitting around the table when I got home. Keith had gone home a few minutes earlier. When I asked about Jane, they gestured in the direction of the deck. Sliding open the glass door, I saw Jane leaning against the rail, and I moved to join her. For a long moment, we stood together enjoying the fresh summer air, neither of us saying anything.

"Was he okay when you dropped him off?" Jane finally asked.

"As good as can be expected. He was tired by the end, though."

"Do you think he enjoyed tonight?"

"Without a doubt," I said. "He loves spending time with the kids."

She gazed through the door at the scene in the dining room: Leslie was motioning with her hands, obviously caught up in a humorous story, and both Anna and Joseph were doubled over with laughter, their hilarity audible even outside.

"Seeing them like this brings back memories," she said. "I wish Joseph didn't live so far away. I know the girls miss him. They've been laughing like that for almost an hour now."

"Why aren't you sitting at the table with them?"

"I was until just a couple of minutes ago. When I saw your headlights, I snuck outside."

"Why?"

"Because I wanted to be alone with you," she said, nudging me playfully. "I wanted to give you your anniversary gift, and like you said, tomorrow might be a little busy." She slid a card toward me. "I know it looks small, but it wasn't the sort of gift that I could wrap. You'll understand when you see what it is."

Curious, I opened the card and found the certificate inside.

"Cooking lessons?" I asked with a smile.

"In Charleston," she said, leaning close to me. Pointing to the certificate, she went on. "The classes are supposed to be top-notch. See? You spend a weekend at the Mondori Inn with their chef, and he's supposed to be one of the best in the country. I know you're doing great on your own, but I thought you might have fun trying your hand at learning some new things. Supposedly, they teach you how to use a carving knife, how to know when the pan is properly heated for sautéeing, even how to garnish the dishes you serve. You know Helen, right? From the choir at church? She said it was one of the best weekends she ever spent."

I offered a quick hug. "Thank you," I said. "When is it?"

"The classes are in September and October—both the first and third weekends of each month—so you can see how your schedule's shaping up before you decide. Then, all you have to do is call."

I examined the certificate, trying to imagine what the classes would be like. Worried by my silence, Jane said tentatively, "If you don't like it, I can get you something else."

"No, it's perfect," I reassured her. Then, frowning, I added, "There's just one thing, though."

"Yes?"

I slipped my arms around her. "I'd enjoy the classes more if we could take them together. Let's make a romantic weekend out of it. Charleston's beautiful at that time of year, and we could have a great time in the city."

"Do you mean it?" she asked.

Pulling her close, I stared into her eyes. "I can't think of anything I'd rather do. I'd miss you too much to be able to enjoy it."

"Absence might make the heart grow fonder," she teased.

"I don't think that's possible," I said, growing more serious. "You have no idea how much I love you."

"Oh, but I do," she said.

Out of the corner of my eye, I saw the kids watching us as I bent to kiss her, feeling her lips as they lingered against my own. In the past, it might have made me self-conscious. Now, however, it didn't matter at all.

Chapter Eighteen

I was less nervous on Saturday morning than I anticipated.

Anna swung by after everyone was up and about and surprised us with her nonchalance as she ate breakfast with the family. Afterward, we all lounged on the back deck, where time passed almost in slow motion. Perhaps we were quietly bracing ourselves for the frenzy that would follow later that afternoon.

More than once, I caught Leslie and Joseph watching Jane and me, apparently transfixed by the sight of us nudging each other playfully or laughing at each other's stories. While Leslie looked almost misty-eyed—almost like a proud parent—Joseph's expression was harder to decipher. I couldn't tell whether he was happy for us or whether he was trying to figure out how long this new phase might last.

Perhaps their reactions were warranted. Unlike Anna, they hadn't seen us much lately, and no doubt each of them remembered how we'd treated each other the last time they'd seen us together; indeed, when Joseph had visited over Christmas, Jane and I had barely spoken at all. And, of course, I knew he still remembered her visit to New York the year before.

I wondered if Jane noticed her children's puzzled scrutiny. If she did, she paid no attention to it. Instead, she regaled Joseph and Leslie with stories about the wedding plans, unable to hide her delight at how well it had come together. Leslie had a hundred questions and nearly swooned over each romantic revelation; Joseph seemed more content to listen in silence. Anna chimed in from time to time, usually in response to a question. She was seated next to me on the couch, and when Jane got up to refill the coffeepot, Anna watched her mother over her shoulder. Then, taking my hand, she leaned toward my ear and whispered simply, "I can't wait for tonight."

The women of the family had appointments at the hair salon at one o'clock and were chatting like schoolgirls on the way out the door. As for me, both John Peterson and Henry MacDonald had called in midmorning, asking if I would be willing to meet them at Noah's. Peterson wanted to check how the piano sounded, while MacDonald wanted to take a look at the kitchen and the rest of the layout to ensure dinner went smoothly. Both men promised to keep the visit short, but I assured them it wasn't a problem. I had to drop something off at the house—something Leslie had left in her trunk—and was heading over anyway.

Just as I was leaving, I heard Joseph enter the living room behind me.

"Hey, Pop. Mind if I come along?"

"Not at all," I said.

Joseph stared out the window and said little on our

drive to Noah's. He hadn't been there in years and seemed
to be simply soaking up the view as we wound along the
tree-lined roads. While New York City was exciting—and
Joseph now regarded it as home—I could sense that he'd
forgotten how lovely the low country could be.

Slowing the car, I turned up the drive, then parked in
my usual spot. When we got out of the car, Joseph stood
for a moment, gazing at the house. It was radiant in the
high summer light. Within hours, Anna, Leslie, and Jane
would be upstairs, dressing for the wedding. The procession, we'd decided, would begin from the house; staring
up at the second-floor windows, I tried and failed to imagine those final moments before the wedding, when all the
guests would be seated and waiting.

When I shook myself from my reverie, I saw that
Joseph had moved from the car and was heading in the
direction of the tent. He walked with hands in his pockets, his gaze roaming over the property. At the entrance to
the tent, he stopped and looked back at me, waiting for
me to join him.

We wandered silently through the tent and rose garden, then into the house. While Joseph wasn't visibly
excited, I could sense that he was as impressed as Leslie
and Anna had been. When he completed the tour, he
asked a few questions about the mechanics of what had
been done—the whos, whats, and hows—but by the time
the caterer pulled up the drive, he'd grown silent again.

"So what do you think?" I asked.

He didn't answer right away, but a faint smile tugged
at his lips as he surveyed the property. "To be honest," he
admitted at last, "I can't believe you pulled it off."

Following his gaze, I flashed on how it had looked only
a few days earlier. "It is something, isn't it?" I said absently.

At my answer, Joseph shook his head. "I'm not just talking about all this," he said, gesturing at the surrounding landscape. "I'm talking about Mom." He paused, making sure he had my attention. "Last year, when she came up," he went on, "she was more upset than I'd ever seen her. She was crying when she got off the plane. Did you know that?"

My expression answered for me.

He pushed his hands into his pockets and looked down at the ground, refusing to meet my eyes. "She said she didn't want you to see her that way, so she'd tried to hold herself together. But on the flight . . . I guess it finally got the best of her." He hesitated. "I mean, here I was, standing in the airport waiting to pick up my mom, and she walks off the plane looking like someone who'd just come from a funeral. I know I deal with grief every day at my job, but when it's your own mom . . ."

He trailed off, and I knew enough to say nothing.

"She kept me awake until after midnight the first night she was there. Just kept rambling and crying about what was going on between you two. And I'll admit that I was angry with you. Not just for forgetting the anniversary, but for everything. It's like you always viewed our family as a convenience that other people expected you to maintain, but you never wanted to do the work required. Finally, I told her that if she was still unhappy after so many years, she might be better off alone."

I didn't know what to say.

"She's a great lady, Pop," he said, "and I was tired of seeing her hurt. And over the next few days, she recovered—a bit, anyway. But she was still dreading the thought of going back home. She'd get this real sad expression whenever it came up, so finally I asked her to stay in New York with me. For a while there, I thought she was going to take me up on it, but in the end, she said she couldn't. She said that you needed her."

My throat constricted.

"When you told me what you wanted to do for your anniversary, my first thought was that I didn't want anything to do with it. I wasn't even looking forward to coming down this weekend. But last night . . ." He shook his head and sighed. "You should have heard her when you left to take Noah home. She couldn't stop talking about you. She went on and on about how great you've been and how well you've both been getting along lately. And then, seeing the way you two kissed on the deck . . ."

He faced me with an expression bordering on disbelief and seemed to be seeing me for the first time. "You did it, Pop. I don't know how, but you did it. I don't think I've ever seen her happier."

Peterson and MacDonald were right on time, and as promised, they didn't stay long. I stored the item that had been in Leslie's trunk upstairs, and on our way home, Joseph and I stopped by the rental shop to pick up two tuxedos—one for him, the second for Noah. I dropped Joseph off at the house before heading to Creekside, since he had an errand to run before the ceremony.

Noah was sitting in the chair as the late afternoon sun streamed through the window, and when he turned to greet me, I knew immediately that the swan hadn't returned. I paused in the doorway.

"Hello, Noah," I said.

"Hello, Wilson," he whispered. He looked drawn, as if the lines in his face had grown deeper overnight.

"You doing okay?"

"Could be better," he said. "Could be worse, though, too."

He forced a smile as if to reassure me.

"Are you ready to go?"

"Yeah," He nodded. "I'm ready."

On the drive, he didn't mention the swan. Instead, he stared out the window as Joseph had, and I left him alone with his thoughts. Nonetheless, my anticipation grew as we neared the house. I couldn't wait for him to see what we'd done, and I suppose I expected Noah to be as dazzled as everyone else had been.

Strangely, however, he showed no reaction when he got out of the car. Looking around, he finally offered the faintest of shrugs. "I thought you said you had the place fixed up," he said.

I blinked, wondering if I'd heard him right.

"I did."

"Where?"

"Everywhere," I said. "Come on—let me show you the garden."

He shook his head. "I can see it fine from here. It looks like it always did."

"Now, maybe, but you should have seen it last week," I said almost defensively. "It was completely overgrown. And the house . . ."

He cut me off with a mischievous grin.

"Gotcha," he said with a wink. "Now come on—let's see what you've done."

We toured the property and house before retiring to the porch swing. We had an hour to ourselves before we had to put on our tuxedos. Joseph was dressed by the time he arrived, and he was followed a few minutes later by Anna,

Leslie, and Jane, who'd come straight from the salon. The girls were giddy as they got out of the car. Walking ahead of Jane, they quickly vanished upstairs, their dresses folded over their arms.

Jane paused before me, her eyes twinkling as she watched them go.

"Now remember," she said, "Keith's not supposed to see Anna beforehand, so don't let him go up."

"I won't," I promised.

"In fact, don't let anyone up. It's supposed to be a surprise."

I held up two fingers. "I'll guard the stairs with my life," I said.

"That goes for you, too."

"I figured."

She glanced toward the empty stairs. "Are you getting nervous yet?"

"A little."

"Me too. It's hard to believe that our little girl is all grown up now, and that she's actually getting married."

Though excited, she sounded a bit wistful, and I leaned in to kiss her on the cheek. She smiled.

"Listen—I've got to go help Anna. She needs help getting into her dress—it's supposed to be real snug. And I've got to finish getting ready, too."

"I know," I said. "I'll see you in a little while."

Over the next hour, the photographer arrived first, followed by John Peterson, and then the caterers, all of them going about their business efficiently. The cake was delivered and set up on the stand, the florist showed up with a bouquet, boutonnieres, and corsages, and just before the guests were to arrive, the minister walked me through the order for the procession.

Shortly, the yard began filling with cars. Noah and I stood on the porch to greet most of the guests before directing them to the tent, where Joseph and Keith escorted the ladies to their chairs. John Peterson was already at the piano, filling the warm evening air with the soft music of Bach. Soon, everyone was seated and the minister was in place.

As the sun began to set, the tent took on a mystical glow. Candles flickered on the tables, and caterers moved out back, ready to arrange the food.

For the first time, the event began to feel real to me. Trying to remain calm, I began to pace. The wedding would commence in less than fifteen minutes, and I assumed that my wife and daughters knew what they were doing. I tried to convince myself that they were simply waiting until the last moment to make their appearance, but I couldn't help peering through the open front door at the stairs every couple of minutes. Noah sat in the porch swing, watching me with an amused expression.

"You look like a target in one of those shooting games at the carnival," he said. "You know—where the penguin goes back and forth?"

I unwrinkled my brow. "That bad?"

"I think you've worn a groove in the porch."

Deciding it might be better to sit, I started toward him when I heard footsteps coming down the stairs.

Noah held up his hands to signal that he was staying, and with a deep breath I entered the foyer. Jane was moving slowly down the stairway, one hand gliding across the banister, and all I could do was stare.

With her hair pinned up, she looked impossibly glamorous. Her peach satin gown clung to her body invitingly, and her lips were a glossy pink. She wore just enough eye shadow to accent her dark eyes, and when she saw my expression, she paused, basking in my appreciation.

"You look . . . incredible," I managed to say.

"Thank you," she said softly.

A moment later, she was moving toward me in the foyer. As she approached, I caught a whiff of her new perfume, but when I leaned in to kiss her, she pulled away before I got close.

"Don't," she said, laughing. "You'll smudge my lipstick."

"Really?"

"Really," she said, and batted my grasping hands away. "You can kiss me later—I promise. Once I start crying, my makeup will be ruined anyway."

"So where's Anna?"

She nodded toward the stairs. "She's ready, but she wanted to talk to Leslie alone before she came down. Some last minute bonding, I guess." She gave a dreamy smile. "I can't wait for you to see her. I don't think I've ever seen a more beautiful bride. Is everything ready to go?"

"As soon as he gets the word, John will start playing the processional music."

Jane nodded, looking nervous. "Where's Daddy?"

"Right where he's supposed to be," I said. "Don't worry—everything's going to be perfect. All that's left now is the waiting."

She nodded again. "What time is it?"

I glanced at my watch. "Eight o'clock," I said, and just as Jane was about to ask whether she should go get Anna, the door creaked open upstairs. We both looked up at the same time.

Leslie was the first to appear, and like Jane, she was the picture of loveliness. Her skin had the dewiness of youth, and she bounced down the stairs with barely suppressed glee. Her dress was also peach colored, but unlike Jane's, it was sleeveless, exposing the tawny muscles in her arms as she gripped the railing. "She's coming," she said breathlessly. "She'll be down in a second."

Joseph slipped through the door behind us and moved alongside his sister. Jane reached for my arm and, surprised, I noticed that my hands were trembling. This was it, I thought, it all comes down to this. And when we heard the door open upstairs, Jane broke into a girlish grin.

"Here she comes," she whispered.

Yes, Anna was coming, but even then my thoughts were only on Jane. Standing beside me, I knew at that moment that I'd never loved her more. My mouth had gone suddenly dry.

When Anna appeared, Jane's eyes widened. For just a moment, she seemed frozen, unable to speak. Seeing her mother's expression, Anna descended the stairs as quickly as Leslie had, one arm behind her back.

The dress she wore was not the one that Jane had seen her wearing only minutes earlier. Instead, she wore the dress that I'd delivered to the house this morning—I had hung it in its garment bag in one of the empty closets—and it matched Leslie's dress perfectly.

Before Jane could summon the will to speak, Anna moved toward her and revealed what she'd been hiding behind her back.

"I think you should be the one to wear this," she said simply.

When Jane saw the bridal veil Anna was holding, she blinked rapidly, unable to believe her eyes. "What's going on?" she demanded. "Why did you take your wedding gown off?"

"Because I'm not getting married," Anna said with a quiet smile. "Not yet, anyway."

"What are you talking about?" Jane cried. "Of course you're getting married. . . ."

Anna shook her head. "This was never my wedding, Mom. It's always been *your* wedding." She paused. "Why do you think I let you pick everything out?"

Jane seemed incapable of digesting Anna's words. Instead, she looked from Anna to Joseph and Leslie, searching their smiling faces for answers, before she finally turned to me.

I took Jane's hands in my own and raised them to my lips. A year of planning, a year of secrets, had come down to this moment. I kissed her fingers gently before meeting her eyes.

"You did say you'd marry me again, didn't you?"

For a moment, it seemed as if the two of us were alone in the room. As Jane stared at me, I thought back on all the arrangements I'd made in secret over the past year—a vacation at exactly the right time, the photographer and caterer who just happened to have an "opening," wedding guests without weekend plans, work crews able to "clear their schedule" in order to ready the house in just a couple of days.

It took a few seconds, but a look of comprehension slowly began to dawn on Jane's face. And when she fully grasped what was happening—what this weekend was truly all about—she stared at me in wonder and disbelief.

"My wedding?" Her voice was soft, almost breathless.

I nodded. "The wedding I should have given you a long time ago."

Though Jane wanted the details of everything here and now, I reached for the veil that Anna still held.

"I'll tell you about it at the reception," I said, draping it carefully over her head. "But right now, the guests are waiting. Joseph and I are expected up at the front, so I've got to go. Don't forget the bouquet."

Jane's eyes were pleading. "But . . . wait . . ."

"I really can't stay," I said softly. "I'm not supposed to see you beforehand, remember?" I smiled. "But I'll see you in just a few minutes, okay?"

I felt the guests' eyes on me as Joseph and I made our way toward the trellis. A moment later, we were standing beside Harvey Wellington, the minister I'd asked to officiate.

"You do have the rings, right?" I asked.

Joseph tapped his breast pocket. "Right here, Pop. Picked them up today, just like you asked."

In the distance, the sun was sinking below the treeline, and the sky was slowly turning gray. My eyes traveled over the guests, and as I heard their muted whispers, I was overcome by a surge of gratitude. Kate, David, and Jeff were seated with their spouses in the front rows, Keith was seated right behind them, and beyond them were the friends whom Jane and I had shared for a lifetime. I owed every one of them my thanks for making all of this possible. Some had sent pictures for the album, others had helped me find exactly the right people to help with the wedding plans. Yet my gratitude went beyond those things. These days, it seemed impossible to keep secrets, but not only had everyone kept this one, they'd turned out with enthusiasm, ready to celebrate this special moment in our lives.

I wanted to thank Anna most of all. None of this would have been possible without her willing participation, and it couldn't have been easy for her. She'd had to watch every word she said, all the while keeping Jane pre-occupied. It had been quite a burden for Keith, too, and I found myself thinking that one day, he would indeed make a fine son-in-law. When he and Anna did decide to get married, I promised myself that Anna would get exactly the kind of wedding she wanted, no matter what it cost.

Leslie had been an immense help, too. It was she who had talked Jane into staying in Greensboro, and she was the one who drove to the store to buy Anna's matching dress before bringing it home. Even more, it was she I called upon for ideas to make the wedding as beautiful as possible. With her love of romantic movies, she'd been a natural, and it had been her idea to hire both Harvey Wellington and John Peterson.

Then, of course, there was Joseph. He had been the least excited of my children when I'd told him what I intended to do, but I suppose I should have expected that. What I didn't expect was the weight of his hand on my shoulder as we stood beneath the trellis, waiting for Jane to arrive.

"Hey, Pop?" he whispered.

"Yes?"

He smiled. "I just want you to know that I'm honored that you asked me to be your best man."

At his words, my throat tightened. "Thank you," was all I could say.

The wedding was all I hoped it would be. I'll never forget the hushed excitement of the crowd or the way people craned their necks to see my daughters making their way down the aisle; I'll never forget how my hands began to shake when I heard the first chords of the "Wedding

March" or how radiant Jane looked as she was escorted down the aisle by her father.

With her veil in place, Jane seemed like a lovely, young bride. With a bouquet of tulips and miniature roses clasped loosely in her hands, she seemed to glide down the aisle. At her side, Noah beamed with undisguised pleasure, every inch the proud father.

At the head of the aisle, he and Jane stopped and Noah slowly raised her veil. After kissing her on the cheek, he whispered something in her ear, then took his seat in the front row, right next to Kate. Beyond them, I could see women in the crowd already dabbing their tears with handkerchiefs.

Harvey opened the ceremony with a prayer of thanks. After asking us to face each other, he spoke then of love and renewal and the effort it entailed. Throughout the ceremony, Jane squeezed my hands tightly, her eyes never leaving my own.

When the time came, I asked Joseph for the rings. For Jane, I'd bought a diamond anniversary band; for myself, I'd bought a duplicate of the one I'd always worn, one that seemed to shine with the hope of better things to come.

We renewed the vows we had spoken long ago and slipped the rings on each other's fingers. When the time came to kiss the bride, I did so to the sounds of cheering, whistles, and applause and an explosion of camera flash-bulbs.

The reception went on until midnight. Dinner was magnificent, and John Peterson was in wonderful form on the piano. Each of the children offered a toast—as did I, to offer my thanks for what everyone had done. Jane couldn't stop smiling.

After dinner, we moved away some of the tables, and Jane and I danced for hours. In the moments she took to catch her breath, she peppered me with questions that had plagued me during most of my waking moments this week.

"What if someone had let the secret slip?"

"But they didn't," I answered.

"But what if they had?"

"I don't know. I guess I just hoped that if someone did slip, you'd think you heard them wrong. Or that you wouldn't believe I'd be crazy enough to do such a thing."

"You put a lot of trust in a lot of people."

"I know," I said. "And I'm thankful they proved me right."

"Me too. This is the most wonderful night of my life." She hesitated as she glanced around the room. "Thank you, Wilson. For every single bit of it."

I put my arm around her. "You're welcome."

As the clock edged toward midnight, the guests began to leave. Each of them shook my hand on the way out and offered Jane a hug. When Peterson finally closed the lid on the piano, Jane thanked him profusely. Impulsively, he kissed her on the cheek. "I wouldn't have missed this for the world," he said.

Harvey Wellington and his wife were among the last to leave, and Jane and I walked with them out onto the porch. When Jane thanked Harvey for officiating, he shook his head. "No need for thanks. There's nothing more wonderful than being part of something like this. It's what marriage is all about."

Jane smiled. "I'll give you a call so we can all have dinner together."

"I'd like that."

The kids were gathered around one of the tables, quietly rehashing the evening, but other than that, the house was quiet. Jane joined them at the table, and as I stood behind her, I glanced around the room and realized that Noah had slipped away unnoticed.

He'd been strangely quiet most of the evening, and I thought he might have gone outside to stand on the back porch in the hope of being alone. I'd found him there earlier, and to be frank, I was a little worried about him. It had been a long day, and with the hour getting late, I wanted to ask him whether he wanted to head back to Creekside. When I stepped onto the porch, however, I didn't see him.

I was just about to go back inside to check the rooms upstairs when I spotted a solitary figure standing by the bank of the river in the distance. How I was able to see him, I'll never be sure, but perhaps I caught sight of the backs of his hands moving in the darkness. Wearing his tuxedo jacket, he was otherwise lost in the nighttime surroundings.

I debated whether or not to call out, then decided against it. For some reason, I had the feeling that he didn't want anyone else to know he was out there. Curious, however, I hesitated only briefly before making my way down the steps. I began moving in his direction.

Above me, the stars were out in full, and the air was fresh with the earthy scent of the low country. My shoes made soft scraping sounds on the gravel, but once I reached the grass, the ground began to slope, gradually at first, then steeper. I found it difficult to keep my balance amid the thickening vegetation. Pushing branches away from my face, I couldn't figure out why—or how—Noah had gone this way.

Standing with his back to me, he was whispering as I approached. The soft cadences of his voice were unmistakable. At first I thought he was speaking to me, but I suddenly realized that he didn't even know I was there.

"Noah?" I asked quietly.

He turned in surprise and stared. It took a moment for him to recognize me in the dark, but gradually, his expression relaxed. Standing before him, I had the strange feeling that I'd caught him doing something wrong.

"I didn't hear you coming. What are you doing out here?"

I smiled quizzically. "I was about to ask you the same question."

Instead of answering, he nodded toward the house. "That was some party you threw tonight. You really outdid yourself. I don't think Jane stopped smiling all night long."

"Thank you." I hesitated. "Did you have a good time?"

"I had a great time," he said.

For a moment, neither of us said anything.

"Are you feeling okay?" I finally asked.

"Could be better," he said. "Could be worse, though, too."

"You sure?"

"Yeah," he said, "I'm sure."

Perhaps responding to my curious expression, he commented, "It's such a nice night. I thought I might take a little time to enjoy it."

"Down here?"

He nodded.

"Why?"

I suppose I should have guessed the reason he'd risked the climb down to the river's edge, but at the time, the thought didn't occur to me.

"I knew she hadn't left me," he said simply. "And I wanted to talk to her."

"Who?"

Noah didn't seem to hear my question. Instead, he nodded in the direction of the river. "I think she came for the wedding."

With that, I suddenly understood what he was telling me, and I glanced at the river, seeing nothing at all. My heart sank, and overwhelmed by a feeling of sudden helplessness, I found myself wondering whether the doctors had been right after all. Maybe he was delusional—or maybe tonight had been too much for him. When I opened my mouth to convince him to come back inside, however, the words seemed to lodge in my throat.

For in the rippling water beyond him, appearing as if from nowhere, she came gliding over the moonlit creek. In the wild, she looked majestic; her feathers were glowing almost silver, and I closed my eyes, hoping to clear the image from my mind. Yet when I opened them again, the swan was circling in front of us, and all at once, I began to smile. Noah was right. Though I didn't know why or how it had come, I had no doubt whatsoever that it was her. It had to be. I'd seen the swan a hundred times, and even from a distance, I couldn't help but notice the tiny black spot in the middle of her chest, directly above her heart.

$\mathcal{S}$tanding on the porch, with autumn in full swing, I find the crispness of the evening air invigorating as I think back on the night of our wedding. I can still recall it in vivid detail, just as I can remember all that happened during the year of the forgotten anniversary.

It feels odd to know that it's all behind me. The preparations had dominated my thoughts for so long and I'd visualized it so many times that I sometimes feel that I've lost contact with an old friend, someone with whom I'd grown very comfortable. Yet in the wake of those memories, I've come to realize that I now have the answer to the question that I'd been pondering when I first came out here.

Yes, I decided, a man can truly change.

The events of the past year have taught me much about myself, and a few universal truths. I learned, for instance, that while wounds can be inflicted easily upon those we love, it's often much more difficult to heal them. Yet the process of healing those wounds provided the richest experience of my life, leading me to believe that while I've often overestimated what I could accomplish in a day, I had underestimated what I could do in a year. But most of all, I learned that it's possible for two people to fall in love all over again, even when there's been a lifetime of disappointment between them.

I'm not sure what to think about the swan and what I saw that night, and I must admit that being romantic still doesn't come easily. It's a daily struggle to reinvent myself, and part of me wonders whether it always will be. But so what? I hold tight to the lessons that Noah taught me about love and keeping it alive, and even if I never become a true romantic like Noah, it doesn't mean that I'm ever going to stop trying.

Please turn this page
for a preview of the book that
started it all…

The Notebook

The unforgettable love story of
Noah and Allie Calhoun

AVAILABLE IN TRADE PAPERBACK

Miracles

Who am I? And how, I wonder, will this story end?

The sun has come up and I am sitting by a window that is foggy with the breath of a life gone by. I'm a sight this morning: two shirts, heavy pants, a scarf wrapped twice around my neck and tucked into a thick sweater knitted by my daughter thirty birthdays ago. The thermostat in my room is set as high as it will go, and a smaller space heater sits directly behind me. It clicks and groans and spews hot air like a fairy-tale dragon, and still my body shivers with a cold that will never go away, a cold that has been eighty years in the making. Eighty years, I think sometimes, and despite my own acceptance of my age, it still amazes me that I haven't been warm since George Bush was president. I wonder if this is how it is for everyone my age.

My life? It isn't easy to explain. It has not been the rip-roaring spectacular I fancied it would be, but neither have I burrowed around with the gophers. I suppose it has most resembled a blue-chip stock: fairly stable, more ups than downs, and gradually trending upward over time. A good buy, a lucky buy, and I've learned that not everyone can say this about his life. But do not be misled. I am nothing special; of this I am sure. I am a common man with common thoughts, and I've led a common life. There are no monuments dedicated to me and my name will soon be forgotten, but I've loved another with all my heart and soul, and to me, this has always been enough.

The romantics would call this a love story, the cynics would call it a tragedy. In my mind it's a little bit of both, and no matter how you choose to view it in the end, it does not change the fact that it involves a great deal of my life and the path I've chosen to follow. I have no complaints about my path and the places it has taken me; enough complaints to fill a circus tent about other things, maybe, but the path I've chosen has always been the right one, and I wouldn't have had it any other way.

Time, unfortunately, doesn't make it easy to stay on course. The path is straight as ever, but now it is strewn with the rocks and gravel that accumulate over a lifetime. Until three years ago it would have been easy to ignore, but it's impossible now. There is a sickness rolling through my body; I'm neither strong nor healthy, and my days are spent like an old party balloon: listless, spongy, and growing softer over time.

I cough, and through squinted eyes I check my watch. I realize it is time to go. I stand from my seat by the window and shuffle across the room, stopping at the desk to pick up the notebook I have read a hundred times. I do not glance through it. Instead I slip it beneath my arm and continue on my way to the place I must go.

I walk on tiled floors, white in color and speckled with gray. Like my hair and the hair of most people here, though I'm the only one in the hallway this morning. They are in their rooms, alone except for television, but they, like me, are used to it. A person can get used to anything, if given enough time.

I hear the muffled sounds of crying in the distance and know exactly who is making those sounds. Then the nurses see me and we smile at each other and exchange greetings. They are my friends and we talk often, but I am sure they wonder about me and the things that I go through every day. I listen as they begin to whisper among themselves as I pass. "There he goes again," I hear, "I hope it turns out well." But they say nothing directly to me about it. I'm sure they think it would hurt me to talk about it so early in the morning, and knowing myself as I do, I think they're probably right.

A minute later, I reach the room. The door has been propped open for me, as it usually is. There are two others in the room, and they too smile at me as I enter. "Good morning," they say with cheery voices, and I take a moment to ask about the kids and the schools and upcoming vacations. We talk above the crying for a minute or so. They do not seem to notice; they have become numb to it, but then again, so have I.

Afterward I sit in the chair that has come to be shaped like me. They are finishing up now; her clothes are on, but still she is crying. It will become quieter after they leave, I know. The excitement of the morning always upsets her, and today is no exception. Finally the shade is opened and the nurses walk out. Both of them touch me and smile as they walk by. I wonder what this means.

I sit for just a second and stare at her, but she doesn't return the look. I understand, for she doesn't know who I am. I'm a stranger to her. Then, turning away, I bow my head and pray silently for the strength I know I will need. I have always been a firm believer in God and the power of prayer, though to be honest, my faith has made for a list of questions I definitely want answered after I'm gone.

Ready now. On go the glasses, out of my pocket comes a magnifier. I put it on the table for a moment while I open the notebook. It takes two licks on my gnarled finger to get the well-worn cover open to the first page. Then I put the magnifier in place.

There is always a moment right before I begin to read the story when my mind churns, and I wonder, Will it happen today? I don't know, for I never know beforehand, and deep down it really doesn't matter. It's the possibility that keeps me going, not the guarantee, a sort of wager on my part. And though you may call me a dreamer or fool or any other thing, I believe that anything is possible.

I realize the odds, and science, are against me. But science is not the total answer; this I know, this I have learned in my lifetime. And that leaves me with the belief that miracles, no matter how inexplicable or unbelievable, are real and can occur without regard to the natural order of things. So once again, just as I do every day, I begin to read the notebook aloud, so that she can hear it, in the hope that the miracle that has come to dominate my life will once again prevail.

And maybe, just maybe, it will.

Ghosts

It was early October 1946, and Noah Calhoun watched the fading sun sink lower from the wrap-around porch of his plantation-style home. He liked to sit here in the evenings, especially after working hard all day, and let his thoughts wander without conscious direction. It was how he relaxed, a routine he'd learned from his father.

He especially liked to look at the trees and their reflections in the river. North Carolina trees are beautiful in deep autumn: greens, yellows, reds, oranges, every shade in between. Their dazzling colors glow with the sun, and for the hundredth time, Noah Calhoun wondered if the original owners of the house had spent their evenings thinking the same things.

The house was built in 1772, making it one of the oldest, as well as largest, homes in New Bern. Originally it was the main house on a working plantation, and he had bought it right after the war ended and had spent the last eleven months and a small fortune repairing it. The reporter from the Raleigh paper had done an article on it a few weeks ago and said it was one of the finest restorations he'd ever seen. At least the house was. The remaining property was another story, and that was where he'd spent most of the day.

The home sat on twelve acres adjacent to Brices Creek, and he'd worked on the wooden fence that lined the other three sides of the property, checking for dry rot or termites, replacing posts when he had to. He still had more work to do on it, especially on the west side, and as he'd put the tools away earlier he'd made a mental note to call and have some more lumber delivered. He'd gone into the house, drunk a glass of sweet tea, then showered. He always showered at the end of the day, the water washing away both dirt and fatigue.

Afterward he'd combed his hair back, put on some faded jeans and a long-sleeved blue shirt, poured himself another glass of sweet tea, and gone to the porch, where he now sat, where he sat every day at this time.

He stretched his arms above his head, then out to the sides, rolling his shoulders as he completed the routine. He felt good and clean now, fresh. His muscles were tired and he knew he'd be a little sore tomorrow, but he was pleased that he had accomplished most of what he had wanted to do.

Noah reached for his guitar, remembering his father as he did so, thinking how much he missed him. He strummed once, adjusted the tension on two strings, then strummed again. This time it sounded about right, and he began to play. Soft music, quiet music. He hummed for a little while at first, then began to sing as night came down around him. He played and sang until the sun was gone and the sky was black.

It was a little after seven when he quit, and he settled back into his chair and began to rock. By habit, he looked upward and saw Orion and the Big Dipper, Gemini and the Pole Star, twinkling in the autumn sky.

He started to run the numbers in his head, then stopped. He knew he'd spent almost his entire savings on the house and would have to find a job again soon, but he pushed the thought away and decided to enjoy the remaining months of restoration without worrying about it. It would work out for him, he knew; it always did. Besides, thinking about money usually bored him. Early on, he'd learned to enjoy simple things, things that couldn't be bought, and he had a hard time understanding people who felt otherwise. It was another trait he got from his father.

Clem, his hound dog, came up to him then and nuzzled his hand before lying down at his feet. "Hey, girl, how're you doing?" he asked as he patted her head, and she whined softly, her soft round eyes peering upward. A car accident had taken her leg, but she still moved well enough and kept him company on quiet nights like these.

He was thirty-one now, not too old, but old enough to be lonely. He hadn't dated since he'd been back here, hadn't met anyone who remotely interested him. It was his own fault, he knew. There was something that kept a distance between him and any woman who started to get close, something he wasn't sure he could change even if he tried. And sometimes in the moments right before sleep came, he wondered if he was destined to be alone forever.

The evening passed, staying warm, nice. Noah listened to the crickets and the rustling leaves, thinking that the sound of nature was more real and aroused more emotion than things like cars and planes. Natural things gave back more than they took, and their sounds always brought him back to the way man was supposed to be. There were times during the war, especially after a major engagement, when he had often thought about these simple sounds. "It'll keep you from going crazy," his father had told him the day he'd shipped out. "It's God's music and it'll take you home."

He finished his tea, went inside, found a book, then turned on the porch light on his way back out. After sitting down again, he looked at the book. It was old, the cover was torn, and the pages were stained with mud and water. It was *Leaves of Grass* by Walt Whitman, and he had carried it with him throughout the war. It had even taken a bullet for him once.

He rubbed the cover, dusting it off just a little. Then he let the book open randomly and read the words in front of him:

This is thy hour O Soul, thy free flight
    into the wordless,
Away from books, away from art, the day
    erased, the lesson done,
Thee fully forth emerging, silent, gazing,
    pondering the themes thou lovest best,
Night, sleep, death and the stars.

He smiled to himself. For some reason Whitman always reminded him of New Bern, and he was glad he'd come back. Though he'd been away for fourteen years, this was home and he knew a lot of people here, most of them from his youth. It wasn't surprising. Like so many southern towns, the people who lived here never changed, they just grew a bit older.

His best friend these days was Gus, a seventy-year-old black man who lived down the road. They had met a couple of weeks after Noah bought the house, when Gus had shown up with some homemade liquor and Brunswick stew, and the two had spent their first evening together getting drunk and telling stories.

Now Gus would show up a couple of nights a week, usually around eight. With four kids and eleven grandchildren in the house, he needed to get out of the house now and then, and Noah couldn't blame him. Usually Gus would bring his harmonica, and after talking for a little while, they'd play a few songs together. Sometimes they played for hours.

He'd come to regard Gus as family. There really wasn't anyone else, at least not since his father died last year. He was an only child; his mother had died of influenza when he was two, and though he had wanted to at one time, he had never married.

But he had been in love once, that he knew. Once and only once, and a long time ago. And it had changed him forever. Perfect love did that to a person, and this had been perfect.

Coastal clouds slowly began to roll across the evening sky, turning silver with the reflection of the moon. As they thickened, he leaned his head back and rested it against the rocking chair. His legs moved automatically, keeping a steady rhythm, and as he did most evenings, he felt his mind drifting back to a warm evening like this fourteen years ago.

It was just after graduation 1932, the opening night of the Neuse River Festival. The town was out in full, enjoying barbecue and games of chance. It was humid that night—for some reason he remembered that clearly. He arrived alone, and as he strolled through the crowd, looking for friends, he saw Fin and Sarah, two people he'd grown up with, talking to a girl he'd never seen before. She was pretty, he remembered thinking, and when he finally joined them, she looked his way with a pair of hazy eyes that kept on coming. "Hi," she'd said simply as she offered her hand, "Finley's told me a lot about you."

An ordinary beginning, something that would have been forgotten had it been anyone but her. But as he shook her hand and met those striking emerald eyes, he knew before he'd taken his next breath that she was the one he could spend the rest of his life looking for but never find again. She seemed that good, that perfect, while a summer wind blew through the trees.

From there, it went like a tornado wind. Fin told him she was spending the summer in New Bern with her family because her father worked for R. J. Reynolds, and though he only nodded, the way she was looking at him made his silence seem okay. Fin laughed then, because he knew what was happening, and Sarah suggested they get some cherry Cokes, and the four of them stayed at the festival until the crowds were thin and everything closed up for the night.

They met the following day, and the day after that, and they soon became inseparable. Every morning but Sunday when he had to go to church, he would finish his chores as quickly as possible, then make a straight line to Fort Totten Park, where she'd be waiting for him. Because she was a newcomer and hadn't spent time in a small town before, they spent their days doing things that were completely new to her. He taught her how to bait a line and fish the shallows for largemouth bass and took her exploring through the backwoods of the Croatan Forest. They rode in canoes and watched summer thunderstorms, and to him it seemed as though they'd always known each other.

But he learned things as well. At the town dance in the tobacco barn, it was she who taught him how to waltz and do the Charleston, and though they stumbled through the first few songs, her patience with him eventually paid off, and they danced together until the music ended. He walked her home afterward, and when they paused on the porch after saying good night, he kissed her for the first time and wondered why he had waited as long as he had. Later in the summer he brought her to this house, looked past the decay, and told her that one day he was going to own it and fix it up. They spent hours together talking about their dreams—his of seeing the world, hers of being an artist—and on a humid night in August, they both lost their virginity. When she left three weeks later, she took a piece of him and the rest of summer with her. He watched her leave town on an early rainy morning, watched through eyes that hadn't slept the night before, then went home and packed a bag. He spent the next week alone on Harkers Island.

Noah ran his hands through his hair and checked his watch. Eight-twelve. He got up and walked to the front of the house and looked up the road. Gus wasn't in sight, and Noah figured he wouldn't be coming. He went back to his rocker and sat again.

He remembered talking to Gus about her. The first time he mentioned her, Gus started to shake his head and laugh. "So that's the ghost you been running from." When asked what he meant, Gus said, "You know, the ghost, the memory. I been watchin' you, workin' day and night, slavin' so hard you barely have time to catch your breath. People do that for three reasons. Either they crazy, or stupid, or tryin' to forget. And with you, I knew you was tryin' to forget. I just didn't know what."

He thought about what Gus had said. Gus was right, of course. New Bern was haunted now. Haunted by the ghost of her memory. He saw her in Fort Totten Park, their place, every time he walked by. Either sitting on the bench or standing by the gate, always smiling, blond hair softly touching her shoulders, her eyes the color of emeralds. When he sat on the porch at night with his guitar, he saw her beside him, listening quietly as he played the music of his childhood.

He felt the same when he went to Gaston's Drug Store, or to the Masonic theater, or even when he strolled downtown. Everywhere he looked, he saw her image, saw things that brought her back to life.

It was odd, he knew that. He had grown up in New Bern. Spent his first seventeen years here. But when he thought about New Bern, he seemed to remember only the last summer, the summer they were together. Other memories were simply fragments, pieces here and there of growing up, and few, if any, evoked any feeling.

He had told Gus about it one night, and not only had Gus understood, but he had been the first to explain why. He said simply, "My daddy used to tell me that the first time you fall in love, it changes your life forever, and no matter how hard you try, the feelin' never goes away. This girl you been tellin' me about was your first love. And no matter what you do, she'll stay with you forever."

Noah shook his head, and when her image began to fade, he returned to Whitman. He read for an hour, looking up every now and then to see raccoons and possums scurrying near the creek. At nine-thirty he closed the book, went upstairs to the bedroom, and wrote in his journal, including both personal observations and the work he'd accomplished on the house. Forty minutes later, he was sleeping. Clem wandered up the stairs, sniffed him as he slept, and then paced in circles before finally curling up at the foot of his bed.

Earlier that evening and a hundred miles away, she sat alone on the porch swing of her parents' home, one leg crossed beneath her. The seat had been slightly damp when she sat down; rain had fallen earlier, hard and stinging, but the clouds were fading now and she looked past them, toward the stars, wondering if she'd made the right decision. She'd struggled with it for days—and had struggled some more this evening—but in the end, she knew she would never forgive herself if she let the opportunity slip away.

Lon didn't know the real reason she left the following morning. The week before, she'd hinted to him that she might want to visit some antique shops near the coast. "It's just a couple of days," she said, "and besides, I need a break from planning the wedding." She felt bad about the lie but knew there was no way she could tell him the truth. Her leaving had nothing to do with him, and it wouldn't be fair of her to ask him to understand.

It was an easy drive from Raleigh, slightly more than two hours, and she arrived a little before eleven. She checked into a small inn downtown, went to her room, and unpacked her suitcase, hanging her dresses in the closet and putting everything else in the drawers. She had a quick lunch, asked the waitress for directions to the nearest antique stores, then spent the next few hours shopping. By four-thirty she was back in her room.

She sat on the edge of the bed, picked up the phone, and called Lon. He couldn't speak long, he was due in court, but before they hung up she gave him the phone number where she was staying and promised to call the following day. Good, she thought while hanging up the phone. Routine conversation, nothing out of the ordinary. Nothing to make him suspicious.

She'd known him almost four years now; it was 1942 when they met, the world at war and America one year in. Everyone was doing their part, and she was volunteering at the hospital downtown. She was both needed and appreciated there, but it was more difficult than she'd expected. The first waves of wounded young soldiers were coming home, and she spent her days with broken men and shattered bodies. When Lon, with all his easy charm, introduced himself at a Christmas party, she saw in him exactly what she needed: someone with confidence about the future and a sense of humor that drove all her fears away.

He was handsome, intelligent, and driven, a successful lawyer eight years older than she, and he pursued his job with passion, not only winning cases, but also making a name for himself. She understood his vigorous pursuit of success, for her father and most of the men she met in her social circle were the same way. Like them, he'd been raised that way, and in the caste system of the South, family name and accomplishments were often the most important consideration in marriage. In some cases, they were the only consideration.

Though she had quietly rebelled against this idea since childhood and had dated a few men best described as reckless, she found herself drawn to Lon's easy ways and had gradually come to love him. Despite the long hours he worked, he was good to her. He was a gentleman, both mature and responsible, and during those terrible periods of the war when she needed someone to hold her, he never once turned her away. She felt secure with him and knew he loved her as well, and that was why she had accepted his proposal.

Thinking these things made her feel guilty about being here, and she knew she should pack her things and leave before she changed her mind. She had done it once before, long ago, and if she left now, she was sure she would never have the strength to return here again. She picked up her pocketbook, hesitated, and almost made it to the door. But coincidence had pushed her here, and she put the pocketbook down, again realizing that if she quit now, she would always wonder what would have happened. And she didn't think she could live with that.

She went to the bathroom and started a bath. After checking the temperature, she walked to the dresser, taking off her gold earrings as she crossed the room. She found her makeup bag, opened it, and pulled out a razor and a bar of soap, then undressed in front of the bureau.

She had been called beautiful since she was a young girl, and once she was naked, she looked at herself in the mirror. Her body was firm and well proportioned, breasts softly rounded, stomach flat, legs slim. She'd inherited her mother's high cheekbones, smooth skin, and blond hair, but her best feature was her own. She had "eyes like ocean waves," as Lon liked to say.

Taking the razor and soap, she went to the bathroom again, turned off the faucet, set a towel where she could reach it, and stepped in gingerly.

She liked the way a bath relaxed her, and she slipped lower in the water. The day had been long and her back was tense, but she was pleased she had finished shopping so quickly. She had to go back to Raleigh with something tangible, and the things she had picked out would work fine. She made a mental note to find the names of some other stores in the Beaufort area, then suddenly doubted she would need to. Lon wasn't the type to check up on her.

~∞~

She reached for the soap, lathered up, and began to shave her legs. As she did, she thought about her parents and what they would think of her behavior. No doubt they would disapprove, especially her mother. Her mother had never really accepted what had happened the summer they'd spent here and wouldn't accept it now, no matter what reason she gave.

She soaked a while longer in the tub before finally getting out and toweling off. She went to the closet and looked for a dress, finally choosing a long yellow one that dipped slightly in the front, the kind of dress that was common in the South. She slipped it on and looked in the mirror, turning from side to side. It fit her well and made her look feminine, but she eventually decided against it and put it back on the hanger.

Instead she found a more casual, less revealing dress and put that on. Light blue with a touch of lace, it buttoned up the front, and though it didn't look quite as nice as the first one, it conveyed an image she thought would be more appropriate.

She wore little makeup, just a touch of eye shadow and mascara to accent her eyes. Perfume next, not too much. She found a pair of small-hooped earrings, put those on, then slipped on the tan, low-heeled sandals she had been wearing earlier. She brushed her blond hair, pinned it up, and looked in the mirror. No, it was too much, she thought, and she let it back down. Better.

When she was finished she stepped back and evaluated herself. She looked good: not too dressy, not too casual. She didn't want to overdo it. After all, she didn't know what to expect. It had been a long time—

probably too long—and many different things could have happened, even things she didn't want to consider.

She looked down and saw her hands were shaking, and she laughed to herself. It was strange; she wasn't normally this nervous. Like Lon, she had always been confident, even as a child. She remembered that it had been a problem at times, especially when she dated, because it had intimidated most of the boys her age.

She found her pocketbook and car keys, then picked up the room key. She turned it over in her hand a couple of times, thinking, You've come this far, don't give up now, and almost left then, but instead sat on the bed again. She checked her watch. Almost six o'clock. She knew she had to leave in a few minutes—she didn't want to arrive after dark, but she needed a little more time.

"Damn," she whispered, "what am I doing here? I shouldn't be here. There's no reason for it," but once she said it she knew it wasn't true. There was something here. If nothing else, she would have her answer.

She opened her pocketbook and thumbed through it until she came to a folded-up piece of newspaper. After taking it out slowly, almost reverently, being careful not to rip it, she unfolded it and stared at it for a while. "This is why," she finally said to herself, "this is what it's all about."